Vanishing Point

Morris West, an Australian by birth, has lived in Italy, Austria, England and the United States. He has written twenty-six novels, as well as screen-plays, radio dramas and works for the stage. His novels have been translated into twenty-seven languages and have sold more than sixty million copies.

ALSO BY MORRIS WEST

MORRIS WEST

VANISHING POINT

HarperCollins*Publishers*

HarperCollins*Publishers*
77–85 Fulham Palace Road,
Hammersmith, London W6 8JB

This paperback edition 1997

3 5 7 9 8 6 4 2

First published in Great Britain by
HarperCollins*Publishers* 1996

Copyright © Melaleuka Investments Pty Limited 1996

ISBN 0 00 649914 7

Printed and bound in Great Britain by
Caledonian International Book Manufacturing Ltd, Glasgow

For my family,
who, like all travelers,
have heard the storm winds rise
and learned the perils of strange shores.
This book—with love.

AUTHOR'S NOTE

This is the novel I believed I would never write. Its genesis was a puffy little piece which I clipped some years ago from a magazine in a hotel room in Zurich.

I did some desultory research on what is in fact a highly developed worldwide service industry: making people vanish. I found I could raise neither energy nor enthusiasm for an idea which seemed to me to belong in another genre of writing than mine.

The impulse to develop the theme came from quite another quarter. I had, over many years, a close acquaintance with the phenomena of depressive illness, the impulse to flight from intolerable reality, and the impulse to absent oneself from the burden of life. The two themes began to knit themselves into a pattern which clamored for expression.

The urge to write this book became as irresistible as that which drove my characters to "the dangerous edge of things."

I offer my thanks to all those who have helped me to write it by sharing their expert knowledge or their very private experiences of suffering.

Morris West

Our interest's on the dangerous edge of things.

—Robert Browning, "Bishop Blougram's Apology"

1

MY FATHER, A FORMAL MAN but a kind one, calls me a certifiable eccentric.

He can call me anything he wants, because it was he who provided me with the freedom and the means to do what I do now: which is to live in a great whitewashed barn in the hills above Cagnes, work during the winter on a history of architectural art, and in spring take to the road with camera, sketchbooks, and canvases to provide another batch of up-to-date original illustrations.

My father is Emil Strassberger, one of the most respected names in New York banking. I am named Carl Emil. I am his only son. Our ancestors came from Alsace, where the business was founded in the mid-nineteenth century to raise money for the Industrial Revolution in Europe. It is perhaps significant to our relations and to our history that I still call him, in the old-fashioned mode, 'Father.'

I know he was sadly disappointed when I chose to break with tradition and follow the gypsy road of the arts. Yet, gentleman that he is, he gave me my liberty on a golden dish. I would retain my shareholding in the company, which would pay me enough in dividends to maintain me in bachelor comfort. The position reserved for me in the company and on the board would pass to my sister Madeleine's husband, Laurence Lucas, Harvard-educated in commercial law, coopted immediately after graduation into the rising band of hopefuls at Strassberger & Company in New

York. My father liked Larry and, more importantly, admired him. In his second year at Harvard, both his parents had been killed in an automobile accident. He was left with a modest legacy and a few distant relatives who lived on the West Coast. Somehow he had managed to survive the ordeal and finish his courses with high commendations and a promising future. On his marriage to Madeleine, my father endowed him with a directorship and a parcel of shares. My sister, Madeleine, made her way, as my mother did, with a quiet grace of care and authority. I treasured them both. They were, after all, my passport to the life I had chosen.

It was a good life, if a completely selfish one. I was thirty-seven years old. I had income to cover all my reasonable needs. I had work that pleased me and earned me both money and a reputation that was growing quietly among a small but influential group of connoisseurs. I liked the rustic life, which kept me healthy and my table well supplied. I had a thirty-foot sloop riding at a safe mooring in Antibes. I had an agreeable and intelligent friend, one Arlette Tassigny, who ran one of the best galleries in Nice with an impressive list of patrons and a stable of respectable talent. She was good-looking, good-tempered, and could summon up a party before you could murmur "Matisse."

She was also a very commonsensical lady. After our first night together she told me; "*Chéri,* I have been married once and had a lot of men on approval. The notion of a permanent arrangement does not appeal to me at all. Tomorrow will be what it will be. Therefore, I am very happy to have a friendship with you. It costs me no effort. You are an agreeable and confident man. We match well in bed. You have your work; I have mine. You can visit me here in Nice; I can visit you in the country. You paint for me there; I sell for you here. If either of us needs a change of company, we say so, *sans blague.* What could be better, eh?"

That was the way things stood when the first winds of spring stirred over the foothills of the Maritime Alps. My father was in New York. My mother, though frail, was still able to preside over his private dinners, for guests he chose with elaborate care. My sister, Madeleine, was kept busy with two young children and a domestic staff in their house on East 80th Street. Larry was commuting to Paris every week as mastermind to a five-billion-dollar takeover of properties owned by the old Suez Company. I, Carl Emil Strassberger, was scoring the final burin strokes on an etching of a Vanvitelli which I had copied in the Palatine Gallery in Florence: a view of the Tiber with the apse of San Giovanni dei Fiorentini in the right foreground and Castel Sant' Angelo in the background.

Then the telephone rang. It was my father calling from New York. He was in what we used to call his high business mode. He wasted no words.

"Carl, we have an emergency. I need you in New York as quickly as you can get here."

"Of course, I'll come immediately. But what's the emergency?"

"Nothing we can discuss on an open line. Just accept that the matter is very urgent. Make your reservations and call me back. You will be picked up at Kennedy. Please come first to the office."

I knew better than to prolong the discussion. I hung up and began to make travel arrangements. They were simple enough. An evening flight on Air France from Nice to London, overnight at a Heathrow hotel, and the first Concorde to Kennedy in the morning, which would put me on the ground at 9:30 A.M. I called my father to confirm the schedule. He was relieved and grateful. That gave me courage to ask him again.

"Please, can you give me at least a hint of what's going on?"

"Let me put it this way. Your mother is well. I am well. Your sister and her children are well. Let me say only that suddenly I don't know as much as I thought I did and I need some help from my son."

"You have it, Father. Give everyone my love. See you in the morning."

I hung up, made the last few strokes on the etching plate, and went into the bedroom to pack. I didn't know then—how could I?—that I was making my first steps toward that dangerous edge of things where all lines and all roads converge to a vanishing point.

3

* * *

My father was waiting for me in his office. He still carried himself straight as a grenadier but when I entered his eyes lit up and he came, arms outflung, to sweep me up into a bear-hug embrace. When finally he released me and held me at arm's length, I saw that he was thinner and grayer and that the fire had gone out of his eyes. His voice was tired and he seemed to have difficulty in framing his story.

"Today is Friday, yes?"

"Today is Friday."

"So your brother-in-law has now been missing for seven days."

He announced it as if it were an item in an auditor's report. I gaped at him foolishly.

"What do you mean, disappeared?"

"Nobody knows what it means yet, Carl, but the chronology begins with this." He turned back to his desk and picked up a heavy file of indexed transcripts. "This is the deal we brokered for the Suez Company. It was signed, sealed, and delivered in Paris on Wednesday of last week. The deal is worth five billion dollars, and our take in commissions, fees, and service charges is something over fifty million dollars. Larry has been going back and forth to Paris every week for the past six months. In the end he put everything together beautifully. He flew in with the documents signed and sealed and laid them on my desk last Thursday. On Friday he was to come into the office again. The members of the board were waiting to offer their congratulations and a handsome bonus for his efforts."

"So?"

"He left home at eight-thirty in the morning. Madeleine kissed him at the door and saw him heading toward Fifth Avenue to pick up a taxi. Nobody's seen or heard of him since that moment."

"Have you told the police?"

"Officially, we have made no report."

Suddenly he was in his negotiating mode, cryptic and cagey. I was angry with him and told him so.

4

"Don't do this to me, Father! You asked me for help. I'm here to give it. Please don't make mysteries."

He shrugged and spread his hands in a gesture of defeat.

"Forgive me. At this moment I make little sense even to myself. We are not trying to make a mystery but to avoid creating a scandal or, worse still, a situation of danger for Larry himself. For the moment Madeleine and I have agreed to keep the police out of it and to entrust the first inquiries to Consec, a security company whom we retain for Strassberger business."

"Why, for God's sake?"

"If you call in the police you get the press as well. Consider a moment: The director of a famous banking house disappears. What are the first thoughts in everyone's mind? He's run off with a woman and possibly absconded with bank funds. As early as last Monday I ordered a secret internal audit. It's almost finished. Larry checks out clean all along the line; there's not the slightest indication of anything criminal or unethical. Next possibility, a kidnapping—but for what? No ransom demand has been made. Our investigators discount the possibility. An accident? A mugging? An amnesiac incident, perhaps? Extensive hospital checks have been made. The results are negative."

"So we are left with the simplest and most vulgar explanation. Larry Lucas has walked out on his wife and children."

"I don't believe that. Larry has just brought off a deal which will make his name in financial circles around the world. From here on, he can write his own ticket. I believe he's too smart and too ambitious to risk his career for any woman."

"What does Madeleine think?"

He had difficulty dredging up his next words.

"Madeleine blames me and only me for Larry's disappearance. The sad thing is your mother agrees with her. Prima facie they have a good case."

"What is their case?"

"This!" Once again he reached for the thick volume of documents on his desk. He held it up before his face as a minister might hold a mass-book or a lectionary. "This, they say, was too much labor to lay on one man. They say I broke him by impossible demands."

"And what's your answer to that, Father?"

"What can I say? It was a big job. I offered him all the help he needed, and he had an open budget to hire the best brains. But I didn't drive him. Madeleine now confesses he had demons of his own that drove him further and harder than I ever could." A tinge of anger crept into his voice. "But what can I say? I'm not prepared to defend myself to my own wife and daughter!"

"I'm sure that's not what they want. They're hurt. They're scared. They're using the wrong words. We all do that sometimes, even you. I love you, Father. We all do. But sometimes you can be very formidable. Tell me what I can do to help."

"Just listen! Listen to all of us! Try not to be angry when they say things you don't expect."

"Like what?"

"That I am insensitive and you are selfish and Larry is a victim of the righteous Strassbergers."

"Does Mama say that?"

"Not in those words. She says I judge people instead of trying to understand them. I tell her everything I do depends on making a judgment of people. She just shakes her head sadly and says, 'Emil, my love, you are a good father, a good husband, but unless you can think differently about Larry, you may well lose your daughter and her children. They will not tolerate you if you treat him as an enemy.'"

Before I had chance to digest that, there was a knock at the door and Madeleine came in. I held out my arms and she came running to embrace me. She was trembling and very close to tears.

"Oh, Carl! I'm so glad you're here!"

"How could I not be? I'm still family."

"How much has Father told you?"

"Just the outline. Larry comes home, delivers the deal, and disappears on the way to the office Friday morning. You decide together not to make a police report but to use private investigators. Father calls for an immediate internal audit of Strassberger.

6

Larry checks out clean, the investigators come up with zero. Father's upset because he thinks you and Mother blame him for Larry's disappearance. He wants you to tell me the rest of the story. I want to tell you that I love you all. I'm a free agent. I'll do anything I can to help."

"How long can you stay?"

"As long as I'm needed."

"Then first you have to understand—"

"Madeleine, my dear." This was now my father the diplomat. "Why don't you take your brother into Larry's office. You can be private there. When you've finished, come back here. Your mother has asked that all three of us join her for lunch at home."

"Fine. But understand I can't stay too long. I need to to be back before the children come from school."

"Of course. I'll phone your mother now and warn her."

"Thank you, Father."

She took my arm and led me across the corridor to Larry's office. She stood for a moment, stock-still on the threshold, looking at the bookcases and the paneled wall space with its quartet of Boudins and the single Matisse sketch which flanked the obligatory display of academic awards and professional licenses. She shivered and clung to me in momentary desperation; then she pointed to Larry's empty chair.

"You sit there, please, Carl! I can't bear the emptiness!"

I sat. She perched herself on the edge of the desk, looking down on me. I waited while she stumbled through the first words.

"I'm very frightened, Carl. I have to stay calm because of the children, but it gets harder every day. I know—or at least I think I know—what's happened to Larry. Mama believes I'm right. Father can't seem to accept it. And yet, it's very simple."

"How simple?"

"Larry's manic-depressive. The illness stems from that tragic time in his youth when his parents were killed and he was left pretty much alone to battle through his first years of manhood and his career studies. He's a highly intelligent, loving man whose life is a continuous roller-coaster ride between peaks of exaggerated euphoria and black pits of the most terrifying depression. The condition is manageable to a certain degree with drugs, and Larry's been good about taking advice and medication. On the other hand, the biggest highs and the worst lows are triggered by stress, and Larry's had more than his share of that over these last months."

"How was he when he came back from France last week?"

"Just off a huge high and heading down into a deep, deep pit."

"You're always sure of your reading?"

"Absolutely. It's as clear as a weather map."

"And you know how to handle it."

"I thought . . . no, I still think I do. The first thing is to make sure he hasn't gone off the medication or, if he has, get him back on it. That isn't always as easy as it sounds, because at the top of the highs and the bottom of the lows, reason seems to go out the window. You can't persuade the sufferer out of the mood. The worst thing you can do is try to argue him out of it. The only thing you can offer is love—and there are moments, Carl, when you just simply run out of that too. You have to take breath and gather yourself again for a new round of giving. Mama understands this. Father doesn't. He can't grasp the irrational element. He has no understanding of it, no sympathy with it."

"But he wants to understand it, Madi, truly he does. I know how he feels. All this is new to me too."

"You've been away too long! You've been living too well."

"So, instruct me. Help me to understand, so I can help *you*. Tell me, first: Is there any violence in the situation, physical violence, against you or the children?"

"No!" She was quite emphatic about it, but she was swift to qualify the negative. "But if he's pushed to extreme frustration, yes, violence is possible. I've seen him drive his fist through a plaster wall. But he's never been violent to me or the children. You have to believe me. Larry is a good husband and a loving father. He's also fortunate that I've got enough sense not to nag him in his exalted moments or his low ones. We can't afford two fares on the same roller coaster."

"So let's talk about the highs and the lows. What happens?"

"In the highs, everything is possible. As Larry explains it, 'You know you can reach up and pluck the stars out of heaven. You can bet a million and win on the turn of a card. You can build empires in your head.' Larry was on a huge high when Father gave him the Suez assignment. He was so sure of himself that Father became quite irritated. He told Mama he would be glad to see Larry taken down a peg. But that's the other side of the coin. Larry is a superbly intelligent man. He knew the commitment he had made. He was determined to deliver and he did—at enormous risk and cost."

"So let's talk about the downside, the slide into the pit. What happens?"

"Larry said to me once, 'It's nothing I can readily describe. It's a moment, a state when the lights go out but you can still see, and what you do see is horror. There is no value left in anything, least of all in yourself. The easiest solution is to kill yourself. The hardest is to stay alive, because there is no tomorrow left to hope for.'"

"Is the death wish real?"

"Oh, yes. It's real for him, for me, for all of us. You have to understand that and believe it. Otherwise you can't help."

"Be patient with me, Madi. I'm trying to take all this in. Are you telling me you believe Larry has committed suicide?"

"I know that he could, that he might, one day. Deep down I've had to prepare myself for the possibility. But this time, no. I believe he's still alive. I've talked at length with the psychiatrist who has been treating him—I admire her and trust her. She works with me, too, because I have to provide the support for Larry and for the family. She believes that this time Larry has attempted to salvage himself by fugue—by a real flight from the real despair which afflicts him. She says the despair is not yet total. He still retains the hope that the upswing will come as it has come before, but the shame of his present condition is intolerable to him. He must cut and run as far and as fast as he can. There is evidence that this is exactly what he has done—and the evidence also points to the fact that he's been preparing for some time."

"So suicide or flight would not be an impulsive act?"

"Oh, no! It would be the act of a rational man, trying to escape from the madhouse in which nature confines him. It's a primal choice: run or die. If you're lucky you'll outrun the demons one more time."

That was the moment when I had to put the question, the hard question.

"Madi, love, you've explained this so eloquently to me, why couldn't you have done the same with Father? Why couldn't Mama have done it for you? He's not a stupid man. He has his funny formal ways, but he's kind and loving and he wants to understand. He feels that a door has been closed in his face."

She sat silent for a long moment, biting her lip, turning her wedding ring round and round on her finger. Then she laid out the explanation.

"Larry was honest with me. Before we became engaged he told me of his problem. We'd had a long bitter quarrel over something quite trivial, and I was sure everything was over between us. Next morning he telephoned, and I agreed to meet him for coffee. He was deeply ashamed and eager to make me understand the nature of his problem and how he was attempting to grapple with it. Later, before we announced our engagement, he took me to meet Dr. Alma Levy, who was and still is his psychiatrist. However, he made me promise that what I had learned would remain a secret between us. He felt that if any word of his condition got out, his career would be compromised. I remember how he put it: 'Money's a timid animal at the best of times, but if word got out that a loony was playing the market . . . ' We laughed about it then. Dr. Levy agreed that discretion even in the family was desirable.

"It worked, too. Larry has done a magnificent job. So until now I've never had to find the words to explain the situation to Father—and when I did find them they were inadequate. Father felt betrayed by our lack of trust in him. I felt frustrated and angry. Mama tried to mediate between us, but even she failed to see Father's own anxieties. Any public disclosure would be disastrous for Strassberger and its clients. That's why he sent for you—and oh, Carl, am I glad he did!"

"Then say it to him. Don't make him stand out in the cold. Meantime, you and I should keep working. You said a few moments ago that there was evidence Larry had been preparing his disappearance for some time. What evidence?"

"When he didn't come home by Sunday I went through his things. I discovered that he had taken his medicine and the renewal prescriptions as well. On the other hand, he had left behind his wallet with his credit cards, his driver's license, and his passport. On Monday morning I telephoned the U.S. bank. We use a Chase private facility on Madison. The manager is a friend. I discovered that, early on Friday morning, Larry had gone to the bank. He had removed his signature from our joint account, leaving me sole signatory. He made no withdrawal. However, he had cleaned out and closed his personal checking account, which had something like fifty thousand dollars in it. His deposit account had been closed out weeks before."

"Which means that this financial genius was taking off into the wide blue yonder with a wad of cash in his pocket, a doctor's prescription, a bottle of pills, and no identification at all. At first glance he's a certifiable lunatic."

"That's what Father said. I called Dr. Levy. She gave me another reading altogether, a much more sinister one. She reminded me first that a manic-depressive is subject to profligate impulses: big splurges at the gambling table, impulsive buying of cars, jewelry, travel. Larry had had some episodes like that—it was only when the credit card bills came in that he truly realized what he had done. Let me say, though, that it was always his own money he spent, never mine or the children's, or our joint housekeeping Dr. Levy interprets what he has done now as an effort to insulate us from the consequences of anything he may do in the future."

"But for God's sake, Madi—"

"Don't say any more, Carl. You don't know enough yet!"

"I'm sorry. Please go ahead."

"Leaving without identification—again according to Dr. Levy—says several things: Larry is not Larry anymore. He has stepped out of his old identity and assumed a new one. Therefore we shouldn't look for the old Larry, but let the new one walk his own road. However, he does cherish some kind of hope that his old self may be available to him again. Therefore he leaves the proofs of it here with me."

"In that case he must have assembled a similar set of proofs for his new identity."

"He could do that anywhere. There's a whole international market for such things if you know where to look."

"And if you have money to pay for them."

"Oh, Larry has money, lots of it: his inheritance, his personal savings, the profits from his own market trading. That was the first thing Father's investigators did—follow the money trail. They found that over the past four months Larry had rearranged all his finances. Two thirds of everything he passed to me and the children by way of a gift within the family. The other third, which is still substantial, he kept for himself and transferred abroad."

"What about his shares in Strassberger?"

"All we know is that so far there is no record of sale or transfer. There is no mention of them in the letter from the attorney in New York advising us of the dispositions Larry made for us. I'll show you that later. It simply says, 'Our client instructs us to inform you. . . . ' That sort of thing."

"What about Larry's transactions on his own behalf?"

"Father's investigators traced most of those. They all ended at the same destination—a small private bank in Geneva, which, naturally enough, refuses to divulge any information."

"How small is the bank? How private?"

"Very small, very private. Its president is one Dr. Hubert Rubens. Father's Swiss colleagues know the man and the bank. Their comment is typical: 'Little is known of the scope of its operations. Nothing is recorded to its discredit. All our dealings have been satisfactory and within the norms of banking practice.'"

"Does Father have any comment?"

"He just frowns and says Larry must have been doing some very offbeat research."

"Have you told Father everything you've told me?"

"Everything. I wish I could be sure he understands the real

12

nature of Larry's problem. He still talks about a 'nervous break-down,' like an old horse-and-buggy doctor!"

"Be patient with him. You'd find the same difficulty if you had to conduct a conversation about modern banking."

"I know. Don't scold me, please."

"My next question's a delicate one. This new, born-again Larry has cut loose. He can be and do whatever he wants. What identity, what lifestyle will he choose? In other words, what are the other faces of the man you married?"

"I have nightmares about that."

"Whom do you see in the nightmares?"

"An actor, Carl." The answer came in a rush of passionate words. "A great actor going through a whole repertoire of parts: rich man, poor man, beggar man, thief, great lover, sad clown. . . . Each role is a mockery of himself—and of me! I know that's unfair, because Larry was never intentionally cruel. Dr. Levy explains that he's had to live half his life behind a mask of urban-ity and sobriety. He couldn't share the wild triumph of the highs. He dared not reveal the squalid terror of the lows. Even with us, his family, there was always some concealment. One day I taxed him with it. He told me, 'I'm trying to cast out my own devils, Madi. I don't want you and the children to share my seasons in hell.' We had to share them anyway. Now he's given me a hell of my own." Then abruptly she ended the interrogation. "Enough for now, Carl! I don't want Father to see me weeping."

"Why not, for Christ's sake? It would do us all good to shed a few tears together."

There were no tears at my mother's luncheon table. Her imperi-ous presence imposed calm upon us all.

According to Berthe Alexandra Strassberger, a meal should be a civilizing ritual, and respect should be paid to the food and to the good appetite of those who share it. She would have no business talked until the coffee was served. Then she surveyed us all serenely and said, "I assume we are all agreed on what must now be done?"

13

It seemed to me a very large assumption, but it was not my place to say so. My father had first right of reply. He was very respectful.

"My dear Berthe, we have not agreed on anything yet. We have had only a couple of hours with Carl. It has taken all that time to give him the information we have."

She turned to me.

"But you are willing to help us, Carl?"

"Of course, Mama."

"Then tell him, Emil! Tell him what is proposed. Then let Carl speak his own mind."

"Very well. Here's where we stand at this moment. The Suez deal has been announced to the financial press. The Strassberger name stands high in the market. No announcement has yet been made about Larry's disappearance. I propose—and Mama and Madeleine agree—that we release a statement to the effect that on medical advice Larry has taken extended leave to recuperate from the labors of the last few months. It's near enough to the truth, and it enables us to invoke medical confidentiality with the press."

"I don't like the idea. Any lie you tell will later carry its own penalties."

"Please let me finish. At the same time, though not necessarily in the same statement, we announce that you, Carl, have rejoined the firm as special assistant to the president. Your assignment will be to review, strengthen, and extend our international operations. In fact you will be searching for Larry, and you will have the name and the resources of the company to support you. Your salary will more than compensate you for any delays or losses on your personal projects. I know this comes as a surprise, but I hope—we all hope—you will agree to the arrangement. If you do agree, you yourself will be the sole arbiter of what is told and to whom."

I should have known that there's no such thing as a free lunch. I should also have known that when Berthe Strassberger lays her silken hand on your wrist and smiles into your eyes, when Emil Strassberger hits you with a sandbag, you drop to the canvas and stay there for the full count.

14

By the time I had my wits together again, Madi had gone home to her children, my mother had retired for her afternoon rest, and I was closeted with my father in his study, plotting the search for Larry Lucas. It was only when we were private that my father put his true thoughts into words.

"If Madeleine is right, you'll come upon Larry sooner or later or he'll drift back when this crisis is over."

"And if she's wrong?"

"Then I'll make an each-way bet. He's dead already, or somewhere along the line he's gone over the edge."

It was too loaded a phrase to let pass.

"What exactly do you mean?"

"Exactly? I can't say. In the most general terms I mean that Larry could step over the edge of acceptable social behavior—he's done it already by this flight—and you could find yourself chasing a rogue."

"But you said he checked out clean with your auditors."

"He did, completely. What bothers me is the degree of premeditation in his exit. If you accept Madeleine's explanation and the opinions of Dr. Levy, it represents a rational act of desperation. I find that hard to believe, against the cyclic pattern of mania and depression which they describe. Remember, I've worked with Larry. I've seen him in highs and lows—and found him equally hard to deal with in either state. That's my fault, not his. But I'm convinced of one thing: Whatever Larry said about himself, on the upswing or the downswing, it was never quite the whole truth. Understand me! I'm not saying he lied. I accept the element of illusion at both extremes of the experience. I can guess, at least, the loneliness of his suffering. But I have to relieve him of his directorship. He's a loose cannon now, with a fistful of our shares in his pocket."

"Have you told Madeleine?"

"Not yet."

"Have you told Mama?"

"I don't have to tell anything to your mother. She reads my mind."

"And what does she say?"

15

"I'll give it to you verbatim: 'Your daughter and her children have to live with what Larry is and what he does. Keep your unhappy thoughts to yourself.' She's right, of course. She's right most of the time. But you're different."

"How different?"

"You're a huntsman now, trying to raise a fox. Just be warned: You may raise a wolf instead."

2

DR. ALMA LEVY WAS WHAT MY elders used to call 'an impressive woman." She reminded me instantly of the Raphael study for the muse Erato, which I had seen years ago in Vienna. There was the same aquiline nose, the same opulent mouth, the strong thrusting jaw. Her black hair was streaked with gray. Her eyes were dark. Her skin was swarthy but smooth as fine leather. I judged her to be somewhere in her early fifties, and I was struck both by the unconscious arrogance and the repose of her demeanor. She might have been a desert princess who had consented to sit for a portrait while she made her own critical study of the painter.

Madeleine, who had made the appointment for me, had also given me a warning: "She can be intimidating. She refuses to waste time fencing. If you're not frank with her, she'll break off the interview."

So I came to Dr. Levy with a whole list of prepared questions. Much to my surprise she began by questioning *me*.

"Suppose you do find Larry Lucas. What will you do?"

"To be quite frank, Doctor, I'm damned if I know!"

For the first time her eyes lit up and a faint smile twitched at the corners of her mouth.

"Do you think you are qualified to deal with him on any level?"

"No."

"But you have assumed that responsibility?"

"That's not quite correct. I've undertaken to search for him. I'll have no hesitation in asking for whatever help I need. I am funded to pay for it."

"How well do you know Larry?"

"Come to think of it, not very well. I was already on my way out of the firm when he came into it. His courtship of my sister began after I had left for Europe."

"How did you feel about his presence in the company and in the family?"

"I was happy on both counts. It seemed to solve a problem for my father. Larry was an asset to the organization. Madeleine was happy. For myself, I had everything I wanted: a reasonable income and the freedom to pursue my own career. Until I was summoned back to New York, I had no knowledge of Larry's ailment. All I know now is what Madi explained to me yesterday."

"You may rely on her explanation. She is intelligent and instructed, but, to put it bluntly, you yourself are not competent to give Larry any help."

"I agree. All I am really able to do is pick up his tracks, using the Strassberger networks and my own personal contacts in a different world altogether. Even if I find him, I can't dictate what he does with his life."

"After we have finished here, what will you do?"

"I'll talk to my father's investigators and try to follow what the newspapers call the money trail, but you must know better than I that I am chasing a phantom. I asked my sister what sort of a profile she could give me on her husband. She told me I was looking for a great actor who could assume any one of a dozen roles. She also told me, by the way, that she had for a long time come to terms with the possibility of Larry's suicide. I'd like to know whether you have any comments on that."

There was another long silence. She raised her hands from the table, putting her fingertips together and touching them to her lips. She seemed to be staring not at me but at some far point on the horizon. When at last she spoke, there was a tone of gentleness in her voice.

"I have given a lot of thought over the years, Mr. Strassberger, to what are called professional ethics, particularly as they touch the privacy of the patient. Sometimes there is a clear conflict between the patient's relative right to privacy and his absolute need of help. I am not talking here in legal terms but in moral ones. I am a healer. I find still that the best guide for me is a line from the Hippocratic oath 'never to do harm or injury.' I agree with the family's decision to exclude the police—for the moment at least. Before you came this morning I knew that I would have to decide on the risks of any communication I made to you. I had to gauge whether you could, now or later, use that information to harm my patient."

"And what have you decided, Doctor?"

"For my patient's sake, I have to trust you."

"Thank you for your confidence."

"I have little confidence in human nature, Mr. Strassberger. I see too many of its frailties. I'm betting on you because you were prepared to confess both ignorance and incompetence. What do you think you need from me?"

"An opinion first. Do you believe your patient is alive or dead?"

"I believe he is alive. I can't guarantee it."

"If he is alive, what role would you guess he is playing?"

Her answer came back sharp as a whiplash.

"The nearest he can get to yours, Mr. Strassberger."

"What do you mean?"

"One of the recurrent themes in my sessions with Larry was what he called 'bond service.' In periods of self-disgust, he felt enslaved, chained by circumstances in his education, by his ailment itself, and by his own talent, to the job and the family he had chosen. Worst of all, his chains were his salvation. He needed the order and the discipline they imposed. They were, in a fashion, the substitute for the parents he had lost. You, on the other hand, had escaped. You had thrown off the bonds and

19

been rewarded for doing it. He saw you sometimes with resentment but generally with reluctant admiration as the miracle escapee from Devil's Island. He despised himself as an animal which could only survive in captivity. The greater his self-contempt, the stronger the urge to flee from the self."

"By hiding behind a fictitious identity?"

"By any means available."

"How many lives can he live, for God's sake?"

"I would guess quite a lot. Your sister estimates his disposable worth at something like five or six million dollars."

"He could have himself quite a party with that sort of money."

"Unless he chose to make some wild gesture of renunciation and throw it all to the winds."

"He knows too much about the money game to strip himself naked like—like an Indian fakir or Francis of Assisi."

"I am trying to tell you"—Dr. Levy was grave but surprisingly patient—"that even I would not dare to predict the extremes of manic-depressive behavior. Once you accept that suicide is a possible outcome, you're left with a big grab-bag of other choices—and all of them will be highly reasoned in the frames of their own distorted logic. The mountain peaks of mania are dizzy ecstatic places, over which the patient, in his illusion, soars like an eagle. The valleys into which he plunges afterward are deep, dark, and noisome with the stink of carrion. He cannot claw his way out because the walls are too steep and too smooth. The horror of that situation is so intense that reason rocks with the pain of it. It is like being manacled to a corpse. The only salvation is in oblivion."

"It sounds like a foretaste of hell."

"It *is* hell, Mr. Strassberger, and the torment is increased because most patients cannot find words to express it. You will understand, of course, that I am describing extreme symptoms. You must understand also that the disease—and it is a disease—is by nature cyclical and progressive. It is also, in a certain sense, infectious because everyone who has any relationship with the patient is touched by it in some fashion."

20

"Madeleine put it another way. She said there are times when you run out of love."

"Your sister's a wise woman. She also has great courage."

"I hesitate to ask this next question, but I have to guess the company Larry may seek out in his exile. What happens to his sex life?"

"In general, the libido is seriously diminished in the depressive phases. On the manic swings it is increased and may assume aggressive forms."

"Aggressive in what sense?"

"At one end of the scale, very assertive demonstrations of desire and potency; at the other, resentful violence."

"Madeleine told me Larry had never been violent with her or the children. She did admit to witnessing violent outbursts."

"Then you should content yourself with that and spare her further questions." It was a clear warning and I accepted it. Alma Levy went on more mildly. "However, on the larger issue of what company Larry may seek out, consider that he has to create a charmed circle within which his new identity will not be challenged. He will, therefore, avoid long-term intimacies and seek the kind of society in which he can assume, like a chameleon, a protective coloration. He will avoid places and events where a chance encounter or photograph may betray him."

"Do you think he's thought through all these risks?"

"Yes. That's what troubles me: the element of premeditation."

"Why does it trouble you?"

This time I was warned very firmly.

"I don't think I'm prepared to discuss that at this moment. It could involve speculation damaging to my patient."

"Then you should know, Doctor, that other people have begun to speculate."

She was instantly alert and hostile.

"What other people? What are they saying?"

"My father, who has worked very closely with Larry, has expressed a fear that he could step over the edge of acceptable social behavior and that, quote, I could find myself chasing a rogue."

21

Doctor Alma Levy sat in silence, considering this proposition. Her eyes were hooded and her mouth was closed like a trap. It seemed a long time before she acknowledged my presence again. Her next words were chosen with meticulous care:

"We are talking here of survival, Mr. Strassberger, survival at the extremity of suffering. The condition of the patient is like that of a victim in a torture chamber. There is no hope of escape. The only hope is that the torturers will tire or that you will die before too long. In this situation there is no morality. No judgment can be passed on what the victim may say or do to win a moment's relief from torment. In that sense your father is right. In another he is quite wrong, because he is passing judgment on a person whose suffering he cannot share and can never, never understand. So, yes! You may find yourself pursuing a rogue, but you must not presume to sit in judgment on him! The kindest thing you can do is bring him back to me as quickly as possible. I am still his physician. He needs my care."

"I believe you, Doctor, but forgive me if I press the point: My father is a shrewd man; he is not a malicious one. His daughter and his grandchildren are involved here. He expressed himself to me in much more serious terms. That suggested, rightly or wrongly, a more active, more hostile situation."

The silence this time was longer; the words, when they came, were less eloquent and more hesitant.

"Mr. Strassberger, please try to understand something. I have certain skills in my profession, but I am not God. I cannot draw you a chart of every human psyche. I walk with every one of my patients through dark and tortuous places. Every new interview brings new perils.

"You talk about hostility. That's a word that covers a whole gamut of attitudes. In the case of the depressive the hostility is directed first against the self, but it is expressed against others . . . sometimes, I regret to say, with tragic results. But this transference is a fact of daily life. The most normal of us understand the 'why me?' reaction when tragedy or disease strikes in our lives. If and when you meet Larry Lucas again, will he be hostile to you? Probably. You will have torn off

22

whatever carnival mask he is wearing. Then again, he may be grateful that the whole charade is ended and that his family has cared enough to mount a search for him and coax him back to a more normal existence.

"Depressive illness can be palliated, if not cured. What can I tell you? Sometimes people do shoot the messenger. Sometimes they even try to kill the healer. I hope you are understanding me, Mr. Strassberger, because there isn't too much more I can tell you—unless you want to listen to an hour of clinical jargon."

Suddenly I was seeing not an arrogant professional but a weary, middle-aged woman carrying the burden of too many muddled lives. The interview was ended. It was twenty minutes past midday, but I felt I should take my leave with something better than a good-bye and a thank you. I asked, hesitantly, whether I might have the privilege of taking her to lunch. She smiled for the first time.

"It's very kind of you, Mr. Strassberger; but whenever the weather's good enough I like to spend my lunch hour in Central Park. I watch the children and envy the lovers and feed the scraps of my sandwiches to the ducks. You'd be bored to tears."

"On the contrary, I'd be honored. I'll buy my own sandwich and I promise not to talk about your business or Strassberger."

"On the other hand, I'd be interested to hear how you live your life."

And that was how I spent my own private, unpaid session with Dr. Alma Levy. We sat on the grass, ate sandwiches, drank lemonade from paper cups, and never once talked of the demons who haunted her life. I did a sketch of her on a cardboard box lid which I picked out of a trash can. She commanded me to keep in touch with her and promised, on my return, to cook dinner for me in her apartment. When I left her at the door of her office she laid a fleeting hand on my cheek and offered something that sounded like a blessing.

"Thank you for my portrait. This has been one of the few hours when I have regretted that I am not twenty years younger. God has been good to you, Carl Emil. Be sure you are gentle with my patient."

* * *

At two-thirty in the afternoon I was given a completely different portrait of Larry Lucas. It was displayed to me on a large computer screen in a conference room in the offices of an organization called Corsec Inc. on Madison Avenue. The man who interpreted it to me was named Giorgiu Andrescu—George for short. He was somewhere in his early twenties, dressed in faded jeans, scuffed loafers, and a tired-looking plaid shirt. He peered at me through thick pebble spectacles. He looked like a very scruffy student, but his tone was that of a faintly patronizing lecturer dealing with a dull pupil.

"Corsec is of course an acronym for corporate security, and we are among the front-runners in the field. We have our own intercontinental networks of surveillance and information. We protect them against hackers with the most sophisticated fire walls available. Strassberger and Company is one of our most valued clients, and I am their account executive. You can contact me on-line through any of our offices around the world. The Lucas file will be updated with any information you send us, while at the same time we can extend our inquiries in any new direction you may indicate."

Without comment he punched up on the screen a number of information items: a series of photographs of Larry, specimens of his signature, and a basic biography up to the day of his disappearance.

"By the use of reimaging techniques we can show you what Lucas would look like with a beard, with spectacles, with his head shaved and so on. Lucas's wife and Mr. Strassberger senior have both checked the biographical details and pronounced them accurate. Do you have any comments on them, Mr. Strassberger?"

The only comment, which I forbore to make, was that Larry Lucas was a handsome devil who could turn the heads of most women in a restaurant. If there was misery inside him, it didn't show in his eyes, and there was a quirky grin lurking at the corners of his upturned mouth. A good companion, you would have said, for work or play; I could understand my father's puritan impulse to take him down a peg.

24

Andrescu then punched up a recall of Larry's career with Strassberger. Again it was a no-comment routine. The records of the internal audit of his activities in Europe were summarized, with an indication that the auditors were prepared to sign off without qualification. Giorgiu Andrescu, however, had a few qualifications of his own.

"You have to understand, Mr. Strassberger, that we have been greatly handicapped in our inquiries by the fact that Lucas is still an active director, and no mention has been made of his disappearance. That's an absolute impediment to any further work on our part. It prevents us from seeking any information from office staff or Strassberger clients."

"I see the difficulty, of course. We may well have to go public in the end. But let's not rush that decision."

"Of course!" Andrescu the good account executive was in instant agreement. "And our fire-wall system is designed specifically to prevent such leaks."

He punched up frame after frame of information—bank records, summaries of legal meetings, credit card statements—explaining each group of items as it came on screen. He summed up wearily. "The guy's an open book. Even his engagement diary checks out. Everything relates to the job he came to do. The IRS would give him a medal for meritorious conduct. Financially he's virgin clean."

"Did he play at all?"

"If he did, it was a long way from the office. But think about it! He spent only four and a half days a week in Paris. Given the size of the job he had to do, he didn't get much playtime."

"No office romances?"

"None we've heard about."

"After hours?"

"He jogged every morning from six to seven and generally had breakfast with one or another of his opposite numbers in the negotiating team. At the end of the day he'd work out at the Apollon Health Club near Strassberger's office. I tell you, Mr. Strassberger, this guy was a good soldier. He kept himself in trim—and, so far as our information goes, kept his hormones under control."

"And he spent all his time in Paris?"

"Most of it. Let's take a look at travel. Here we are. There were regular trips to London to confer with British attorneys. Most of those were day trips: out early morning, back in time for dinner. There were, let's see, four trips to Geneva, all except one of those was a same-day return. That's where Dr. Hubert Rubens pops into the record. The appointments were made in each case by Claudine Parmentier, who was—I guess still is, technically—Lucas's secretary in Paris. They're recorded in Lucas's diary and hers, but they were charged to him and not to the company; that was established in the office audit."

"Any other variants like that?"

"A couple. There are two overnight visits to Milan. The diary notation for these is an acronym, SVEEO. Claudine again made the bookings and charged them to Larry Lucas. He did not explain what the acronym meant. She didn't ask him. He was that kind of guy. He could be very brusque if you caught him on the wrong day."

"How does she feel about him?"

"We haven't asked. We haven't done that sort of intelligence roundup yet. How could we? We were supposed to be doing just a snap audit on the office, not on the individual. However, apart from indicating that Lucas was exacting—the impression was that she respected the guy, even liked him."

"No surprise in that. Larry was a very likable fellow."

Suddenly, a notation on the screen caught my eye: a ten-day absence from the office, not covered by travel vouchers. I asked what that meant. Giorgiu Andrescu had the answer on the tip of his tongue.

"Mr. Lucas had invited the principals from each side, with their own advisers, to a week's cruise round the Balearic Islands: Majorca, Minorca, Ibiza. Apparently a logjam was building up and he thought this might be a good way to clear it."

"Who made the charter arrangements?"

"I assume Lucas did."

"But the charter doesn't show up in the audit. That would have had to be a largeish item."

"I agree; but the fact is, neither the contract nor the payment is recorded. There is, however, a diary note: *Out-of-Paris conference authorized by Mr. Emil Strassberger*. One has to think that for some reason settlement was made through the New York office."

I made a note of the dates and told Andrescu I would refer the matter to my father. I asked whether he had anything more to show me.

"No. What you've seen is all we've got. I'll give you a print-out before you leave."

"Thank you. Meantime, keep the file active. I'll feed you whatever new information I get."

"May I make a suggestion?"

"Go ahead."

"At the moment, under our existing instructions, we're hand-icapped and grossly underused. Believe me, Mr. Strassberger, all you've seen today is old-hat junior-grade storage and retrieval. But once you give us a free hand, you'll be surprised at the information we can deliver. You don't ask and we don't tell you where it comes from; but we do guarantee its authenticity. Think about it, Mr. Strassberger. Talk about it with your father."

I promised him I would think about it. I also thought very seriously that before Giorgiu Andrescu was thirty he and his peers would be running the world, because they would control access to all the world's secrets. I had the uneasy feeling that no matter how much we paid them to serve our interests, they would always be holding a spare ace up their sleeves.

When I went to his office in the late fall of that Monday afternoon, my father was in a dark mood. The stock market was falling dangerously fast, and he had spent all day trying to hedge his positions around the world. Tokyo, Hong Kong, Sydney, and Singapore had all shut up shop. New York had steadied a little before the close of business. The West Coast was still fluttering about within a narrow margin. When I asked him how he was faring, he shrugged unhappily.

"We're holding, Carl, but it's a goddamned bazaar out there: pimps, harlots, hucksters, and sellers of snake oil. No sooner do you find yourself a foothold than the raiders move in and try to cut it out from under you. . . . I'm getting tired, son, beginning to think it might be nice to have someone mount a raid on me. Right now, if the price was right, I'd take the money and run."

"Would you really?"

"Try me!" He summoned up a reluctant smile. "A drink to say good-bye to a lousy day. Join me?"

"Thanks. I could use one too."

While he was pouring the liquor he talked to me over his shoulder.

"Tell me about your day."

I told him about Giorgiu Andrescu and the missing vouchers for Larry's ten-day cruise. My father burst out laughing. He laughed so immoderately that the decanter shook in his hand and some of the whiskey splashed on the glass top of the liquor cupboard.

"There! That's exactly what I mean. It's a crime what we pay the Corsec people for what they are pleased to call security. They're like the old sorcerers, peddling black magic! The reason there's no financial record of Larry's charter cruise is very simple: He never made the trip. He talked about it with me. I told him he could do whatever he thought best for the deal. I did say to him, however, that he ought to think twice about such a maneuver. I've been in that position many times. Everything seems to grind to a halt. Nobody's got a single new idea. The gears are frozen.

"I suggested to Larry that, instead of taking his troubles away with him, he should walk away from them and be private for a while: unwind, free up the gears. I couldn't put a name to it then, as I can now, but obviously he was in a deep depression. He talked about coming home for a week. I talked him out of that. I suggested he give himself a total break from business and family. The deal was on track, it wouldn't hurt to let it coast awhile. . . . The reason there are no vouchers is that Larry finally accepted my advice but insisted on paying for his own holiday."

"Wherever he went, none of the reservations were made from his office."

"I can understand that. If you want a complete break, you don't let anyone know where you're going. What else did Andrescu tell you?"

"Nothing you don't already know. He gave me the same printout you have. But he did suggest that if we gave them free hand and didn't ask questions about their sources, they could deliver a lot more information."

"And how much more does that cost us? Already we have them on a fat retainer."

"Why not offer a reward for information leading to the discovery of Larry Lucas?"

He thought about it for a few moments and then nodded his agreement.

"If they'll come at it, fine—but it has to be a handshake deal, no documents. We can't risk an invasion-of-privacy suit. We depend on them for clean information, they depend on us for prompt settlement."

"How much are you prepared to offer?"

"A quarter of a million, tops."

"I'll try it; but there's something else you and I have to decide right now. What are we going to tell your senior people here? What am I going to tell the staff in Paris?"

"The truth—part of it, at least. Larry has done a big job for the house of Strassberger. Everybody profits from that. His financial records are impeccable. Larry, however, has succumbed to a depressive illness and on the advice of his physician has taken extended leave to recuperate. This is not a business scandal but a painful family misfortune. The press response will be minimal, because no crime has been imputed or committed. There is an element of personal tragedy in the situation of a successful man, stricken in a moment of triumph. Our staff will be discreet, because they've all got deals cooking and the Strassberger name is their shield and protection.

"Once that news is planted and circulated, then you, Carl, can gently insert the supplements—what may happen in such episodes: suicide, flight. . . . I know it's a handicap in your inquiries, but any other course could damage us and would certainly be ruinous to Larry's later career—if he has one."

As always, I had to admire the swift, pragmatic fashion in which he had summarized and addressed the situation. At the same time I noted how much the experience—and perhaps the guilt—had aged him: nevertheless, I could not spare him Dr. Levy's blunt message. I tried to phrase it as tactfully as I could, but he waved me on impatiently.

"Say it, Carl! Say it! Otherwise it will stick like a fishbone in your craw."

While I was talking he crossed to the cabinet again, splashed more Scotch into his drink, and tossed off half of it at a gulp. It was the first time in my life I had ever seen him take refuge behind a highball glass, and I was curiously shocked. He heard me out in silence and then perched himself on the corner of his desk while he sipped slowly at the rest of his liquor. Finally, phrase by deliberate phrase, he set down his confession.

"Dr. Levy is quite correct. In one sense, I have no right at all to judge Larry. I can't share his suffering because I can't even conceive of its nature. I'll admit, too, that I drove him too hard and offered him too little praise or credit. You'll never know, Carl, how much I hated losing you from the business and the family. In certain lights, in certain moods, I tended to see Larry as an intruder, taking over my daughter and your birthright in the business. Sure he was paying with toil and blood for his interest, but I couldn't admit that to myself, let alone confess it to him. Right here and now there's a small, nasty voice reminding me that I might even be glad of what's happened to Larry if it brought you back into the company."

I knew what he needed from me at that moment: some gentling words, some expression of understanding, if not hope, for the dynastic survival of the Strassberger family. He wasn't asking for oaths and promises, just enough reassurance to lighten the burden of the moment. I couldn't give it to him. The same niggardly imp which plagued him was whispering in my ear too, telling me that I should not, could not, make any concession that might later be held against me as a pledge of service. So—God help me!—I let the moment pass and the good words remained unsaid.

The rest of our talk was banality: who among senior staff should be informed first; who were the stout hearts, who could be trusted with secrets, and who were the gossips in the market-place; how I should answer questions about my function with the company; what authorities and documents I would need for Paris—and was Paris the right place to begin my inquiries? We debated that one until it was time for the pair of us to go home and share the cocktail hour with my mother.

After that, I was committed to dinner with Madeleine and a last walk with her through the thickets of a difficult marriage.

The evening was a long-drawn-out affair. First there was my bed-time story for the children: Marianne, a blond beauty, five years old but endowed with the wisdom of centuries, and Laurence Emil, two years her senior, already complaining about the tyranny of the women in his life.

The stories I told them were Aesop's fables. They are very short and they are also easy to illustrate with quick cartoon sketches: the fox and the grapes, the greedy dog dropping his bone into the water. Each child was tucked under the covers with a good-night kiss and a private icon from Uncle Carl perched on the bedside table. Uncle Carl crept out of each room enriched by a brief vision of innocence and haunted by the image of another man fleeing headlong across a plague-stricken landscape.

Dinner was an easy meal. The same mother had trained us both to honor the cook and enjoy the food, so we left the skele-tons hanging in the cupboards and talked lightly of pleasant matters: childhood memories, old friends and their new adven-tures in love or out of it, what I was doing and why I wasn't planning to get married, and how easily I could turn into a gray-beard laboring over an interminable manuscript in a wintry barn.

By the time the meal was over, we were both a little manic on memories. The sound of the mantel clock chiming ten imposed a sudden prickling silence on us both. Madeleine stood up, led me into the drawing room, then curled up defensively in the armchair opposite mine.

"You look just like Father, when he's playing Grand Inquisitor," she said.

"I feel like an invader. Please, try not to be angry with me."

"I'm not angry, but I can't help feeling embarrassed."

"You said Larry left all his documents here in the house?"

"Yes."

"His pocket diary? His address book?"

"They're both here."

"What about his clothes?"

"Part of his wardrobe's in Paris."

"Where?"

"At his hotel—Le Diplomate. They store personal effects for regular guests."

"I thought he was finished in Paris."

"He knew he'd have to go back on business arising out of this recent deal, as well as on routine company matters. It was something we all took for granted."

"Has anyone checked Le Diplomate to see if the clothes are still there?"

"Yes. They're still in storage, as he left them."

"Have you been through his clothes here?"

"Every garment that has a pocket in it—nothing, nothing, nothing!"

"His study, his desk, his files . . . ?"

"Those too. The Corsec people have been through everything. That Mr. Andrescu was like a ferret in a rabbit hole!"

"To the best of your knowledge, are there any other women in Larry's life? Any affairs?"

"To the best of my knowledge, no. But if there were—"

She broke off. I waited a moment, then prompted her.

"If there were. . . ?"

"I hope I'd be able to cope with it. Dr. Levy has taught me to understand that at certain critical moments Larry has no sense of

32

moral responsibility at all, to me, the children, or anyone else. He's not joined to us in any social sense. He is simply a spectator. We are like actors on a movie screen."

"But when we first talked, you described him as a highly intelligent man: a good husband, you said; a loving father."

"I also said that at certain moments reason goes out the window, that he's an actor playing one role after another—and watching himself as he does it. . . . And since we're talking about women, let me tell you that Larry can be a wonderful lover. The problem is he knows it—as a good actor knows how to handle an audience, while remaining detached from it."

"Does he act like this with you too?"

"Occasionally with me—but not when he's himself. You may not believe that; but I can distinguish one state from the other."

"But you do admit Larry's a manipulator?"

"Yes."

"How can you bear that?"

"Sometimes I can't."

"What sort of women attract him—at a party, for instance?"

"When he's on the climb, it's the aggressive beauties, the challengers. When he's on the downward run"—she gave a small rueful laugh—"it's the tender ones, the comforters, the old-fashioned motherers like me! Even in his wildest moments he needs to know there's a safety net, because he knows that sooner or later he'll come tumbling down from the mountain."

"So where do I look for him now?"

"On the high slopes and the wild side."

"That doesn't tell me much."

"I think you have to start in Paris."

"Why?"

"He's been working there all these months. He planned this exit, his escape, from there. My guess is that's where he procured whatever new documents he has."

"But why would he go back on his tracks?"

"Carl, all this is a guessing game, but there are things Larry used to say about the city and the people that contain a clue. One phrase he used stuck in my mind. He said, 'Paris is a haunting place. It's as I imagine Rome must have been, drowning in the backwash of a vanished empire . . . Algeria, Africa, Indochina, the Americas, the Pacific Islands—the whole world is different when you look at it from the Eiffel Tower.'"

"So you're saying he'd start his flight from there?"

"I can't be sure. I've talked this out with Dr. Levy. She believes that this act of fugue—of desperate retreat—will turn into a macabre adventure. The adrenaline will start pumping again, the brain chemistry will change, and he'll be launched into another manic episode."

"And how long could that last?"

"I don't know." She faltered but managed to hold her composure. "It seems I don't know anything anymore. Look! You've never experienced a manic episode. You may have seen one but not been able to identify what it meant." She was instantly animated, an actress eager to demonstrate a scene. "This is Larry on a high. The day's over, it's been a good one. He comes home almost at a run. He sweeps me into his arms, demands that I make the drinks. While I'm doing that, the kids are swarming all over him, thrilled to be in his company. He's a whole circus in himself. I'm drawn into the performance. He drives us all along like a ringmaster. . . .

"I see what's happening: I try to slow down the whirl of action. I can't. Larry's out of control. The kids are getting hysterical. Something is bound to happen—it always does—a glass is broken, Marianne falls and hurts herself, the game ends in tears. Larry goes off to bathe and change. I am left to clear up the mess and calm the little ones and wonder which Larry will be down for dinner: the happy one, oblivious of the chaos he has caused, or the other one, perched on the cusp of change, moody, withdrawn, resentful, afraid of the dark which he knows will soon envelop him again. I have to be ready to treat with either one on a plane of normality. The children are settled. I remind him to kiss them good night. I ask him to uncork the dinner wine, to try a spoonful of the sauce, tell me if there is enough spice in it. . . .

"It's hard labor, Carl. If he's on the downturn it's labor lost. If he's still on the upswing, he resents the distraction. All my attention must be focused on him—'To hell with the sauce and the spices, I've got the most wonderful plans!' They do sound wonderful. So it's easier to go with the swing than to fight it, and the lovemaking afterward is so wonderful I can almost forget the fear that came first and the grief that will follow sooner or later. . . . "Would you pour me a brandy, please?"

I was pouring the liquor so I didn't have to meet her eyes as I asked the next question.

"Are you sure he'll come back?"

"No. I'm not sure. After all, he did make a settlement on me and the children, which is more or less equivalent to the amount we could get in a divorce. So maybe that's what he wants: to cut clean and start again. On the other hand, abrupt changes are symptoms of the illness. What he wants today he will reject tomorrow."

I handed her the brandy and tilted her chin up so that she was forced to look at me.

"I need a straight answer to this one, Madi," I told her. "Do you want Larry back in your life, in this house, as your husband?"

When she did not answer immediately, I returned to my own chair. She sat, eyes downcast, twisting the wedding band on her finger as I had seen her do at the office. There was a chill in her answer like the first breath of winter.

"I know what you're asking, Carl, and why you have to ask it. Dr. Levy warned me long ago that Larry would infect me with his own disease. That's exactly what has happened, in the sense that I'm forced to live in his rhythms. But deep down, I know the price I'm paying for the occasional joy is too high. There are too many agonies and uncertainties. But don't you see? The children need him, need what he can still give them as a father. I can't deny them their right to him. He loves them, they love him. Besides, he's a sick man. I can't let him be put down like an ailing animal. I can't bear the thought that he's somewhere out there trapped in his private hell with nobody to open the door for him."

She broke then. She covered her face with her hands and huddled in her chair, weeping quietly. I knelt beside her, stroking her hair, murmuring small words, remembering how much, even as a child, she had needed the comfort of physical contact. Finally, when her tears were spent, she dried her eyes with my handkerchief, demanded another brandy, and led me upstairs to inspect the relics and personal effects of Laurence Lucas, missing in action on some far frontier of human experience.

3

MARC ANTOINE VIANNEY, our executive director for France and the Low Countries, met me at Orly Airport. He was one of the new breed of Eurocrats, young, lean, and fit, impeccably groomed, fluent in several languages and all the jargon of modern business. He was also faintly disdainful of American modes and manners and supremely confident that it was the destiny of France to revitalize Europe and civilize the barbarians beyond the Urals.

All this he managed to convey to me between his first cool handshake at the gate, a hair-raising drive in his Porsche from Orly to Paris, and a highly ceremonious arrival at Le Diplomate, where, he told me, I was booked into the suite recently occupied by my brilliant colleague, Larry Lucas. He suggested that I might prefer to rest a little before lunch. I told him I wanted to begin immediately and continue our discussions over coffee and sandwiches. Fine! Marc Antoine Vianney was as eager as I was to *faire le branle-bas,* clear the decks for action. But first there was a statement he felt duty-bound to make. I invited him to speak with absolute freedom; what he gave me was a barrage of bitter complaints—a firestorm of angers.

"Your father has written and spoken to me but I still have no precise idea of why you are here. I am told you will explain everything to me, but first I have things to explain to you. This company is about to be destroyed—by a collapse of confidence in itself and possibly by a mass defection of its members. Just at the moment when they should be celebrating a commercial triumph, they feel themselves insulted, demeaned, placed under degrading and totally unjustified suspicion."

I opened my mouth to speak but he silenced me with a gesture.

"No! You will hear me out first, Mr. Strassberger. Consider this, consider it carefully: In cooperation with your Mr. Larry Lucas, this office has just brought off a financial triumph of the first magnitude. Everyone down to the humblest file clerk contributed to that triumph. Before he left for New York, Mr. Lucas gave an office party. He paid compliments and handed out personal gifts to everyone. He expressed in glowing terms the thanks of your father and the other principals in New York. He left, trailing clouds of goodwill, with the completed documents in his briefcase. That was—let me remember—on Wednesday. The next day your father sends me a personal note of commendation and a recommendation for special payments at bonus time. That was Thursday. On Sunday night he calls me at home and informs me that a snap audit and a general security check by Corsec will begin on Monday morning. He promises that he will make a full explanation in due course. I am troubled, yes, but I am not yet angry. I have respect for your father. I owe him much in my career with Strassberger and Company; but, when the Corsec people present themselves, it's like a police raid."

"Can you be more specific?"

"Certainly! They were brusque, and impolite. They made demands in a manner that was almost threatening. They gave no explanations. They accepted what they were told with cold reserve, as though we were suspected of a crime."

I knew exactly what he meant. More and more this has become the American way. Money business is conducted with a hard face and a big stick. It gives offense to a lot of people. It certainly would have offended me. Vianney pressed on with his complaint. "This is not our way, not here in this office. We feel, as I have said, insulted and degraded . . . I call your father, he apologizes for any unfortunate impression that may have been created but does not wish to explain the situation over the telephone. He is sending you as a special emissary to make everything clear to us. Frankly, we do not know whether to regard this as an apology or another insult. We have always understood that you are a scholar and an artist living and working here in France. We hear good things of you in your profession. Our common sense tells us that you are not an experienced banker. . . . What more can I say? I hope you understand our position. I hope most fervently that you understand ours and that you will be able to explain the meaning of these extraordinary happenings, not only to me but to my colleagues. Service in Strassberger has always been a matter of pride. We hope—against hope—that our pride may be restored."

In the silence that followed I had to take the measure of the man and of the situation he had described to me. I had no doubt that his grievance was real. On the other hand, I had very strong doubts about my father's handling of the situation. He was a paragon of business rectitude, but in this case, it seemed that his tactics went hopelessly astray. He wanted to preserve at all costs the integrity of the Strassberger reputation. He was trying to protect Larry Lucas as well. He had failed on both counts, because he had refused to trust his own executives and had handed them over to poker-faced investigators from a hard-nosed security outfit. More than this, he had ignored the sensibilities of the French themselves and their long memories of enemy occupation and financial dependence on the United States. Now I had to tell them the truth and try to persuade Vianney to accept it at face value.

"Mr. Vianney, I was not in New York when this affair began. I was in my studio in Cagnes, working happily on a new etching. My father called me, told me he was in the middle of a family crisis, and asked me to come to New York. That, I gather, was more or less what he told you. He didn't want to talk on the phone. He would explain later. Yes?"

Vianney nodded but said nothing. I pressed on, a little more confidently.

39

"As for myself, you're absolutely right. I have no real talent for banking. I became an artist by choice. I can tell you the difference between a derivative and a debenture, and that's the extent of my interest. However, I can see quite clearly the color of the events as you have described them to me. My father is a man of principle but he is not always tactful and he works sometimes in the modes of another generation. So I understand your distress and that of your colleagues. I will see that my father is informed of it as soon as we have finished our talk. You are welcome to be present while I speak to him. I hope by then you will have understood the real reason for these unfortunate events, which is a conflict of interest between family and business. This is a long story. Please be patient and feel free to ask any questions you wish. After that, if you want me to address your colleagues, I shall be happy to do so."

Vianney was puzzled now but still wary. He had expected argument, a spirited plea for the defense. In the same low-key style, I told him the story of Larry Lucas's illness, of his disappearance, and of our fears for his safety. I explained that my presence in Paris was based on pure guesswork, and I quoted Larry's remark to Madeleine: "Paris is a haunting place . . . drowning in the backwash of a vanished empire."

When my story was done, there was another silence, a long one this time. Vianney heaved himself out of his chair, walked over to the window, and stood staring out into the empty air. When he turned to face me, he was as pale as death and his lean features were like a stone mask. His voice was studiously neutral.

"I am glad that you have been open with me, Mr. Strassberger. I believe what you have told me. My only regret is that your father did not place the same trust in me from the beginning."

"I've already explained his dilemma."

"I am beginning to understand it, just as I am beginning to understand Larry: his wild enthusiasms, his passion in argument, his sudden angers. I respected his talents but I could not bring myself to like him or be close to him. We consulted, of course, at every stage—indeed almost every day—but I could not offer him friendship. I left that to others."

"And how did others react to him?"

"The men were divided. Some found him arrogant and abrasive, others were attracted by the very things that repelled me."

"And the women?"

"The women were drawn to him. Almost without exception they described him as charming and considerate."

"What about his angers?"

"Brief but tolerable. That seemed to be the general opinion."

"Did he work closely with any particular woman?"

"When he arrived, I appointed Mademoiselle Claudine Parmentier to act as his personal assistant. She is very good at her job; she has paralegal training; her English is excellent."

"And how did they get along?"

"In the first weeks, not easily. Later they settled into a good working relationship."

"Was the relationship confined to the office?"

Vianney gave me a swift, suspicious look. "Why do you ask that, Mr. Strassberger?"

"I have to find, if I can, someone who was close to him, someone who, perhaps only for a single moment, may have been admitted into his confidence or given a hint of his future plans. There is nothing sinister in my question."

"Then I think you should ask it directly of Mlle. Parmentier. Once again I warn you that our people are sensitive about inquisitors from across the Atlantic."

"Which brings me to the next decision we have to make. You want me to address the staff; how much do I tell them? From this moment we can't afford any mistakes."

"I agree. After listening to you, I recommend a direct personal appeal for help. Your French is fluent—if rather tainted by your residence in the midi." He gave me a ghost of a smile. "No offense, Mr. Strassberger, but I am Parisian born and bred and we too have our parochial prejudices."

I grinned and let the comment pass.

"How much do I reveal?"

"The whole truth. Nothing less will satisfy them. Nothing else will encourage them to offer you information."

"When can you get them together?"

"Shall we say four o'clock this afternoon? Then, if someone wants to talk with you, you can either have coffee in the office or an aperitif elsewhere. As I said, the decision to send in the auditors has left a taste of lemon in everyone's mouth."

"Including yours?"

"Of course, including mine."

"Do you object to my presence in the workplace?"

"Not at all. It's only common sense to work from here. We have, in fact, put you in Larry's old office."

"I'll probably need an assistant."

"That too we can provide." He glanced at his watch. "It's after midday. I don't think I can face coffee and sandwiches. May I offer you lunch at my club?"

"It's a kind thought, but do you mind if I take a rain check? I'd like to shower and change and set a few notes in order before I face the lions at four o'clock."

"Are you afraid of them, my friend? You shouldn't be. They are just ordinary people, good at what they do, resentful that their jobs can be threatened by decisions made on the other side of the Atlantic."

This time the humor was lost on me. I was tired of playing mind games in another language.

"No, I'm not afraid of them, Mr. Vianney," I told him curtly. "If they all walk out at five o'clock tonight, Strassberger will still be in business—and I know at least enough to hold the fort until reinforcements arrive. What I'm really afraid of is a poor bastard with a bee in his bonnet, scuttling around somewhere between here and kingdom come. He's my sister's husband. He's got two small children, and he's got a caring psychiatrist who is herself very fearful of what may happen to him. I'm paying you and your people a compliment. I'm trusting you to think about the threat—the many threats—which hang over Larry Lucas. He's a walking time bomb and I've got to find him before he explodes. This is not a bullfight, so I don't need anyone sticking pics in my hide to soften me up for the matador!"

He was shocked by my outburst but he managed a calm-enough answer.

"I have offended you. I apologize. Before you arrive at the office this afternoon, I shall have briefed the staff, so that you will not be obliged to give long and painful explanations."

"I appreciate that. Thank you."

"I have been angry, yes, but never enough to play games with a man's life. You see, I have experience of Larry Lucas's illness. My eldest brother was a brilliant violinist with a great career before him as a concert performer. He killed himself the night before his first big concert."

"My God, I'm sorry."

"You owe me no sorrow, Mr. Strassberger. But please believe I am not a matador who wants to provoke you first and then kill you in a public spectacle. People purge their grief in many ways; mine is by anger and irony. I'll see you at four o'clock."

Before he walked out, we shook hands. It wasn't exactly an entente cordiale; but at least it was a gesture toward a possible one.

Bathed, changed, and refreshed with coffee and a *croque-monsieur*, I still had two hours to kill before my encounter with the Strassberger staff. I decided to try my luck with one Gerard Marcel Delaunay, doyen of the concierges of Paris, who, like all senior members of the brotherhood, is a very important fellow indeed. He is discreetly rich, and his wealth is daily increased by cash gifts from satisfied clients, by tributes from his staff, and by commissions from all those whose services he mediates: airlines, travel agents, florists, escort agencies, hirers of limousines, operators of bus tours. His power is great and widespread. His arrangements with taxing authorities are also a matter of discreet agreement, because there is no way they can check on all the currency which passes through his hands and they have to content themselves with a reasonably estimated share of the very large revenue.

So my approach to M. Delaunay had to begin with a demonstration of sincere respect. I called his office, introduced myself as the latest occupant of the Strassberger suite, and asked if he would grant me the privilege of a fifteen-minute interview in private as soon as possible. His condescension was almost regal. He was inordinately busy, but he would be happy to receive me in twenty minutes. I thanked him and hung up.

Among the luggage which I had brought from New York was a small packet of leaflets which Dr. Levy had given me. The title of the leaflet was "Mood Swings—Coping with Manic-Depressive Illness." The note she had attached to the packet said simply, *If you can get people to read this, it will save you a lot of painful and wearisome talk. A.L.*

I took out one of the copies and marked the passages which I thought might help me most in my discussion with Delaunay. One paragraph dealt with increased sexual activity; another described the profligate spending of money; a third was concerned with the reduced sense of danger and the susceptibility to gambling, dangerous sports, and indiscriminate sex encounters.

I tried to prepare myself for the interview with a worst and best prognosis. At worst, the concierge could decline all discussion. He supplied his clients' needs but could not betray their confidence. Neither would he be too much inclined to reveal any of the sources of his service revenue.

At best, he might unbend enough to give me a carefully edited outline of Larry Lucas's off-duty life in Paris. He could not, in any case, refuse me access to whatever clothing and effects were still being held in storage. Finally, since my concerns could best be expressed in financial terms, I put five hundred dollars into an envelope, put the envelope inside the brochure, tucked both into the inside pocket of my jacket, and rode downstairs to talk to the great man.

He was not, at first sight, impressive. He was middle-aged, running to fat, with a ruddy moon face, a crown of white hair, and a benign smile. His eyes were cornflower blue. They sparkled when he smiled and were alert when he listened. I had the impression that after one glance he would have been able to recite every detail of my dress and deportment.

His welcome was formal. He and his staff were wholly at my disposal at any time during my stay. He was more than interested

44

to hear that I was Mr. Lucas's brother-in-law and that I was in Paris on temporary assignment to fill his place. He had the most pleasant recollections of Mr. Lucas, who, he understood, would still be a fairly regular visitor. He was indebted to Mr. Lucas for some good financial advice which had enabled him to turn a useful profit on the bourse. If, therefore, I needed any special service, he would be happy to offer it.

It was the best cue I would get; I still moved tentatively.

"It's a service I hesitate to ask."

"Please, Mr. Strassberger, we have a wide variety of clients, with a wide variety of needs!"

"My brother-in-law, Larry Lucas, has disappeared. His family and his colleagues are all concerned for his health and safety. My father and my sister have asked me to trace him if I can. I ask whether you, who served him over a period of many months, can give me any information about his habits, his associations, his places of resort during his stay in Paris."

Delaunay's ruddy cherub face expressed concern and regret. His limpid eyes were wary.

"You have, of course, informed the police?" he asked blandly.

"We have not. No crime is involved. Mr. Lucas is as free to come and go as you are; but there is an element of personal and family tragedy. His physician describes him as in a state of fugue—a brilliant man in a manic flight from reality. That state will inevitably shift to deep depression, in which suicide is a constant possibility."

He picked up a letter opener from his desk and began toying with it like a dagger, testing its point against the ball of his thumb.

"I have a real problem with this," he said gently. "I serve thousands of people in a year. All of them rely in some fashion on my professional discretion. Mr. Lucas has no less right to his own privacy than anyone else."

"I understand."

"I need time to reflect on this and check back through my records. There may, of course, be nothing to tell you."

"Of course; but I'm sure you understand the urgency of the matter. A man's life may be at stake here."

"All the more reason to make careful inquiries first. Yes? I'll be in touch with you before nine tomorrow morning."

"Thank you. This envelope contains a small expression of my gratitude."

"You are very kind. Mr. Lucas also was very kind. He merits any service I can offer. Until tomorrow, then!"

He ushered me out with ceremony, the perfect servant attending the distinguished client. I was so impressed that I forgot to ask him to have Larry Lucas's clothes and effects taken out of storage and delivered to my room. No matter. I still had a busy afternoon ahead of me. Morning would be soon enough.

Before I left the hotel, I called my father in New York. I told him of my meetings with Vianney and with the concierge and how I proposed to address myself to the staff. He objected strongly: The staff were servants of the corporation; they were directed, they didn't dictate. I disagreed. An unhappy staff was a threat. He had to leave the job to me. He bristled for a moment and then gave me a grudging assent.

"Do what you want; but make it clear that you will not be manipulated. Vianney is a good man but he has a stiff neck and a certain vanity. As to the concierge fellow, I do not wish you to demean yourself by these inquiries. Now that the word is out, you might consider employing a private investigator; I am sure the Corsec people can offer you someone suitable."

I didn't tell him that I had certain doubts about the Corsec people. I promised to think about his suggestion and act upon it when the time seemed right. Then—true to form, God bless the man!—he suggested I might take the opportunity to make myself familiar with the workings of the Paris office. He didn't want, of course, to preempt any decision I might later make, but it was a good opportunity to extend my experience. There was a protest on the tip of my tongue but I swallowed it.

"First things first, Father," I told him. "I'm trying to cover a lot of ground in a short time. Besides, the last thing they need is a junior Strassberger trampling through their melon patch."

Once again, he gave me a grudging agreement. Once again, I felt a pang of guilt. His need for support was very great. My need for personal liberty was great too. I began to wonder whether Larry's flight might not have been prompted by the need for liberty rather than by illness. The thought nagged at me through the jolting taxi ride from the hotel to the offices of Strassberger et Cie. It inserted itself into the litany of names and titles which Vianney recited as he introduced me to the staff and which were instantly erased from my unstable memory. It lingered like an uneasy counterpoint to the words I spoke to the small assembly.

"I beg you not to be offended by the sudden and unexplained invasion of the Corsec audit team. My father sends his apologies, to which I add mine. I trust you will understand that his prime concern was to protect the good name of the company and everyone connected with it. You didn't like the Corsec style. I didn't like it much myself. However, they have signed a clean bill of health, which puts you all in line for a healthy bonus on the recent Suez deal.

"That's the good news. The bad news is that Larry Lucas has disappeared. He is a sick man. The symptoms of his illness include wild risk-taking and a detachment from the norms of daily conduct, followed usually by a plunge into deep depression where the danger of suicide is always present.

"I have to find him and try to persuade him back to the care of his physician and to treatments which can help him, as they have helped in the past. I don't know where he is. He could be in Patagonia or Tokyo. All I have to work on is one fact: He was here in Paris long enough to prepare for his flight, to supply himself with documents, to make friends or contacts on a number of levels in a very mixed society. For the rest, I'm working by guess and by God. All of you had some association with him. Some of you obviously were closer to him than others. He may, at some moment, have offered you a confidence about his attitudes, plans, or tastes. Please don't withhold it and please don't delay in coming forward. Understand that time is against Larry and against me.

"Finally, let me emphasize: There are no crimes involved

here. We are concerned with one man under threat from himself. At this moment I feel very inadequate and very afraid. Larry Lucas has two small children. He is part of my family. Please, help us, if you can. I'll be available here or at Le Diplomate."

As I walked from the room with Vianney I felt strangely shaken. For the first time in my life I understood what it meant to be totally dependent on the goodwill of strangers. At that moment they were indeed strangers, their faces blank, their eyes averted in embarrassment, their emotions masked. When I sat down at Larry's desk, my face was clammy and my hands were trembling. Vianney opened a cabinet, brought out a bottle of whiskey, and poured me a generous dose.

"That wasn't easy, but you did well. You cleared the air for me. You touched them with your appeal for help. Now you can only wait."

"Thanks for preparing them. Thanks for the drink."

"The least I could do. I have another piece of news for you."

"Good or bad?"

"Good, I think. Delaunay, the concierge, called me from Le Diplomate."

"The hell he did!"

"I didn't know you were going to talk to him, otherwise I could have warned you. He's a client of ours, a reasonably substantial client. He was checking up on you and, incidentally, on the stability of his banker! He told me you were quizzing him about Larry's off-duty habits."

"And you told him—?"

"He could trust you and believe you."

"Thank you again."

I raised the glass in a silent toast and took a long, grateful swallow. Delaunay's call was a small but significant incident. It reminded me that, like Larry himself, I was now the stranger, blundering around in territories with whose customs and relationships I was totally unfamiliar. I had to depend on spontaneous understanding and spontaneous kindness. I had to depend also on my own tact and instincts, in both of which, like my father, I lacked a certain delicacy of perception.

"I'll see you before I go home," Vianney told me quietly. "Best I leave the approaches to you open and clear."

His hand was already on the doorknob when I stayed him.

"This was Larry's office?"

"Yes."

"Has anything been changed or taken away since he left Paris?"

"Nothing. The Corsec people went over it as if it were a minefield. They didn't find anything useful but you're welcome to examine it." He gave me again that thin, crooked grin of his. "It's Strassberger territory anyway."

"You're a bastard, Vianney—but I could get to like you."

"Take your time," said Marc Antoine Vianney. "There's a proverb I seem to remember about making love to a porcupine. One has to be slow and careful!"

He walked out, closing the door behind him. The sudden silence in a strange room troubled me. Caught in a moment of poignant melancholy, I was aware of the picture I should present, slumped behind a desk with a glass of liquor in my hands. I had again the curious sensation of being in another man's skin and contemplating myself through a glass screen. My father's warning hovered at the fringes of memory like a haunting refrain. *You're a huntsman now, trying to raise a fox. Just be warned: You may raise a wolf instead.*

I tossed off the lees of the drink and began to move about the room, opening drawers and cabinets, flipping through the desk diary, as if the simple contact might provide a psychic link to Larry himself. Once again I found myself contemplating what I was doing and telling myself at the same time that it was a pointless and foolish exercise.

A knock at the door jolted me back to reality. When I opened it I was confronted by a young woman I had seen in the front row of my audience. At first glance, she looked to be in her late twenties, a perfect model of the new-age Gallic woman: trim, tailored in black with a white lace jabot, hair cut pageboy style, and olive skin molded over a classic bone structure. Her manner was relaxed.

"You've probably forgotten all our names. I'm Claudine Parmentier. Mr. Vianney has appointed me to assist you during your stay. If you'd prefer someone else, don't be afraid to say so."

"On the contrary, you're probably the person I need most at this moment. Please come in. Sit down and let's talk."

She sat. She waited.

"Do you prefer that we speak French or English?"

She gave me a shrug and the hint of a smile.

"The choice is yours, Mr. Strassberger. I'm comfortable with either."

"English, then. You understand all our concerns about Larry Lucas?"

"You expressed them very clearly."

"So, after working with him all these months, what can you tell me about him?"

"He was brilliant at his job. I admired that. He drove himself like a racing car. He drove us too. One sensed always a certain . . ." —she hesitated over the phrase—"a certain fragility, which fits your description of his illness."

"Did he ever discuss his illness with you?"

"Not immediately. At first—how shall I say it?—he tried to preempt friction. It was as if he wanted to apologize in advance for any sharpness or anger. He asked me several times to explain him and his requirements to other staff. 'Put out the fenders so we don't scrape the paint.' I would try to do that. You understand that he had someone other than myself for routine secretarial duties."

"What sort of work did he demand of you?"

"I translated for him at conferences. His French was adequate but he tired quickly in conversation. He insisted that I check all his correspondence and all documents that came back from our legal department. He wanted to understand every nuance. It was exhausting work but, again, I admired his stubborn attention."

"Did you have any relationship outside the office?"

"When he gave business dinners he would ask me to act as hostess. At cocktail parties I was his escort and, as I told you, his interpreter."

"You were comfortable with that?"

"Most of the time, yes."

"Most of the time?"

"Occasionally Larry would want to play on, go nightclubbing with colleagues, that sort of thing. I did it once. After that I declined."

"It was an unpleasant experience?'

"No, a boring one. Most businessmen at play are boring anyway. I explained to Larry that I live with my lover. She is a senior official in the Ministry of Foreign Affairs. We both have busy careers. We try to reserve as much time as we can for our private lives."

"How did Larry react?"

"Much as you are reacting, Mr. Strassberger. He was obviously surprised. He assured me he understood perfectly—and he made no more demands."

"And how did that affect your working relationship?"

"It removed a barrier. It gave us the chance to be friends. He asked me to bring Anne-Louise to dinner with him. The encounter was a success. We invited him to our apartment. We found we could be comfortable together. We began to exchange confidences. Larry talked about his illness and the sense of alienation it produced. He asked us how we coped with what he called our 'difference.' Anne-Louise didn't like the word. She gave him a fairly cryptic answer: '*On s'arrange....*' He accepted it with a smile; but he had the wit to turn the phrase about: 'It's simple to make an arrangement: one has very little control over a *de*rangement.' Anne-Louise said there was a warning in that for all of us: *we* should not make ourselves too vulnerable to the derangements of other lives. She scored that point; but afterward there was always a certain caution in his friendship with her."

"But not with you?"

"No. Anne-Louise is inclined to be jealous. I am less dependent than she. I have had other lovers, not all of them women."

"And you told Larry that?"

"Of course, but he had already guessed. With him you didn't have to spell the words. What he found hardest to accept was

51

himself, but he had much pride and on his bad days he tried hard to mask his depression."

"And you? How much did you understand of his condition?"

"Not nearly as much as I do now. I regret that. I might have been able to reduce some of the pressures."

"Did he ever ask for help with his personal problems?"

"I think he was trying to ask. . . ." For the first time she faltered over her answer. "One day, in a quiet moment, he asked me how Anne-Louise and I ran our lives before we decided to settle down together. I had to explain about the Sapphic sisterhood, about lesbian clubs, certain resorts where we could be ourselves. Anne-Louise has always been reticent about that part of our experience. She calls it the auction ring and she has painful memories of it. It doesn't bother me in the same way, though I'm glad I don't have to depend on it anymore. Larry's comment touched me deeply: 'Like you, I've arrived at love. I give it and I get it in my marriage, but I've got to find someplace where I can close the door on my doppelgänger.'"

The words were like cold water dashed in my face. I was suddenly at a loss for words.

"It shocked me too, when I heard it first," Claudine Parmentier said. "I asked him to explain it to me. He turned it into a black joke. When I went home that night I looked up the word. It refers originally to the 'double,' the image of a person which is said to present itself just before or just after death. . . . So, when you spoke today of the possibility of Larry's suicide, I felt I had to tell you. . . ."

Once again I had to prompt her.

"Tell me what?"

"Larry did come back to Paris from New York."

"Are you sure of that?"

"I'm sure."

"When?"

"Three days ago. He called me from Orly and asked me to pick up the clothes he had left at the hotel and take them back to my apartment."

"Why didn't he pick them up himself?"

"He said he didn't want anyone else to know he was in Paris. He came to the apartment later that night. He stayed only long enough to say good-bye and thank us for our friendship. Then he left."

"How was he traveling?"

"He arrived in a black Peugeot. The driver was a woman."

"Did he tell you what brought him back, where he was going?"

"I asked. He said he was going on a long vacation—and this time even the doppelgänger wouldn't find him. He kissed me good-bye and went out loaded with hotel hanging bags and a cardboard box full of clean laundry. The woman got out of the car to help him stow the stuff in the trunk. Then they drove off."

"Did you get the number of the car?"

"No. The thought didn't enter my head."

"The woman?"

"I wondered who she was. I admit I was piqued that Larry hadn't taken me into his confidence. But then, why should he? We were office friends, not lovers. I suppose what upset me more was that Anne-Louise underlined the incident in red ink. We quarreled about it. . . . Now I'll have my own small victory. One needs those from time to time in any partnership, yes?"

"I guess so."

"Obviously you're not married."

"Does it show?"

"In this place, the history of the Strassberger family is an open book, much discussed, variously interpreted by senior staff."

At that moment, the telephone rang. I asked Claudine to answer it. After a brief dialogue she passed the instrument to me.

"Your father, calling from New York. I'll wait in my office."

Then she was gone and my father was demanding to know what had happened in the last two hours. I was annoyed and told him so.

"You've broken into my first important interview."

"I apologize. There's something I felt you should know. The Corsec people called. They were responding to your proposal

53

about extending their inquiries on a handshake arrangement with a contingent fee."

"And?"

"They want us to increase our offer to half a million, plus operational expenses—and an indemnity against any suits for breach of privacy or trespass in the U.S. or in Europe."

"Tell 'em to go to hell! And tell Andrescu their current contract is in jeopardy because of their crass handling of the Paris assignment."

I gave him a short account of my meeting with the staff and my unfinished interview with Claudine Parmentier. He was skeptical as always.

"You'll check her story, of course. She could be colluding with Larry."

"I doubt it—but I'll be checking as soon as I get back to the hotel."

"What shall I tell Madi?"

"Just what I've told you. Our first guess was right. But please, Father, don't call me at the office. I'll phone you from the hotel. You're six hours behind us. So I'll get you either at the office or at home. Agreed?"

"Agreed. Do you have any thoughts on the woman driving the Peugeot?"

"It's too early to speculate."

"I have a suggestion."

"Tell me."

"Ask Vianney who handles the *carnet de bal*."

"The what?"

"The *carnet de bal*, the dance card. I know there is one. I know there's someone in the office who handles it."

"That doesn't tell me what it is."

"Work it out for yourself—my compliments and good luck. Madi will be relieved and the children will be happy."

"Don't build too much hope on me yet."

"Little or much, Carl, we all need hope. Once it goes, there is only grief to be endured. Again, I apologize for disturbing you. Good luck!"

The line went dead. I sat there with the receiver clamped to my ear cursing my father for a provocative mischief-maker and thanking my lucky stars I was not bound to him forever and a day. Then the humor of it took hold of me and I began to laugh. I put down the receiver, picked it up again, and dialed Vianney's office.

"I've just been talking to my father in New York," I told him. "He suggested I ask you about the *carnet de bal*. Who handles it now?"

There was a sudden silence on the line, then a very formal answer.

"I am in the middle of dictation. This is something we should discuss at the end of the day, in private. I'll drive you back to your hotel about six."

"Fine."

"You have spoken with Mlle. Parmentier?"

"We're just about to continue our conversation."

"Until later then."

I looked at my watch. It was already ten minutes after five. I called Claudine back into my office. I told her I needed to clarify some notes given to me by the Corsec people. She was not amused.

"It's late. I have mail to sign and an appointment at six. May we continue in the morning?"

"This won't take long. Larry made four visits to Geneva to see a certain Dr. Hubert Rubens. What can you tell me about him?"

"He is what the Swiss call a *Treuhänder,* a trustee. I gather he handles a small list of big clients."

"Of whom Larry was one?"

"I don't know."

"Is there any correspondence with Dr. Rubens in the files?"

"A series of faxes confirming appointments Larry made by phone. Nothing else."

"Next, two overnight visits to Milan. The diary note has an acronym, SVEEO. You told the Corsec people you didn't know what it meant."

"I was lying."

"Why?"

"Because I didn't like the gorilla who was asking the questions, and it was Larry's private business anyway."

"Will you tell me what the letters mean?"

"It's a travel agency: *Simonetta Viaggi, Europa ed Oltremare*—Simonetta Travel, Europe and Overseas."

"Paris is full of travel agencies. The concierge at Le Diplomate could send you to the moon if you asked him. Why would Larry go to Milan?"

"He didn't tell me. I didn't ask."

"Were you afraid of him?"

"No, but I learned fast that when he was frayed and tired he could be as prickly as a rosebush. I never asked unnecessary questions. In this case, however, I was interested enough to find out for myself. I have a colleague who works for the Banco Ambrosiano in Milan. I called her. She told me that Simonetta is a boutique agency specializing in exotic tours for rich clients, male and female. There is no Simonetta. The director is a man; he has a team of attractive young people to tout business for him."

"Sometime after his visit to Milan, Larry went on a ten-day holiday. Where did he go?"

"Again, he didn't tell me. Again, I didn't ask."

"Who made the travel arrangements?"

"I don't know."

"I understand your lying to the Corsec people. How do I know you're not lying to me?"

If she was startled by the question, she gave no sign of it. Her answer was faintly contemptuous.

"You don't. But the old test still applies. *Cui bono?* Who profits from a lie, if there is one? Larry and I were not lovers. He was a respected colleague, an agreeable friend. How do I profit from his distress? On the other hand"—she thrust in fast, like a duelist—"on the other hand, Mr. Strassberger, you could be lying to us, setting up some elaborate fiction to protect your family interests. The Corsec invasion could have been the first move to

56

soften us up. Then you follow in with a beautifully scored cry from the heart for the lost lamb and the afflicted family."

"The same question to you then. Who profits?"

"Simple answer. Disappearing bankers make world news and big dents in the stock market." She gave a small dismissive laugh. "Don't worry! I believe you. You can believe me. You'll find my signature on the receipt for Larry's clothing and laundry."

"You understand I had to ask the question."

"You did it very clumsily."

"I apologize."

"I forgive you; but you shouldn't try to frighten me, Mr. Strassberger. I was blooded in the battle of the sexes."

She was out the door and gone before I could utter another word.

4

"IT'S A JOKE," SAID MARC Antoine Vianney, "a stale office joke!"

We were sitting over drinks in my suite at Le Diplomate, waiting for the concierge to call us as soon as the evening scramble around his desk was over. Vianney was commenting on my father's cryptic phrase, the dance card.

"Your father invented the term. I remember the occasion very well. I had just taken over this job. Your father had come from New York to preside at my installation. I was looking to him to define company policy on various matters. What I got was a flea in my ear. 'We deal in money,' your father told me. 'Money and moneyed people. We wine them, we dine them: we entertain them, at the racetrack, at the casino, at the theater. Nobody notices that we are doing it with their money.'"

Vianney grinned in self-mockery.

"I asked him then how we were to act on the question of sexual entertainment. He cocked his head at me like an old owl contemplating a fat mouse. He said, 'We are bankers, Vianney! We are not pimps or procurers or brothel touts, and none of our clients, male or female, is going to thank us for an HIV infection or a dose of the pox. Every concierge at every major hotel runs a dance card of call girls and houses of appointment. So you refer your clients to the concierge at their own hotel. But before you do, write the concierge a discreet note introducing our valued client and asking him to use his best efforts to render the client's stay in Paris comfortable. Enclose a generous offering—in cash.

After that you take no further role in the matter. And if you happen to be playing on the bordello circuit yourself, never, never mix your pleasure with our clients' business!'"

I laughed aloud. I couldn't help myself. He had my father down pat: the tone, the gestures, the peremptory 'never, never!' I raised my glass in salute.

"Bravo! Now you've got five-star hotels handing out the dance cards to Strassberger clients!"

"Not quite." Vianney had something more to add. "I decided later that the spread of risk was far too great. In sexual commerce there are no guarantees. Too many accidents can happen between contact and consummation: so now we work only through Delaunay at this hotel. He has his own rules. No rough trade, no violent games. His escorts are already in the health industry."

"And what is that supposed to mean?"

"They are surrogate partners employed by a large consortium of doctors engaged in the sex-therapy business. They coax the patients, male or female, back to normal function. As Delaunay reasons it, the doctors themselves have a vested interest in the health of the surrogates. He figures that's the best insurance he can offer. So far—touch wood—we've had no complaints either."

"Which brings us full circle, doesn't it?"

"How so?"

"Did Larry Lucas have a dance card?"

"I never asked but I presume so. Delaunay would be able to tell us. He is the one who makes the appointments for clients."

"And presumably collects his commission?"

"Oh, no! He's much too shrewd for that. We pay him a certain sum for general services. The clients pay him for pointing them to a safe address. To collect anything from the girls would be as distasteful for him as it would be for us, who are 'all, all honorable men.'"

Twenty minutes later, Delaunay, that honorable man, was sitting with us, taking the edge off a very hard day with a shot of Glenfiddich. He was cordial now, relaxed, even amiable, but the edge of caution never left him. He confirmed that Mlle. Claudine Parmentier had signed for Larry's clothing and laundry. He confirmed also what Giorgiu Andrescu had told me in the Corsec office in New York that Larry Lucas was not a great chaser of women, that he jogged every morning and worked out at the Apollon Club most evenings after work. He did occasionally have Delaunay call up women on the dance card as escorts for himself and his clients. There was certainly no history of continuity with one woman or of overnight visitors at Le Diplomate.

When I asked him to hazard a guess as to the woman who drove Larry Lucas to pick up his clothes from Claudine Parmentier's apartment, he shook his head.

"I'm afraid I can't help you. I suggest, however, that the woman may not have been a sexual partner at all. It may well have been a person paid to cooperate in his flight."

"Why do you say that?"

"Because the girls on the dance card work from their own apartments and are transported at the expense of the client. They do not use their own vehicles even if they have them. A minor traffic accident, after a party, with alcohol consumed, could spell big trouble for them."

This made sense. There was no way I could argue the issue. I switched to a new tack.

"Monsieur, you have, naturally, a large number of dealings with travel agencies?"

"Of course."

I handed him a slip of paper on which I had written *Simonetta Viaggi, Europa ed Oltremare, Milan*.

"What can you tell me about this one?"

He hesitated a moment and then hedged the answer.

"Not a great deal. They have an office here in Paris. Sometimes one of their representatives calls on me to remind me of their existence and the special services they offer."

"And what is the nature of these special services?"

"Luxury travel to exotic places, with or without escort, as the client chooses. Their clients are middle-aged to elderly, but they are always rich. The agency people, on the other hand, are young men and women, very polished, very persuasive."

"Did you ever make any arrangements with them for Mr. Lucas?"

"I made him aware of their existence. I gave him their telephone number and recommended he make his own arrangements."

"What, in fact, did he ask you to find for him?"

"In his own words, 'a quality agency specializing in exotic locations—but nothing either too vigorous or too extreme in climate.'"

"Do you know whether he made contact with Simonetta Travel?"

"I have to assume so. I saw him on occasion in the lobby, deep in conversation with one of their young ladies."

"Do you know her name?"

"At this precise moment, it escapes me."

"Would you try to remember, please? You understand how important this is."

"I do understand, yes; but may I ask a very personal question, Mr. Strassberger?"

"Please!"

"What are your feelings toward your brother-in-law?"

It was on the tip of my tongue to tell him that my feelings were none of his damn business. I realized just in time that I had made them his business. If I wanted his help, I had to pay him deference. So, as calmly as I could, I put together the answer.

"My feelings are, naturally enough, very mixed. Larry is family. He is married to my sister. He has two beautiful children. He is a brilliant banker and extremely important to our firm. He is suffering from an illness that is little understood and which can put him at extreme risk. So my first feeling is deep concern. We

61

are his family. My next is anger, which I can neither justify nor suppress. Larry Lucas walked out on his family and his business and has disrupted a working summer for me."

Delaunay threw back his head and laughed.

"That's a very open confession, Mr. Strassberger!"

I had the sudden notion that Delaunay was playing out an old comedy in which he was the clever Parisian and I was the fall-guy American, who couldn't tell a *clochard* from a cloche hat. I decided that I didn't like the script and I told him so.

"I'm a stranger here. I'm tired and I'm worried. This isn't *Monsieur Hulot's Holiday*. It's an old fashioned dead-or-alive manhunt. Can you help me or not? If you can't, say so and we're done here. If you can, then don't make me beg like a poodle for dinner scraps."

There was a long moment of silence; then Vianney confronted me.

"Cool down, Carl! Try to understand what you're hearing. M. Delaunay owes us nothing. How would we react, if suddenly he were knocking on our door with intrusive questions about our financial dealings—no matter under what pretext? In fact, he's trying to help, as I am, if not for the same reason. As I told you, I was not attracted to Larry Lucas. I respected him; I could not warm to him. M. Delaunay counts Larry a friend. He feels very protective of his interests. He is not hostile to you or to us. He is simply exercising a proper personal and professional caution with a man he does not yet know very well—yourself."

"Thank you." Delaunay acknowledged his advocate with a nod, then sat, hands folded placidly in his lap, waiting for my reaction. The words pieced themselves out slowly.

"M. Delaunay, I'm desperate. Therefore I am less than gracious. I apologize. I understand your professional reticence. I respect it. I shall be grateful for whatever help you can give me."

"*Eh bien!*" Delaunay smiled and raised one plump hand in absolution. "Let us talk about Simonetta Travel. I have told you I know these people. I am, however, unsure of them. Therefore, I do not recommend them to my clients. I did not recommend them to Mr. Lucas. On the other hand, I do not ignore or conceal their existence and the services they offer. A concierge, like a banker, must be—or at least appear to be—all things to all men and women."

He fished in his waistcoat pocket and brought out a business card, attached to a folded clipping. He handed them to me.

"The card is that of the young woman from Simonetta Travel who most often calls on me. She is the one whom I have seen in conversation with Mr. Lucas. The cutting comes from one of those magazines which you will find in your own suite in this hotel. It advertises luxury travel, luxury lodgings, like this place. Its editorial content is addressed to the idle browser, to be read in the bath. Read it, please!"

The piece was obviously patched together from an interview by a very pedestrian journalist.

Simonetta Travel (Paris, Milan, New York, Los Angeles) is, by all accounts, a discreet success in the gadabout trade. It must be successful to afford the services of the beautifully turned out young men and young women who haunt the best hotels in search of clients. Presumably the clients are satisfied, because they've got exactly what they paid for—they've dropped out of circulation, disappeared completely, stepped off the sidewalks of their home place into a special nowhere, discovered, recommended, and tailored to their personal needs by Simonetta—who, by the way, isn't Simonetta but a certain Francesco Falco, who commutes round the world in search of secret retreats where his wealthy clients may literally disappear.

Mr. Falco has a long list of heavenly havens in the Philippines, Costa Rica, Brazil, Madagascar, Morocco, the Windward Islands. You name a place you'd like, he can point to it on the map and recite the services his agency has available there: luxury housing, abundant domestic help, companionship, male or female, in a whole range of colors, medical services, discreet financial arrangements to break the money trail between the client's old world and the new one.

Who are the clients? At this point Mr. Falco wags a chiding finger. "That's the whole exercise, isn't it—absolute discretion!"

He will admit, however, that there are typical profiles: men between forty-five and sixty who are bored, lonely, or simply in flight from a bad marriage; women, some damaged by marriage or a love affair, some bored, some chasing the retreating romance of youth.

Criminals perhaps? Mr. Falco shrugs eloquently. How would one know? One takes paying clients at face value. He points out that criminal organizations everywhere have their own travel arrangements, their own vanishing tricks. All that Simonetta demands is that the clients have solid credit and a sincere desire to step permanently from one life to another.

Documents? Mr. Falco shrugs again. "Many countries offer special arrangements for moneyed people. Every nation in the world welcomes a well-heeled immigrant." Nice work if you can get it, we thought—and Simonetta Travel is obviously getting enough of it to stay in business in four very expensive cities.

I handed the clipping to Vianney. He scanned it swiftly, then passed it back to me.

"May I keep this?" I asked.

"Of course."

"How long has Simonetta Travel been in business?"

"Seven, eight years to my knowledge. But under Falco's administration, in this kind of business, less than three years."

"Next question: Are the documents he provides real or forgeries?"

"My guess would be that they are real but bought at premium prices from the consulates of the countries which offer this hospitality."

That made sense to me. I could not imagine Larry building his new identity and his new existence on a forgery. I knew, or thought I knew, the answer to my next question; nonetheless I wanted to hear Delaunay's version. I pointed to the passage in the clipping about "discreet financial arrangements to break the money trail between the client's old world and the new one."

"From your own experience in the hotel business, what kind of arrangements would suggest themselves?"

Delaunay, in his bland fashion, chose to be discursive rather than specific.

"An interesting question, Mr. Strassberger. Let's suppose I am the service provider in one of Mr. Falco's havens. I'm a banker, a merchant, an *hôtelier*. I am working probably in an area of debased currency, Brazilian cruzeiros, Philippine pesos, Turkish lire. Anybody who can offer me hard or even reasonably solid currency is automatically my friend. No way in the world am I going to ask how or where the funds originate. Once a pattern of prompt remittance is set, I lean over backward, dance on a high wire, to keep my clients happy. I become also their strongest advocate with the police and the many-headed dogs of local government. I am concerned with their health. The longer they live, the more they spend, the richer I become."

"And where does the original travel agent, our Mr. Falco, figure in all this? I can't imagine his being satisfied with a one-time commission while you and all the locals dine for years off the plump bird he has sent you."

"My guess would be—and mind you it is only a guess—that before he starts using our facilities, Mr. Falco already has a scale of contingency contributions arranged and a local collector in place."

"So, one more question, again pure theory. The happy dweller in this happy paradise falls sick. Who provides the nursing care, the specialist attention which may be needed?"

"You mean"—Vianney amplified the question—"even though the patient may be able to afford the necessary treatment, it may not be available or, worst case of all, it could be deliberately withheld."

"It's possible." Delaunay's voice took on a musing, meditative tone. "In fact, the more one dwells on it, the more likely it seems that the real rewards of this curious enterprise come from the source funds—the client's own money safely parked with a trustee or banker in Luxembourg, Liechtenstein, Switzerland, Hong Kong, or the Netherlands Antilles. That trustee has to have full discretion, because his client has surrendered his identity and disappeared from the planet."

"My guess would go further," said Vianney. "The travel agent and the trustee would work hand in glove together to manipulate the estate."

Bingo! There it was, all laid out, all numbers filled, the whole scam. Only one question remained, and Delaunay asked it.

"Why would anyone be crazy enough to take a risk like that?"

Neither of us answered him, but I heard Alma Levy's voice echoing out of memory, clear as a bell in high mountain air.

The mountain peaks of mania are dizzy ecstatic places, over which the patient, in his illusion, soars like an eagle. The valleys into which he plunges afterward are deep, dark, and noisome with the stink of carrion.

The thought must have been written on my face, because Marc Antoine Vianney said very quietly, "Remember, Carl, this is all speculation, guesswork, the great *perhaps*."

Delaunay was the first to challenge him.

"It is, however, simple to prove, one way or the other!"

"How?" The question was mine.

"You yourself become a client of Simonetta travel. You yourself become the fugitive, looking for the key to a fool's paradise."

When they had gone, I called my father in New York. He was having another rough day in the markets, so it took him an extra few minutes to focus on my report. His reaction was predictable.

"It's too pat, too easy! This Delaunay fellow is blowing himself up like a bullfrog, and Vianney's happy to let him do it. It gets him off the hook!"

I reasoned with him as patiently as I could. It was he who had pointed to the dance cards as a possible lead. The dance cards inevitably involved Delaunay. I reminded him also that the first clue to Simonetta Travel had been given to us by Corsec, who had also noted the Swiss connection with Dr. Hubert Rubens.

Prima facie, at least, a pattern was emerging. We could not afford to ignore it.

By this time my father's attention was off the market and wholly concentrated on the question of how I should proceed.

"If the guesswork is right, you're talking about heavy criminal activity. You can't go into it without careful preparation. You'd need a new identity, a visible source of funds other than Strassberger. You'd have to break off all open connection with our company and establish a whole new set of provenances for yourself—a new career history, in fact. Again, if your reasoning is sound, these people are playing for very high stakes. They can't afford to risk a wild card in the deck. Therefore, you have to assume that while they take ordinary travelers for granted, their screening of potential scam victims will be very thorough. Let's not forget that in a real sense Larry could become a hostage and a possible casualty of any mistakes you make."

"I agree, Father. I haven't had time yet to do any planning."

"I know that. And you shouldn't make any plans in a rush or at the end of a long day. However, there are a few things you might consider. . . ."

I found myself grinning into the phone. As a banker and a man, Emil Strassberger always ran true to form: Reason with the worst, reduce the risks to a minimum, then plan the campaign like Clausewitz—textbook all the way! He was spelling it out for me now in curt sentences. "We'll supply the funds; we'll use the quarter of a million we were prepared to pay Corsec, and we'll scratch up some other funds from here and there. Maybe even from the bonus Larry declined to collect! When you've chosen your new name and your identity, we'll arrange for you to access the monies through Morgan Guaranty. They owe me a favor or two. Talking about identity, You've got one ready-made. You're an artist. You're a natural runaway like Gauguin. You're going through a switch of styles and outlook. All you need is a set of works in another mode and a new signature on the canvas. Your *curriculum vitae* may present some problems, but I'm sure between us here and your girlfriend in Nice, we can manage. . . ."

He was as hard to halt as a river in flood, but finally I had him silent enough to listen to what I had to say—which at that moment wasn't too much.

"I hear what you're telling me, Father. I'll accept all the help you can offer. Right now I want space to breathe and reason through this myself. Like you, I'm uneasy about Delaunay, and I can't get a clear reading of Vianney. In both cases, it's probably a question of idiom. They're the locals, I'm the outsider. I sense that they're putting me over the jumps to see how I perform against the Parisians."

"They do it every time, by God!" My father was happy to vent his frustrations at being so far away from the action. "But they'll learn, Carl! They'll learn! Why don't you relax and give yourself a night on the town—use the dance card if you want. Meanwhile, I've just thought of someone who could help us greatly. Let me brood on it and I'll talk to you again, same time tomorrow. How much of this can I tell Madi and your mother?"

"You explain it to Mother. I'll call Madi myself."

"Good! But please don't make any more moves until I get back to you."

"It would be useful to know what you have in mind."

"It would be a waste of time to discuss it if it can't be done. Be patient and trust me. Good night, son."

"Good night, Father."

My conversation with Madi was longer and more stressful. She was living in a nightmare of fears, angers, and jealousies while trying to keep a brave face for the children. They, it seemed, were less troubled than she by their father's absence, which they accepted as a normal pattern of life. First I had to talk her through an outburst of emotions and then walk with her through every possibility, good and bad, of Larry's situation. Finally, I was able to focus her attention on my immediate need.

"I've seen you and Larry sitting on the floor of your living room planning your holidays. You were surrounded by travel brochures and magazines. Cast your mind back and see if you can recall where Larry was interested in going and what attracted him. Don't confuse his choices with places you finally visited. Don't let your own preferences cloud your mind. Put it another way. If Larry had followed his own impulses, where would he have chosen to go? Try to remember his exact words. Think about it. Make some notes."

"How will that help? It's just another piece of guesswork."

"The guesses have been right so far, because they've been based on reasoning. I'm just running with the luck. What else can I do?"

"You could do me a big favor."

"Anything."

"Call Dr. Levy. She's eager to know what's going on, and she's strong as a rock, holding me up. Also, she may have something to contribute to your guessing game."

"I'll do it now. You dig out your travel brochures and start work. Give my love to the children."

"They love you, Carl. So do I."

I loved her, too. I shared in a special family fashion her rages and fears and frustrations. At that moment I could cheerfully have murdered Larry Lucas. It was a singular relief to talk to Dr. Levy, who demanded a calm and clinically precise narration of all that had happened since my arrival in Paris. She wanted word portraits of all the characters involved and an account of my relations with each one. Her verdict made me feel better.

"So far, I think you have done well. I believe you should follow this line of inquiry through the travel agent. However, I caution you again: Larry is a very intelligent man. It will be much easier for him to use people than for them to use him. So do not expect continuity in this or any other line of inquiry. Be prepared always for a fracture point, followed by tangential behavior."

"I'm not sure I understand you, Doctor."

"Let me put it another way. Larry has established a brilliant career in banking. Suddenly he quits. He has a good wife and a stable marriage. He quits that too."

"Has he ever quit you, Doctor?"

"Clever Carl!" said Alma Levy with dry humor. "Of course he has quit me, many times, as he has done now. Always he has come back like a penitent schoolboy. This time—if what you tell me is true—it may not be possible for him to return. He may find

69

himself captive to those who have helped him disappear. It will not happen at once. It may not happen at all, but it could: oh, indeed it could!"

Which brought me back to the same question I had put to Madi. "Where in the world might Larry choose as his place of exile?" I asked her.

Alma Levy was silent for a few moments.

"I can give you no ready answer," she said at last. "I shall have to replay certain tapes of my interviews with Larry. But again, I warn you, those indicators may no longer be reliable, or if they are reliable, they may not be permanently so. I remind you to be prepared for abrupt changes and destructive discontinuity. You tell me Larry is moving only a few days ahead of you. You must try never to lose the scent of him, otherwise you may lose him altogether. Call me again tomorrow and I'll tell you what I've been able to dig out of the tapes. Now tell me, Carl, how are *you* holding up?"

"Don't ask me, Doctor. I might be tempted to tell you."

She laughed. "You've a long way to go before you need me! I'll drink a toast to you."

Which left me hungry, thirsty, and restless, alone in my hotel suite in Paris, holding a blank dance card for the evening.

I would have welcomed company but I was too edgy to go looking for it. There were friends I could have called, but I shied away from the simple action of contact and explanation. I could have used Delaunay's network of squeaky-clean concubines, but that would have required a minimal interest to begin with and raised the old end-game question, "What do you say to the girl afterward?" Finally I decided that the least stressful company would be my own.

I changed into jeans, sneakers, and a well-worn windbreaker, shoved a small sketchbook and a clip of colored pencils into one pocket and a wad of francs into the other, locked my wallet and documents in the small combination safe in my suite, and marched out into the night.

My destination was a place I had discovered during my post-graduate sojourn at the Beaux Arts. Tucked away in a dingy alley between the Quai des Augustins and the Boulevard Saint-Germain, it presents a great wooden porte cochere framing a small wicket gate, over which a carved wooden sign announces *BOITE DES COULEURS*—the Paint Box. Once inside the wicket gate, you find yourself in a large courtyard paved with ancient cobbles which still bear the tracks of iron-rimmed coach wheels. The walls on either side are pierced by narrow windows, barred and heavily curtained. The end wall is broken by two larger mullioned windows, glowing with the colors of ancient stained glass.

Inside, there is a great barnlike space, part bistro, part bar, part studio. It is full of steam, cigarette smoke, and the smell of rich country soup, which with bread, cheese, and wine is the full menu in the Paint Box. The guests are artists of one kind or another who come for cheap food, congenial company, and a companionable workplace. The models, male and female, are extras. The guests make a contribution for their services whether they use them or not.

This is one of the pleasanter relics of *la vie de Boheme* which are still to be found in odd corners of Paris. The atmosphere is relaxed. It is your privilege as a guest and a fellow artist to stroll about, peer over people's shoulders, and offer comment, criticism, or an invitation to after-supper diversions in another place. This is Bohemia still and it can get rowdy and bawdy, but Madame Lutèce, wielding a heavy iron ladle, makes a very formidable watchdog, while her husband, Louis, is an old legionnaire with a stone head and fists like hams.

I am known and accepted here, which means I'm entitled to a grunt from Louis and a wave from Madame while I find a place for myself among the clutter of tables, easels, and the motley of guests who are either drawing, eating, drinking, or engaged in the preludes to lechery which, Madame insists, must be consummated in some other place.

I chose first a place at the bar. Louis poured me wine and brought me food. I was eager for both and I paid little attention to the models or the table guests or the small passing traffic between them. It was a relief to be in my own element again, unnoticed, anonymous, free—at least for a while—from the briar patch of other lives. When I had finished eating I turned my stool around and sat with a glass of wine in my fist, watching the next model on the rostrum.

She was one of the old identities of the artists' quarter, a big swarthy woman with a Rubens body and the fluid movements of a onetime belly dancer. She was wearing a silk dressing gown, which she peeled off slowly to a chorus of whistles and rhythmic handclaps, then used as a drapery for a series of well-timed poses. She was a wonderful subject—all curves and deep shadowy creases and an arrogant indifference to everything but her own body.

I set down my drink, took out my sketchbook and a charcoal pencil, and began to sketch her. I moved away from the bar, changing my position each time she assumed another pose, until I was down on one knee trying to deal with an image foreshortened from her foot soles to the mane of coarse dark hair trailing across her breasts.

The sketch was still unfinished when she ended the short session, put on her dressing gown, and glided back into the shadows. I remained kneeling, making the last shadow strokes, when I breathed a drift of familiar perfume, felt a hand on my shoulder, and heard Arlette Tassigny's mocking voice.

"Not bad, not bad at all! I'd buy it if you weren't such a *salaud!*"

She was smiling, but she was not amused. I lurched as I stood up but she made no move to steady me. She demanded an instant accounting.

"So! You make a big dramatic exit from Nice. Family business, you tell me! Suddenly you're back in Paris and I don't hear a word from you! How long have you been here—or did you leave at all?"

"I arrived this morning—and I apologize for not calling you. Things are in crisis mode just now."

"Obviously! A blind woman could see that. And what better place than this to enjoy a crisis! Tell me about it."

"I will, when you've finished scolding. And what, pray, are you doing here?"

"What I always do in Paris: buying stock for the summer trade, sniffing for new talent."

"Do you have any talent with you tonight?"

"In fact, I do—except it's not new. It's old Jules Beaudouin. He's a fine painter, but he's been out of fashion for ten years, living on hope and cabbage stalks. I've agreed to buy half a dozen canvases, take a dozen more on consignment, and see what sort of a market we can make for him this season. Come and meet him—unless of course you have other plans."

"Introduce me to Beaudouin by all means. Afterward, if you're still interested, we'll have a late supper at my place and I'll tell you my story."

"And where, my negligent one, is your place?"

"Le Diplomate."

"Oh-la-la! Aren't we grand! You're not living there on what I'm making for you."

"It's the company suite. I'm here on business for Father. You're welcome to share it with me."

"For how long?"

"I don't know. I told you there's a crisis. I may have to move elsewhere very quickly. But tonight, at least, I can tell you bed-time stories."

"How can I refuse? But first you'll have to help me with Jules Beaudouin. He's a good painter. He just needs someone to give him back his courage."

It should have been easy. It wasn't. Jules was garrulous and eager to impress. After an hour, my composure was beginning to wilt and Arlette's patience was fraying around the edges. It was after midnight before we set him on his way and walked back to Le Diplomate with a river mist rising about us. As I explained what had happened to Larry Lucas and how I was trying to deal with it, and the possible role of Simonetta Travel, Arlette became more and more uneasy.

"You are swimming in dark waters here, Carl. France is not America. The Côte d'Azur is not Coney Island. Oh, yes, I know you have more gangsters and crooks than we do, but ours is a different mode—how do you say it?—a different idiom. I live in Nice. I run a modest art gallery, but even I make my contributions to the Corsicans who run everything right along the coast from Ventimiglia to Marseilles. It's dressed up as a voluntary contribution to the Traders' Association Promotional Fund, but it's still protection money. And if you think you don't need protection, they'll teach you very quickly that you do. This disappearing trick you talk about doesn't surprise me at all; but you're not talking about amateurs here. They traffic in people all the time, all over the world: girls, boys, drug mules, illegal immigrants, criminal types on the run. The moment you step into their territory you'll be as conspicuous as a bug under a microscope. And they'll squash you without a second thought."

"But do I have to be conspicuous? All we're talking about here is a travel agency. I'm a traveler, looking for an exotic holiday."

"You're a traveler without a history. A man without a shadow."

"So we create the history. It's the oldest routine in spy novels. Even professionally it works. I'm an artist; I can create respectable pastiches in any style I want. You can represent my new work under my new name."

"But don't you see, that puts you in exactly the same position as your brother-in-law. You're a new person, yes; but you're a person nobody knows. You can drown without a ripple. And even I can't shed a tear for you because I don't know, do I?"

It was too grim a thought to dismiss lightly. We talked it over as we trudged through the river mist toward the hotel. Arlette was too much a hardhead to accept easy assumptions.

"Can you guarantee that your family or your business associates won't drop a word out of place? Can you be sure that international computer records at frontiers, in banks—in travel agencies, for instance—match all along the line? If they don't, lover, you'll be hung out to dry with the laundry."

"Everything I'm doing is a calculated risk."

"Calculated on what?"

"On Larry himself. Unless these people see him as a real

prize—not just as a tourist with exotic tastes—they have no reason to move against him or to expect an intruder like me."

"Wrong! Wrong! Wrong!" She was already burying herself in the bed. "They've spotted him as a mark. They've hooked him into the service network. His funds are already lodged in Geneva. He may be smart enough to play their game and quit when he's ready, but he's targeted already, make no mistake. Now come to bed, lover. Let's not waste the rest of the night on things we can't change until tomorrow!"

Arlette is a happy and enthusiastic lover, so it was easy to stifle the dark imps of foreboding; but when I woke at four in the morning they were perched on my pillow, mocking me. Arlette was sleeping, as she always did, deeply and calmly. I clawed myself into a dressing gown and went into the lounge, closing the door behind me.

In New York it was ten in the evening of yesterday. My father, I knew, would still be up, reading in his study. I called him. He answered instantly.

"You're up late, my boy!"

"I just woke up. I needed to talk to you."

"Go ahead."

"I suggested you call Corsec and tell them their contract is in trouble. Have you done it yet?"

"Not yet. I hate to hurry into hostile action. Why do you ask?"

"I think I have a use for them."

"At a much revised price, I hope."

"At my price, which we'll negotiate after I tell 'em about the foul-up in Paris. Then I want to commission them on my own account, so Strassberger isn't involved. The company can pay me later—ex gratia."

"Do you want to tell me what you have in mind?"

"I'd rather not."

"As you choose, of course. Now I have something for you. I want you to remain in your hotel suite until midday. You'll have a visit from a certain Oskar Kallman. Receive him in private and listen carefully to what he tells you."

75

"Who is he?"

"An old friend, well regarded in high places, although he's retired now. By the time he's briefed you fully, we'll have funds at your disposal with Morgan Guaranty in Paris. Call me after you've talked with Oskar. Oh, one other thing. Madi was much cheered by your call. She's working tonight on the matter you discussed."

"Dr. Levy is doing the same thing."

"I'd like to meet that woman one day."

"That's simple enough. Ask Madi to arrange it. I'll have to leave you now. I have another call to make."

"Good night, Carl. Telephone me after you've spoken with Kallman!"

I opened my briefcase and fished out the Corsec card on which Giorgiu Andrescu had written his contact number. I dialed it and waited through what seemed an interminable series of switching operations. Finally Andrescu himself answered with a noise of chatter in the background. He sounded irritable.

"Who is this?"

I told him. He was immediately attentive.

"What can I do for you, Mr. Strassberger?"

"I need some special service, George. And I need it billed to me personally, not to Strassberger."

"That's easily arranged." He laughed. "Your credit's good."

"I should tell you, George. Corsec's credit is a little tarnished. I'm telling you as a friend because I don't want the same problem on my job."

"What happened, for Pete's sake?"

I told him at length and in detail about the hostile reactions in Strassberger's Paris office. He listened in silence until I had delivered the final punch line.

"So as soon as I hit Paris, I was faced with the real possibility of a walkout by senior staff and the specific instance of one person who admitted lying because, and I quote, 'I didn't like the gorilla who was asking the questions.'"

Giorgiu Andrescu swore explosively and obscenely. He was too bright to give me an argument. He apologized.

"I'm sorry. We were asked to work fast. We had to scratch up an investigating team in a hurry. The man who led 'em is a hard-nosed interrogator but not a leader or a diplomat. The foul-up is clearly my responsibility. I'll write your father a letter of explanation and apology and we'll discount the charges. Now, please keep talking while I move to my desk. Tell me what I can do for you."

"When we met in New York, you told me that with a free hand, you could deliver much better information."

"I remember the conversation, yes."

"In your records you'll find the acronym SVEEO."

"I remember that too."

"The initials stand for a Milan travel agency: Simonetta Travel, Europe and Overseas. It's run by a man called Francesco Falco. It has branches in Paris, New York, and Los Angeles. They specialize in exotic destinations and specifically advertise a service for wealthy dropouts. I believe that Larry used their service in Paris and Milan. My question is—"

"Don't ask the question." Andrescu cut in brusquely. "The answer is, yes we can. We can tell you who, when, where, how much. You fax me everything you've got. I'll get some action moving right away. Where are you staying?"

"Le Diplomate, but I may have to move shortly. I may be signing up myself for a trip with Simonetta—in which case it would be nice to think you were following my bouncing ball on your charts as well as Larry Lucas!"

"Give us departure dates and transport details; we'll do the rest."

"Next question: Who handles it and how much?"

"I'll handle it myself. Strassberger is important to us. You're important. I'd like to clean the slate."

"And the cost? This is me, solo, remember."

"Give me half a minute."

He was back on the line in twenty-five seconds.

"Fifty thousand on signing, fifty each on the closing of each case, yours and Lucas's, plus twenty-five thousand in each case for delivery of a live body. That's everything, capped at two hundred thousand."

"No extras? No overheads?"

"None at all."

"You've got a deal. I'll remit the first funds tomorrow, bank to bank. Do you want me to sign a contract?"

"In this case, better we don't. You can't really give me an effective list of requirements. I can't specify how we'll meet them. So we're both working by guess and by God."

"What's the first step?"

"You send me everything you have on Simonetta Travel. We'll start immediately building our own file. I wish we'd known this ten days ago."

"You could have—except you had a gorilla asking the questions."

"Don't rub it in, please! We've got a team of juvenile geniuses running our electronics, but we're still recruiting our investigating staff from auditors and the offices of district attorneys. Old Romanian proverb: 'The best wine is drunk from golden cups, but you still need mules to haul the barrels.' Besides, we're starting fresh, remember? I assume this cancels out the handshake deal your father proposed?"

"It does."

"Then I'll expect your fax and I'll get busy."

"I'm sorry if I spoiled your party."

"Party? That's not a party. It's work time. We're surfing and trawling the networks for information. We'll be doing the same for you very soon. You'll be surprised at what we can turn up when we put our minds to it."

As I set down the receiver, I was vividly conscious of the irony of the situation. Here we were, the Strassberger clan and all our extended family of friends and retainers, committing our lives and our money to the search for a man who had, of his own free will, in his own wisdom or unwisdom, opted to leave his wife and children to make a new life for himself alone.

Every great city in the world has its own garbage dump of disposable humanity—men, women, children of all ages. All the money in the world could not buy them out of their bondage of poverty, ignorance, and dead-end despair, but we could alleviate some of it, give hope to a few, save some at least from an extension of horror.

Yet here was Larry Lucas, playing his loony tune, dancing his crazy jig, and leading us all on his merry dance to nowhere. It made no sense at all. It was, if you stared at it long enough, a blasphemous abuse of the privilege which our family enjoyed, and which we might at this very moment be putting to better use.

"Come back to bed," said Arlette from the doorway. "I'm cold, and you look angry enough to start a fire. Let's do a little heat exchange, eh? Afterward, if you must, you can explain about these four-in-the-morning phone calls!"

In those small, dark, vulnerable hours of early morning, I felt a special gratitude and a new surge of affection for Arlette Tassigny. I was, let me say it plain, beginning to be afraid. I was resenting Larry because he had exposed me to fear and made me ashamed of my spoilt, protected self. Arlette understood. Her passion restored my damaged self-respect, bolstered my wavering courage.

Long after dawn, when we sat over coffee and croissants, she told me in her terse, pragmatic fashion, "You're easy to read, Carl. You've been brought up in the nice, tidy, controllable world which your father built for you. You left it, but you were able to set up an equally tidy world for yourself: scholar, artist, well-organized gypsy with markets for his wares. Now that world's out of joint. You're scrambling around in strange country—and suddenly it hits you that your brother-in-law may not be worth all the trouble he's giving you."

"Do you believe he is?"

"Listen, Carl! You took on this job. Right or wrong, ready or unready, you're stuck with it."

"You don't think I'm ready, is that it?"

"I told you last night, you've got a lot to learn. Don't be angry. It's true. Up till now, you've managed very comfortably to ignore the needy of the world. I don't think you have any right to start drawing distinctions between them. Larry is family. You're asked to find him, not deliver a judgment on him. You made promises which maybe you shouldn't have made, but you have to

79

keep them. Because we're friends and I love you more than a little, I have to keep you honest. You understand that, I think?"

I understood it, but the taste of the truth was sour in my mouth. I had no argument against it. I wanted no contest with Arlette. I kissed her and thanked her and set her on her rounds of the galleries. She promised she would be back at the end of the day and bring her luggage with her. I was absurdly pleased at the prospect. Never before had I felt so great a need of her presence.

5

AT TEN-THIRTY THAT MORNING, the man called Oskar Kallman presented himself at my door. My first impression was that he was a beautifully groomed specimen in late middle age. His gray hair had been trimmed by a first-rate barber; his lean, tanned face was freshly shaven. He was wearing a gray suit, cut by a Savile Row tailor, with a bow tie and a fall of blue silk handkerchief at the breast pocket. His accents in French and English were Canadian. His eyes were shrewd, his smile open and friendly. He carried a small but expensive leather briefcase. His handshake was firm and dry.

"I'm Oskar Kallman. You're Carl Emil, and you're the image of your old man—but just for the record you'd better show me some identification."

I opened the room safe, took out my passport, and handed it to him. He studied it closely for a moment, then laid it face down on the coffee table. He sat down. I sat facing him and waited in silence. He explained briskly.

"Your father and I are old friends. In the cold-war days I worked for Canadian Intelligence. Strassberger was one of our several bankers. Your father proved himself a man of singular discretion. He asked no questions about the operation of our accounts. He executed the orders we gave him with good sense and understanding. I'm a document man by training. A lot of lives depended on the acceptability of my papers: identity cards, passports, family histories, professional dossiers, everything. I was—come to that, I still am—very good at it. However, I'm retired now. I accept occasional assignments only. I've invested in a perfume enterprise, quite near where you live. So, that's me. My name isn't Oskar Kallman, but it serves me well enough in part-time activities.

"Your father telephoned me. He explained your situation and the dangers of your involvement with this Simonetta Travel organization. He expressed the view that you needed complete cover—a whole new identity, in fact. Do you agree? Please don't hesitate to argue the matter. It's your life on the line."

I thought about that for a moment.

"You're the professional. How does my plan look to you?" I asked him.

"As far as I can see, you don't have a plan. You've just got an idea."

"I think it's more than just an idea."

"Convince me of that."

"Item one: I already have a flexible identity. I'm a temperamental artist, who wants to broaden his horizons. I read about Simonetta in a hotel magazine. It sounded like an interesting starting point for my travel inquiries."

"But their routing and your first choice may lead you a thousand miles away from Mr. Lucas."

"That brings me to item two: I am hiring an international security firm, which Strassberger employs, to tap into the computer systems of Simonetta Travel and see if we can identify any one of their clients as Larry Lucas."

"I like that. Go on."

"My father is lodging funds for me with Morgan Guaranty. They'll be sufficient to make me a possible target, like Larry."

"In my view you're very much alike. Each of you is going like a lamb to the slaughter."

"For different reasons."

"I don't know either of you well enough to comment on that. Certainly you're both waving money around like drunken sailors."

"It's bait for the bears."

"Maybe." He frowned dubiously. "However, the essential person in all this is you: your own capacities and instincts, how flexible you are, how comfortable you can be with a new persona. Before we go any further, I'd like to examine this question with you. It isn't a game, you see. It isn't just a piece of acting. It's a surgical operation. You're divested of one self. You acquire another. You will experience trauma. Contrary instincts will begin to work in your unconscious mind. There will be moments when you will feel caught in quicksand, when you will know that you can kill yourself in the struggle to find a foothold. I could tell you a lot of stories about such cases. I won't bore you with them; but the message is constant. You will face some kind of crisis in your own identity. You will risk becoming a casualty, as your brother-in-law has done."

It was a curious moment. In a few minutes this dapper fellow had confronted me as an authority figure. I saw myself sitting before him meek and dumbstruck, incapable of protest. Finally, I found words to assert myself.

"You talk of trauma and crisis. If the identity you provide for me is comfortable enough, why should there be trauma?"

Oskar Kallman smiled and shook his head.

"It isn't quite as simple as it sounds. On the one hand the client must be comfortable in the suit his tailor makes for him. On the other, any deception creates a fault line in the personality. Under extreme stress it will crack along that fault line. Of course, one hopes that such extreme stress may be avoided. . . . Now take off your jacket and tie. Stand over there against the blank space between the pictures. Just relax and look straight at me."

He opened his briefcase, fished out a camera, and took a series of flash exposures. Then he put the camera back in his briefcase and brought out a manila folder, which he laid beside my passport.

"Now let's be comfortable and discuss this great sea change.

83

You were born in the United States and educated there and in Europe. You've visited Canada on a number of occasions. You speak French comfortably, with a pronounced regional intonation. I think a Canadian identity would sit quite well on you. We could construct a biography which would fit the major circumstances of your life—and which, therefore, would be easier to sustain. The documents for it are easy for me to obtain. Also, and most importantly, it provides a reason for your change of lifestyle, your desire for exotic locations and fresh experience. The Canadian climate is harsh, the light is bleak, the landscape often unutterably boring, yes?"

His good humor was infectious. I was, at last, prepared to relax with him. I asked him whether he would like coffee. He declined.

"Not for the moment, thanks. Let's discuss names which would suit you. Take a sheet of notepaper and write your normal signature several times. Then show me how you sign your canvases."

My normal signature is a long emphatic scrawl in which the capital letters dissolve suddenly into two dark bars broken by the downstroke of the g and ending with a small fillip on the final r. My works are signed with an elaborate calligraphic S in the form of a striking serpent. It has references to the old illuminators whose texts were one normal element in my architectural studies. Kallman studied the two signatures for a moment and then delivered his verdict.

"It's always tempting to stay close to the client's original handwriting style. The danger is that in a moment of inattention you may begin to use your own signature instead of the fictitious one. I have known people caught out by that. In your case, we have to control your emphatic impulses which display themselves in your writing. We have to slow you down, force you to reflect before you sign even a credit card. So let's stay well away from cursive scripts. You've obviously studied calligraphy?"

"I have."

"Choose a script with which you are comfortable but which is dissimilar to your own. Something preferably which will make you deliberate for a second or two. Are you ready?"

"Yes."

"Now write, in your chosen script, the following: Edgar Francis Benson. Francis Edgar Benson. Florence Georgina Smith."

I wrote, as he directed, in an old-fashioned Gothic style which one of my early masters had taught me. I was out of practice, so I wrote slowly and carefully in the manner of an elderly person. Oskar Kallman nodded approval.

"Excellent! Now take a clean sheet of paper and do me six specimens of Edgar Francis Benson. That's you. The others are the names of your parents. They will complete the biographical record, which I'll put in your hands same time tomorrow, together with your Canadian passport."

"You work fast, Mr. Kallman."

"I hold reserve stocks," he told me blandly. "This sort of merchandise holds its value. To set your mind at rest, the background information for Edgar Francis Benson will be authentic. Your job will be to memorize it and be able to render it verbatim, if and when it is required—which, please God, will be very rarely.

"Once the documents are ready, I'll take you down to Morgan Guaranty, who will arrange drawing facilities and fit you out with credit cards and travelers' checks. You'll surrender your own documents into their safe custody. From then on you function as Edgar Francis Benson. Now let me go through the rest of the list. You check out of here tomorrow."

"Where do I go?"

He handed me a typed card and explained the location.

"It's a full-service apartment near the Étoile. They cater to up-market transient tourists. No one will bother you. Clothes? New York tailor-mades are a dead giveaway. You'll need to buy—"

He was going too fast for comfort. I cut him off in mid-sentence.

"Hold it a moment, Mr. Kallman. I have to think this through before I start living it. I surrender all my documents—"

"Everything, passport, credit cards, address book, diary."

"Suppose I'm knocked over by a truck, how will anyone know whom to contact?"

"My name and my accommodation address will be written under the 'please notify' line in your passport."

"But you could be off making lemon-scented aftershave."

"I'm a very well-organized man," said Oskar Kallman mildly. "You really can trust me. When do you propose to make contact with the Simonetta agency?"

"I thought I'd stroll around to their office today."

"No! Wait until you have all the paperwork done and you've moved into new lodgings."

"That means I'm losing time."

"You're also insuring your life—and the life of Larry Lucas."

"Are you saying, Mr. Kallman, that you believe my theory about Larry's disappearance?"

"Once your father laid it out for me, I had no doubts at all that you were on the right track. It happens I have more than a nodding acquaintance with Francesco Falco. He's been trading in warm bodies for many years now—Pakistanis into England; Koreans and Chinese into Canada and the United States—only big-money clients, though. No boat people, no raggedy-ass refugees—"

"So read me the next chapter, please. How and why would Larry walk away from a million-dollar bonus package in my father's company and put himself in the hands of an international rogue?"

"The how is easy. He'd been living here for months. He was friendly with the concierge—what's his name?—Delaunay, who profited from his patronage and introduced him to Simonetta Travel."

"Delaunay says he never uses them."

"Delaunay's a professional. He serves the interest of the hotel and his own, conjointly. He offers all care and minimal responsibility. Read the little notice on the back of your door and you'll find it's a very wide disclaimer of liability. I saw you take your passport out of the room safe. The management, you will find, does not accept any liability for loss if you use it. It accepts responsibility only for what you lodge in the central safe-deposit boxes."

"But it was Delaunay who suggested that I try to trace Larry through the agency."

"He's good at his job. He makes two-way bets. He serves Strassberger, his client and banker. To you he demonstrates clean hands and good intentions—as well as a neutral attitude to commerce! What can you prove, you or your colleague, Vianney, except that Delaunay was obviously trying to be helpful? You'll never budge a man like that. He's anchored in concrete."

"But I can't trust him either?"

"Only to serve his own interests. Once you move out of Le Diplomate he'll wash his hands like Pilate and file you away with the rest of his case histories. Another important matter. Your father has told me that you have a girlfriend in France?"

"I have."

"You've no doubt confided in her?"

"Up to this point, yes."

"Then explain to her clearly that everything she knows exposes her to danger. That's the last thing you—"

At that moment, the telephone rang. Madi was on the line from New York. She had news of a sort.

"I've been up half the night, going through boxes of old travel brochures and playing the memory game you suggested. Two things keep popping up in my mind. Larry was very health-conscious, as you know. He worked hard at keeping fit. Whenever he discussed holiday locations he would say, 'Let's set a minimum standard of hygiene. I don't want to be eating pig food. I don't want to be running back and forth to the john with the Curse of the Incas. I don't want to have an accident in Africa and wake up with an AIDS infection from contaminated blood.' He used to chant the motto 'The Lucas family likes healthy holidays.'

"The other thing was that he, personally, was always attracted to the idea of working on an archaeological dig in the Mediterranean or the Middle East. He never did it because it didn't fit the family needs. I found that he'd marked places in

Anatolia and Mesopotamia and even as far away as China, where the last Roman Legions were reported to have settled. I've marked the places on a sketch map and faxed it to your office. That was right, wasn't it?"

"Right, and wonderfully helpful. Thanks."

"What are you doing now?"

"Working through the next steps—which we shouldn't talk about on the phone. Keep your courage up, and say a prayer or two."

"I'm holding up, Carl—old family training!—and the kids are keeping me sane. I try to bluff myself that this is no different from Larry's absences in Paris. Sometimes, though, I get the feeling that he is fading far too quickly out of my life. I dream of him like that: a figure receding to infinity across a long bridge."

The phrase had an ominous ring and it raised again the question that had begun to gnaw away at my confidence: Was Larry worth any of the risks I was taking for him? If and when I found him, would he greet me with a handshake and a thank you or spit in my eye and walk away?

"That's a dark thought you're harboring," said Kallman, after I had hung up. "It might help to share it."

I told him what Madi had said. He was interested.

"The concern about his health is important. It argues against sexual promiscuity and excludes places where health risks are high. I attach less importance to his interest in archaeology. It would not seem to suit his present purposes of concealment. It would make him prominent in a small elite group with international connections, so I'd discount it somewhat. But that wasn't the thought that was troubling you, was it?"

"No, it wasn't."

"Tell me, please."

I told him with a certain embarrassment. He took it quite seriously.

"That's a symptom of the trauma we were talking about: the sense of futility, of wasted effort, of resentment against the person who got you into all this. It's normal. It's useful as a danger signal, but don't let yourself brood on it. You've agreed to search for your brother-in-law as a family duty. It's a debt of honor. Pay it, don't question it."

Kallman did not linger on the subject. He went on brusquely.

"I'll meet you here tomorrow morning and provide you with documents. We'll go together to Morgan Guaranty, to make sure their financial routines are watertight. After that, I suggest you move out of here and operate from the apartment for as long as you need to be in Paris."

"What do I tell Vianney and the people at Strassberger?"

"Just that you're on the move and you'll check in from time to time for messages and mail."

"And Delaunay?"

"Give him a handsome tip and tell him to refer all messages and information to Vianney."

"He'll ask about my plans. He'll want to know about Simonetta Travel."

"You've developed a sudden strong reservation about the whole idea. The more you think about it, the less you like it."

"Ain't that the truth, Mr. Kallman!"

"The truth is always much easier to tell." Oskar Kallman looked like a schoolmaster smiling tolerantly at a thick-headed pupil. He bade me a brisk farewell and was gone.

When he had left I felt oddly restless and uneasy, as if I were surrounded by spies and eavesdroppers. When I brushed my hair and knotted my tie I was relieved that there was no face looking over my shoulder. As I passed through the foyer on my way out, I had to force myself to smile and salute Delaunay behind his counter. On the way to the Strassberger office I found myself rehearsing my dialogues with Vianney and Claudine Parmentier as if their roles had changed overnight from supporters to enemies.

This paranoid mood was still on me when I arrived at the office. The map Madi had faxed me was in an envelope on my desk. As I studied it, I found that my hands were clammy and there was a film of sweat on my forehead. I sat for a few minutes, eyes closed, palms flat on the desk, breathing deeply and slowly, trying to clear the nameless phantoms from my brain. Finally, they were gone. I felt as though I had wakened from a bad dream. I shoved the sketch back into the envelope and put it in my breast pocket.

I called Vianney in his office and asked if he was free to talk with me. He had clients with him. He would be free in twenty minutes. I reflected for a while before calling in Claudine Parmentier. I liked the woman. She was good to look at. She had a certain to-hell-with-you-Jack approach that pleased me. There were no sexual complications. There was no way in the world I was going to double in brass in a modern version of the Sapphic odes. On the other hand, she had lied to a company investigator. Her relations with her lover were ambivalent. She was sympathetic with Larry and his plight. Could I trust her as an ally? I called her in, sat her down, and put the question to her directly.

"I'll be leaving Paris in the next couple of days. I need a personal and private contact in Paris, here in the office and after hours."

"And you'd like me to be that contact?"

"If you're willing, yes."

"Do you trust me?"

"If you tell me I can."

"That's a big risk."

"Bigger than you know. There may well be two lives on the line. Larry's and mine."

"Have you told Mr. Vianney about this? I can't do it if he objects. I have a good position here."

"If you agree, I'll ask his consent. Your career won't be hurt."

"Why can't he help?"

"He can, but what he can do for me is limited by the nature of his job. You were closer to Larry than any other person in the office. That means we can work in shorthand if necessary. Situations may arise when there's no time to spell the words."

"I won't be a spy. I won't peddle gossip."

"I'm not asking that."

"Explain then what you will ask."

"Fine! Today, now! I want you to make a casual call on Simonetta Travel. You are making inquiries about exotic holidays. You are what you choose to be: single or in a lesbian relationship. You can invent what you are looking for, or you can use this as a guide."

I laid out Madi's faxed map of archaeological sites and explained its context. She was dubious.

"I don't know enough. I'm not interested enough to follow that line."

"It doesn't matter."

I handed her the clipping Delaunay had given me. She read it swiftly and was as swiftly involved.

"Yes! This I can play with."

"They'll ask you how you came by it."

"I read it in a magazine in a dentist's waiting room."

"Which magazine?"

"I can't remember. I tore it out and copied it."

"Good! Then you ask all the questions you can think of about their travel packages. Let it be known, discreetly, that money is not a problem. I'll be interested to know how they deal with you, how much personal information they try to get out of you, how the staff impresses you. The only things you should not reveal are your real name, your home address, and your connection with Strassberger. Come straight back here with your information and I'll buy you a very good lunch."

I saw—or thought I saw—a new gleam of respect in her clear eyes. Without a word she stood up and smoothed down her skirt.

"Do I have a choice of venue for lunch?"

"Of course. Anywhere you say."

"I'd like to go to the Vert Galant."

"Done! Make the reservation on your way out. Any special reason for the choice?"

"Half a reason, yes. When we met yesterday I was not impressed. I thought that for an American and an artist you were rather stuffy and old-fashioned—*un vert galant,* in fact. I've changed my mind. One might even say. . . ." She smiled and shook her head. "On second thoughts one had better not say anything. I'm on my way. "

When she had gone, I sat doodling on a sheet of office notepaper, practicing the Gothic signature of Edgar Francis Benson and

91

memorizing the names of his parents. Then I set about designing a monogram with which to sign the pictures that Edgar Francis Benson would have to paint to verify his temporary existence as an artist. When Vianney buzzed from his office to tell me that he was ready to see me, I tore the paper into little pieces and dumped them in the wastebasket. I had the momentary comic thought that, perhaps, I should have swallowed them.

Before I reached Vianney's office I had composed my brief. Vianney had been mortally offended by the Corsec affair, and he was too important to my father and to the company to risk another alienation. He was prickly, but he was honest, and I had to demonstrate respect. On the other hand, he had to know my doubts about Delaunay. I decided to leave that little gambit until last.

First I thanked him for his contribution to yesterday's discussions, then I told him of my decision to take the underground route suggested by Delaunay. His reaction surprised me.

"The more I think about that, my friend, the more it troubles me. When I reflect on what Larry has done and how he has done it, I believe even less that anyone should interfere. Suppose the reverse were true, that your sister had walked away from him; would you intervene, to the extent that you are doing now? I think not. I believe you would decide that both parties had the right to a certain privacy. I leave aside all the other considerations—the expense, the risk which you personally are assuming. You are leaving the man no room to move or to recover. We have already determined there is no crime here. Larry has more than honorably discharged his obligations to the company. He has, at least in financial terms, taken care of his family. So, I tell you frankly, I disagree with what you are doing."

"I respect that. Thank you for telling me. I'll advise my father that I've agreed to sideline you from any further participation in the affair. I shall emphasize that you have a valid point of view and have the company interest at heart."

"I appreciate that. I confess it will not absolve me from my doubts and from a certain guilt about my dislike of the man."

"I'm sorry I can't offer you absolution. I'm not feeling so

good either. Now I have two favors to ask. The first is that you tell Delaunay nothing of my plans."

"I know nothing, therefore I can tell nothing."

"If the question is asked, I'd be happy for you to tell him you are no longer involved."

"I can do that, very easily. It would be much more difficult to lie to him. He is a good client. He serves others of our clients. Our relationship is formal, but it has been in existence for a long time. I'm sure you understand that."

"I do. My second request is that Claudine Parmentier remain as my personal contact inside and outside the office."

"Have you spoken to her about this?"

"I have. She will accept, subject to your approval. Your only involvement would be to make any payments I recommend for her activities and expenses."

"I can do that, certainly; but may I ask how much you know about Mlle. Parmentier and her background?"

"Only what she has told me herself."

"Before you leave me, you should take a look at her dossier. She's a talented woman—not everyone's cup of coffee but a highly efficient member of the staff."

"Trustworthy?"

"So far as I know. Erratic, sometimes. She has a fierce temper if she is crossed."

"I can believe that."

He leaned back in his chair and gave me a slow, quizzical smile which transformed his saturnine face.

"You are not, perhaps, romantically interested in Claudine?"

Now it was my turn to smile.

"No. I can read. The sign says KEEP OFF THE GRASS."

"Sometimes, I am told, the sign changes."

"I've been told that too, by the lady herself, but I won't be around to see it. As from tomorrow I'm on the move. Messages and mail should be passed to Claudine. I'll check in from time to time. Just one more thing. This hasn't been the best beginning to a friendship. Once this business is behind us, you might care to come down to Cagnes and spend a weekend with me."

There was a moment of silence between us; then Marc Antoine Vianney stood up and held out his hand.

"I'd like very much to get to know you better, Carl Emil Strassberger. Go with God, and come safely home."

Lunch at the Vert Galant was an event which never happened. I waited in the office until two o'clock. I had a ham sandwich and a cup of coffee. I talked with my father in New York and reported my meeting with Oskar Kallman. He had just finished breakfast and was in a hurry to get to his office. He told me that he would be pursuing his own inquiries on Dr. Hubert Rubens of Geneva. I should call him back before close of business in Paris.

I called Dr. Alma Levy. She had spent a long night going through her tapes on Larry Lucas. Her secretary would be typing up the material and her notes during the morning. She would fax them to me at my office. She was not too hopeful about their value. The geography was vague, the images specific to states of mind but not necessarily to an identifiable earthly paradise—lost, regained, or imagined. She would, however, scan them once more before transmitting them.

At two-thirty I called Giorgiu Andrescu at Corsec and told him my change of plans and residence. He was happy with both. He asked me to let him have further details—numbers of passport and credit cards—as soon as the documents were in my hands. In his high-noon style he informed me, "We'll track you like a satellite. We'll know every move you make." So far, however, he and his people were still feeling around the walls of Simonetta Travel. They hadn't yet opened a window on its operations. I had just put down the phone and tossed my luncheon wrapper into the wastebasket when Claudine Parmentier walked in. It was five minutes past three. I snapped at her.

"As I remember, we had a lunch date at the Vert Galant."

"We did. Please don't be angry. There was no chance to call. I'm sorry I stood you up; but this was an opportunity I dared not miss. Will you let me explain, please?"

"That depends on what you're about to tell me. Sit down."

94

She sat down, a little less gracefully than normal.

"Have you been drinking?"

"Yes. One certainly—maybe two—glasses more than I should."

"Where?"

"At the Vert Galant, of course."

"Tell me about it."

With slightly tipsy abandon, she acted it, scene by scene.

"Where to begin? Simonetta Travel maintains an office on Saint Honoré, second floor. There is no display window on the street, just a brass plaque, very reserved, very chic. The reception area also is very discreet, modern furniture, pastel walls, no posters, no magazines, just a Chagall and a Giacometti and a stunning piece from a Mexican painter I've never heard of.

"The receptionist matches all this: black hair, tailored suit, a voice like golden honey. She asks if I have an appointment. Regrettably I do not. I tell her I am obeying an impulse. I have read about their agency. I wonder if they can offer me the kind of service I need. She asks where I have read about them. I say, in a magazine, don't ask me which one. I was struck by the name of their director—two *f*s—Francesco Falco. Very romantic. Ah, yes. She remembers that article. They have had many inquiries from it. If I would be so kind as to wait a few moments, one of their consultants will be at my disposal. I ask, with a certain reserve, whether I may deal with a woman consultant. There is an intimate side to travel matters which many agencies do not understand. But of course! I think I catch a gleam of understanding in her eyes. She speaks quietly into the telephone.

"I wait perhaps three minutes when the consultant enters. Now this is where a miracle begins to happen. I have seen this one before with an older woman at Elle et Lui, which, in case you haven't heard of it, is a lesbian club. She is beautiful and—you will not laugh!—still as desirable as she was when I first set eyes on her. She does not recognize me. We had not spoken that first time. My Anne-Louise is very possessive, so in company I'm careful. Anyway, here is the consultant, fresh, well-groomed, infinitely obliging. Her name is Liliane Prévost.

95

"She presents her card, formally like a Japanese. I pretend to have forgotten mine. She leads me into her office, which is furnished to accommodate four people. There are comfortable armchairs, a display screen, a tray with coffee cups and mineral water. She seats me beside her within hand's reach. Her chair is equipped with an index and a computer keyboard. She moves smoothly into an obvious routine. Can I give her my name, my address, my marital status, *et patati et patata*! It's basic information that helps them to make recommendations that suit the client. I decline gently. She understands surely that one prefers to keep all personal details to oneself until one has established a personal rapport. Of course she understands! She's been in the auction ring herself. First names only until you're ready to get acquainted. She compromises by handing me a printed form and asks me to fill it out at my leisure. I agree. She hands me the form which I now hand to you. She pats my hand and asks how I think she can help me. . . . Are you reading me so far, Mr. Strassberger?"

"I am reading you loud and clear, Mademoiselle. Take your time. I don't want to miss a single grace note of this opera."

"I tell her, with carefully modulated emotion, that I have certain problems in my life. My lover is very possessive. She insists on an exclusivity, which I feel is unreasonable. I'm young. I have the means to enjoy myself. I want to do just that. . . . Of course I don't want to break up our relationship—but I want to think about choices: a restorative vacation for both of us, or in the last resort we break up and I go traveling alone for a while.

"Instantly the atmosphere changes. Liliane is infinitely sympathetic. She explains the workings and the policy of Simonetta Travel. This is not mass tourism. This is haute cuisine for the gourmets of travel. The menus are designed and prepared by their eminent director, M. Francesco Falco. He is constantly seeking new locations and preparing them to receive the distinguished clients of Simonetta. Sometimes he himself, or one of us, travels with the clients to see them installed and marshal the local services they need. He functions from Milan but he is always on the move. Two weeks ago he made a transatlantic trip to settle a lady on an island in the Caribbean.

"That's my cue to tell Liliane I've never been to the Caribbean. She moves immediately into selling mode with her computer and the display screen. I tell you they have everything beautifully organized. All the relevant facts pop up on the screen: accommodation, routings, costs, and beautifully sanitized film clips. When I begin to make notes, she stops me. There is no need. She will supply printouts and photographs of anything I want.

"Then we begin to be a little playful. I name a place at random and we search the screen for details. Then we play the game in reverse, fitting places to people. I push the game a little further—whom would I like to send where. All the time Liliane is loosening up. I am becoming more and more the eager client and I have to confess I'm enjoying Liliane. So I ask her to join me for lunch at the Vert Galant. She accepts with pleasure."

"How did you pay for lunch, by the way?"

"In cash. You didn't think I'd be stupid enough to use a credit card!"

"So what did the lunch produce?"

"Intimacies, mostly. The prospect of an affair if one wanted to pursue it, which for the moment I do not want at all. I believed also that I might pick up more useful information."

"You didn't think she might have had the same idea?"

"Of course. That was the spice of the game. The more she pressed me, the more emotion I had to spend on the scene. I played it like Bernhardt, believe me. I had debts of love and honor. But yes, yes, yes, I would be back to her. By way of distraction I asked if it might it be possible for her to travel with me to my chosen destination."

"And her answer?"

"Was strictly business. It would be a pleasant idea. It could work if the money I was spending with the agency were substantial enough, and if I paid her expenses as well. However, things changed from day to day. The number of clients was increasing. Each one required special personal attention. For example, only a few days ago she had been appointed to escort a male client who was spending a week in Paris before she sent him on his way to his next destination. He had to pay very expensively for that. How did she feel about this kind of escort service? That depended. This one was young, agreeable, obviously wealthy, and Mr. Falco had planned a big journey for him. He wanted him kept happy and interested. It wasn't as if it were a romance. But he was exciting to be with and generous. I pressed her for a description and a name. I had to make a joke of it. You know, girlish giggles over the wine. I didn't get a name, but she came up with a reasonable facsimile of Larry Lucas."

"Then she could have been the woman driving the black Peugeot when he came to pick up his clothes."

"I believe she was. I want to check my diary so I can be sure of the date and time of the incident. However, I hadn't been near enough to see her—and thank God she hadn't seen me. You have to remember I'm stringing out a game here, because I can't ask the big direct question. I ask where the client was going. She just smiles and touches my lips with her finger. I shouldn't tempt her. I might be her client very soon. She might have to protect my privacy too. I tease her then. I don't want to be just a client. I hope we might be friends. Besides, what was so secret about a man going on a holiday? Most travel agents were very happy to talk about satisfied clients. She is quick to point out that the article I had read emphasized a confidential relationship. I pouted a little. She relented and told me strictly *entre nous* there was some sort of mystery about this one. Her own opinion was that he was in the middle of a divorce and didn't want anyone to know where he was.

"Finally, the last drink did the trick. His name wouldn't mean anything because it wasn't his real one. The night he left he gave her a handsome present. She drove him to Orly Airport. They stopped on the way to pick up some luggage. He was ticketed to Milan. Falco was meeting him there and driving him to a villa the agency operates near Sirmione on Lake Garda. It's called the Villa Estense. Liliane had taken a woman client there once. According to her it was a place of great luxury, with attentive staff and all sorts of services on call. I ask whether she'd recommend it for me. She shrugs. For me and my lover perhaps, if we wanted to be quiet together. For me alone, or me with Liliane, no! There were much better choices. She didn't think this man would be staying too long. Mr. Falco himself was arranging his onward ticketing. She didn't know where.

"Then she asked again when I thought I might decide about my own arrangements. I told her I wanted to think about it, talk to my partner. I didn't want to be rushed. Of course not! It was just that there was constant pressure for performance inside the agency. Simonetta's consultants were paid a retainer, but their principal income came from commissions. By that time I knew we'd had one glass too many and Liliane was pressing too hard for comfort. I called for the check and had the doorman call me two taxis. Liliane and I kissed as we parted. Then we went our separate ways—and here I am, still a little *grise* and waiting for you to tell me I've been a clever girl and that you forgive me for standing you up for lunch."

"I do forgive you. And you have been a *very* clever girl. I'm going to bring you some coffee."

"And then you're going to read me a lecture, aren't you?"

"Would it do any good?"

"No."

"Then no lecture."

"Thank God for that."

"But there is a caution. It may be fun for you falling into the tender trap with Liliane Prévost, but you could drop both Larry Lucas and me into a tiger trap!"

For the first time her composure was shaken. She wasn't just squiffy; she was in aftershock. There was a whole wave of emotion behind her half-humorous narrative. Her face paled and she fumbled in her handbag for a tissue.

"You'd think I'd learn, wouldn't you?" she said.

I had no answer to that, so I went out to the machine to make her a cup of very strong coffee. By the time I got back with the coffee, she had repaired her makeup and her old persona was firmly in place; ironic, mocking, and defiant. After a few mouthfuls of coffee she challenged me.

"Go on, say it. I got randy and made a fool of myself."

"Enough that you know it. I was the one who put you at risk. You did better than I hoped—or you deserved. You opened a door into Simonetta Travel. You may well have identified Larry's first port of call after Paris. But you can't go back to Simonetta, unless you sign up either for travel or a love affair. Either way, you end up in Liliane's computer. So you bail out, now!"

"How do I do that? If I ignore the girl I make an enemy."

"You may never see her again."

"I never expected to see her today, did I? Women like us tend to move in fairly tight circles."

"So make it formal. Write her a gentle note without your address: *Dear Liliane: Lovely lunch. Thanks for your time and trouble. The plans we discussed don't work for me just now. When they do you'll be the first to know. Affectionate salutations.* That way it's done, it's over. If you ever meet again you meet with a smile—even though she will be disappointed over the commission! Which, if you're thinking about love, is also a cautionary thought."

It was the first time I had seen Claudine Parmentier blush. She nodded a reluctant agreement.

"That's true. But you didn't have to say it. Very well. I'll wait for a couple of days and then write the note. Talking of notes, have you told Vianney about our arrangement?"

"I have; but I'm going to cancel it."

"Why?"

"You represent a risk I can't afford."

"I understand. I'm not very proud of myself either. I'm a silly bitch who doesn't know enough to come out of the rain. What about my job here?"

"That's between you and Vianney."

"What are you going to tell him about today?"

"Only that I've reconsidered. I think it's better for everyone that I work alone and outside."

"You're a hard man, Mr. Strassberger."

"And you're a bright woman, but you're also reckless; and I can't cope with that right now."

As she walked out, she looked so dejected that I was tempted to relent. God knows, I needed an ally at Strassberger; but this one was already away and winging with the bat people.

I sat for a long while studying the document which Claudine had handed to me: the personal details and the vacation wish list which Simonetta Travel required from all those who wanted to use its exotic services. Whoever had designed the two-page form had done a very clever job. It elicited information for a complete identity and credit check as well as a profile of private tastes, recreations, and sexual orientations. Somewhere along the way—and before his change of identity—Larry must have filled out one of these forms. I would obviously be required to do the same before I embarked on my underground journey in search of him. Both forms would be loaded into the computer system; both could therefore be extricated from it.

I scribbled an explanatory note to Giorgiu Andrescu at Corsec and told him I'd call him later. I sent the note and the form on the private fax in my office. Then I folded the originals and shoved them in my briefcase to show to Oskar Kallman when he delivered the documents of my new identity.

I debated for a few moments what I should say to Vianney. To honor my promise, I made it as brief as possible.

"About Claudine Parmentier. I've had second thoughts. I've decided against using her."

"I assume you're not asking for a comment from me?"

"No. I'm asking a personal favor. Will you receive and hold all messages for me until further notice?"

"Of course. Is there anything else I should know—anything that might touch the interests of Strassberger?"

"No. There's a credit Claudine should have. She uncovered some very useful information about Larry's possible movements."

"On the other hand?"

"There is no other hand. There is only the sound of one hand clapping—and that's a very small, sad sound. Hardly worth mentioning, in fact."

"But something to remember, yes?"

"Yes indeed. I'll be in touch."

"*À bientôt*, my friend—and good luck!"

6

IT WAS TWENTY TO FIVE in the afternoon when I left the Strassberger office. I was glad to be out of the place, where I was now isolated and unwelcome. I could not quarrel with Vianney's desire to distance himself from the Larry Lucas affair. He had a business to run, and the last thing he wanted was to tangle with the Strassberger oligarchy.

I was less troubled by Claudine Parmentier's performance than by my own defective judgment of her character—or was it my subconscious desire to play mind games with an ambivalent woman? I didn't like that thought either. It reminded me too sharply of Alma Levy's warning that psychic illness was by its nature infectious. Claudine Parmentier, randy and reckless, was an image of Larry in his moods of wild elation. I myself was suddenly trapped in his other world, a winter landscape of self-doubt and fear of the future into which I was about to launch myself.

These were thoughts too dark to entertain in a hotel suite with a whiskey bottle for company; so I crossed the river and gave myself the simple pleasure of a browse along the bookstalls of the quai. There are few treasures to be found there nowadays, but there is always a double challenge in the hunt. You may just stumble on a treasure, and the *bouquiniste* may just be ignorant of its value. The odds against either event are enormous. The real pleasures are in the handling of forgotten texts with yellowed pages and scuffed leather bindings, in ruffling through folios of foxed prints and sheaves of student drawings pawned for the price of a breakfast.

Today it seemed, my luck was out. The only object that caught my fancy was an 1893 edition of *Les Trophées*, the only book of verse published by José-Maria de Hérédia, a disciple of Leconte de Lisle and one of the greats among the Parnassians. The book was in poor condition, but I wanted it for a sentimental reason, the famous last quatrain of the sonnet on Antony and Cleopatra, which in my youth I had tried vainly to render into English.

I asked the price. The bookseller named an exorbitant figure. I tried to bargain. He would have none of it; this was a rare and valuable piece. I pointed out that it was in very poor condition. It would fall apart in my hands after a couple of readings. He would have none of that either; the price was fixed. I shrugged and handed it back. What did I need it for anyway? I would still have my boyhood vision of the two lovers, clasped in each other's arms, seeing in each other's eyes that "immense sea on which the scattered galleys were in flight."

It was at least a romantic thought on which to end a lousy day. I turned away from the miserly bookseller and headed in the direction of the Pont Royal.

Back at the hotel I paused at reception to tell them of the arrival of Arlette Tassigny and of our departure next morning. Delaunay was busy with a pair of clients. I waved to him and went upstairs to pour myself a drink and make my telephone calls.

My father had news for me.

"I called an old friend of mine who has just retired from the Union Bank. He knows everybody who is anybody. I asked him about this Dr. Hubert Rubens in Geneva. He's an old man now and apparently in his dotage. His son, who has the same name, took over the business, which was founded on deposit funds from German bigwigs during the war years: runaway Nazi money and funds plundered from Jews and other victims of the Third Reich. Some of the depositors didn't survive the war, so their funds still remained in trusteeship in Geneva. Those who got away to Brazil, Argentina, Uruguay, and the other South American republics continued to invest with Rubens. It's a tight, very quiet, very discreet business involving much personal service which the big banks don't really want to touch. Rubens himself is described as very reserved but very punctual in his dealings with the major institutions. He's respected, too—which is understandable, because he has a high credit rating. He doesn't need to play games."

"But apparently he does."

"I'd put it another way. He's continuing the old game his father played. You are trustee to major estates. A number of them must pass into your unfettered control—just by the accidents of mortality."

"Or by premeditated arrangement."

"The evidence is that Larry made his own arrangements. You, Carl, premised the sinister interpretation."

"Could this old friend of yours arrange a meeting with Rubens?"

"For you? I think that would be a mistake. If you pursue this plan of yours—"

"I am pursuing it, Father."

"And if your premise is correct, then sooner or later Rubens will come to you. Or you will be introduced to him."

"You're probably right. I confess I'm not too confident of my own judgment just now."

"That's healthy."

"I've had an odd sort of day."

"Tell me about it."

I told him at length and in detail about Vianney and Claudine Parmentier. As usual he listened in silence, asked a few curt questions, and then delivered judgment.

"Vianney is right. He is not part of the family. He doesn't believe we should be pursuing Larry. Therefore, he declines to be involved. He's running our business in Paris and running it well. Let him do that. Demand what service you need and forget the rest of it. As for this Parmentier woman, are you sure you weren't tripped up by your male vanity?"

"Very probably. How would you have handled it, Father?"

He laughed, a big full-bellied chuckle.

"To tell you the truth, Carl, I don't know. I've managed men all my life. As for women, your mother has always managed me. As a bachelor you're a natural prey to women who are much cleverer than we are. But if you're open to a little advice, I'd suggest you make your peace with Mlle. Parmentier before you leave Paris. You can't afford—we can't afford—a declared enemy in the camp. Besides, whom else do you have?"

"No one except Arlette, and I refuse to involve her."

"You have Corsec. Already we're paying them a lot of money, which they're eager to keep. Squeeze them for every service you can get."

"I'll be talking to Andrescu after we've finished this call. Make sure to note that I check out of Le Diplomate tomorrow morning. I pick up my documents and then go underground. We won't be able to have this kind of conversation too often."

"Be careful, Carl, and remember always we love you—I love you!"

"I love you too, Father."

Confessions of love were rare between us. This one had its own special poignancy. It was an acknowledgment of risk and danger, which were the more threatening because they were too vague to be defined. They came into much clearer focus when I talked to Alma Levy. I had to tell her not to send any documents to the office in Paris but to give me the gist of them on the phone. She had little to add to her first summation. Larry's reveries and fantasies were a geography of soul states, not of voyages he would choose to make. The surprise came when I told her Larry's suspected location was a villa on Lake Garda. There was anxiety in her voice too:

"If we are talking of foul play, of Larry as target and victim, he is most vulnerable of all in a clinical situation. If acute symptoms of either mania or depression are demonstrated, drugs can be used, quite legally, to control the patient. In unscrupulous hands drugs then become a weapon."

I reminded her of the opposite argument which she herself had put to me. Larry had a chameleon talent for evasion and manipulation. Would not the survival odds favor him?

"They would—unless he is hit for any reason by an acute episode."

"Could such an episode be induced?"

"Only by someone who understood how fragile he is—a nagging wife, an importunate lover, a professional psychiatrist like myself."

"It's only a short time since his disappearance. He's still on the move. I doubt anyone would have had time to set the scene for that kind of drama."

"Unless the scene were already set for similar cases . . . which, I agree, is pushing the laws of probability. Now tell me about yourself."

"I'm fraying at the edges. I'm beginning to start at shadows and see villains behind every bush. I could use a good laugh and some happy loving."

"Then grab it while you can, Carl Emil. You can spend so long in a sickroom that you forget the fresh air and sunlight on the lawn!"

I was beginning to be bothered by the elegiac tones of these farewells. It was a relief therefore to hear the brash trumpeting of Giorgiu Andrescu.

"We're in, my friend! We're in and living with the Simonetta family by way of their New York operation! It was easy. We're asking them for travel and accommodation quotes on client conferences, individual vacations, incentive executive packages. We're working on-line with them from our own terminals. Our continental people will have similar access in the European area. We can keep them interested for quite a while, while our hackers go searching their files. Give us a few days and we should have a movement pattern for Larry Lucas as well as his new alibi. We'll put you into the system as soon as we have your document numbers and a travel schedule."

"You're clever fellows, George! Now see what you can tell me about the Villa Estense, near Sirmione on Lake Garda, Italy. It's supposed to be a luxury resort owned and operated by Simonetta. It's possible Larry is staying there before moving on. His itinerary has been arranged by Falco himself. He had someone to look after him in Paris, a young woman from the Paris office, Liliane Prévost. Obviously the rest of the itinerary was arranged from Milan. I'm heading there as soon as I've got my new papers and established my banking arrangements."

"Good! We have an office there. Use it. I'll contact Sergio Carlino and tell him to expect you. He'll also inform us and you about the Villa Estense. If you need a companion for cover or for company, he'll arrange that too."

"I'll keep it in mind. Thanks, George."

"All part of the service. This is only the beginning. Fun, isn't it?"

It was on the tip of my tongue to tell him that I could think of better ways to enjoy myself; but at least he was ending the day's drama on an up beat. I thanked him with warmth and sincerity and hung up.

There remained only one nagging thought: How to tidy up the situation with Claudine Parmentier. I was still toying with it when my telephone rang. Arlette was on the line.

"*Chéri*, the end of my day is a mess—but a beautiful mess. I want you to share it with me. It will do you enormous good. I am at the Galerie Céline. There is an exhibition which begins at eight. Céline Audran, the patronne, is an old friend of mine whom you haven't met. The artist is a young Tahitienne who has been studying at the Beaux Arts. This is a talent to knock your eyes out: wild colors and figure drawings like the best of the Baroque and a sensuality which will have the viewers chewing the carpet.

"Céline has asked me to introduce her work on the Côte this summer. I think I'll do better there than Céline will in Paris. You know what competition is like here, and the snobs will give this artist a rough time at the beginning because she's young and a woman and a colonial from the Pacific. Also, they won't like the feminist dialectic, which is a little heavy in places. "Please will you come? We'll have champagne and canapés and a late supper afterward with Céline and the artist and a few friends. At least it will get you out of that business suit which I hate. Say yes."

"Yes! Yes! Yes! I'll be happy, happy, happy! Now where do I find this Galerie Céline?"

"It's in the rue de Montalembert. Number nineteen. You can't miss it. There's a quite splendid Polynesian nude in the window. She's been getting a lot of attention from the passersby. It'll be good to see you! Don't let me forget my valise when we go to supper. See you at eightish. *Je t'aime, chéri.*"

I was only too happy to go. I was sick of the business world I had been inhabiting under sufferance, sick of Larry Lucas, and sickest of all of my own crotchety company. It would be a treat to slip back into the casual anonymity of a *vernissage* at a less-than-fashionable gallery where a bad review wouldn't break an artist and a modest sale or two might make a big career. Besides, an eight o'clock rendezvous gave me time for a shave and a long hot bath, with a sip or two of whiskey to lift the heart and open it to young encounters—even with a feminist dialectician from Polynesia!

Even with all that I arrived early. Arlette was happy to have me at her side. Her colleague, Céline, welcomed me and then handed me over to the artist herself, a big Gauguinesque beauty whose explanations were only a shade less vivid than the paintings themselves.

"In the tropics there is a perpetual problem for the painter. In clear weather the sea is so vivid, and by comparison the rain forest is so dense and shadowy, they tend to cancel out the contrasts, even while you are observing them. The sea becomes like a tourist postcard. The forest is dark, lush, and oppressive. Life slows down. Distinctions blur. One becomes sluggish. But here in Paris, away from it all, I have been able to hold it in my mind's eye, clear and fresh, the forms distinct—especially the woman forms and the flow of the bodies hidden under those ugly great colored sacks which the missionaries brought. You are a painter, they tell me. You come from America, how does all this hit you? Be open with me, please! I can't bear to be patronized!"

She was a prickly one, as Arlette had warned me—and the

Parisians were going to be nibbling like piranhas at her fragile self-esteem. I chided her gently.

"Why should you think I'd patronize you? I'm an academic architectural painter. This work of yours is free, open, alive. You're managing to do what Van Gogh and Gauguin did and, strangely enough, the Englishman Turner. You've caught the light and fixed the color and you've rendered the body forms beautifully. My compliments!"

"If you were a buyer, which one would you choose?"

"If you wanted me to remember you—painter to painter—which one would you choose for me?"

"That's not fair."

"Your question wasn't fair either."

"I know. I'll have to get used to keeping my mouth shut and waiting on the pleasure of the clientele. It's hard when you come from the colonies to the big city. They make it hard—even your peers at art school."

"Smile and ignore them and hang on to the belief in your own talent. Think what you do. You're offering people a hand-hold on the mystery of creation."

"I wish I could believe that."

"You do it. Therefore you know it."

We paused by a small canvas: a young woman naked, leaning on the carved prow of a ceremonial canoe, staring across a sunset ocean, her body lighted from the side by the last rich glow. The painter watched me in silence as I studied the canvas. She asked no questions. She waited until I asked her.

"Would you have Céline put a sticker on that for me, please?"

"You like it that much?"

"Enough to want to live with it. That's the test, isn't it, for a picture or a lover?"

"You're my first buyer."

"That's my privilege."

She laid her big hand lightly on my wrist and went hurrying back to Céline. The gallery was beginning to fill up now. I took a glass of champagne and moved into a quiet angle next to Arlette to watch the new arrivals. It wasn't what you would call a buying audience. There was a scattering of second-string critics, a few older artists, mostly local denizens, and a gaggle of young intellectuals eager for free champagne and the chance to air their opinions.

"You bought the canoe girl," Arlette said. "That was a good choice. It was also a generous encouragement."

"Can you take it back to Nice with you, please? We're moving out of Le Diplomate tomorrow, and I'm going to be on the road soon after."

"And of course you're going to explain why!"

"But not here."

"Very well. So tell. Am I right or wrong to take on our young Tahitienne?"

"Absolutely right—so long as she can run the gauntlet and last the distance. If you're handling her, why not bring her down to the coast during the summer and let her soak up some clean sunlight?"

"That's a great idea! I'll talk to her about it—and to Céline." She cast a knowing eye about the room, which was rapidly filling up. "It's a good turnout, but I don't see too much real money. A couple of good reviews would help—but I'll bet my summer sales will be three, four times Céline's."

Just at that moment a new group of guests arrived at the door. As they paused to sign the visitors' book and grab a glass of champagne, I recognized Claudine Parmentier with a woman companion. I retreated into the shadowed corner and drew Arlette with me toward Céline's small office. Arlette protested.

"What are you doing, Carl?"

"Don't ask questions! Just come with me."

The door of the office was ajar. We sidled through and closed it. Céline and her staff of two were busy receiving guests and working the room. I explained hurriedly to Arlette.

"Claudine Parmentier from our office has just come in. I don't want her to see me here until I know whom she's with. I want you to go out again, check the visitors' book, and tell me the names above and below hers."

"But why, for God's sake?"

111

"Please, *chérie*. I'll explain everything later. Just do as I ask, now!"

It seemed an age before she came back. She had identified the name above that of Claudine Parmentier. It was a male, Philippe Cardamatis. The one beneath it was female, Liliane Prévost. I uttered an angry curse and tried to reason with this sudden mischance. Arlette stood watching me in silence, waiting for my explanation. I had no time to frame one. I had a simple choice: confrontation or flight. Confrontation was out of the question. All my carefully constructed cover would be blown in the first encounter with Liliane Prévost and Claudine. Flight meant an immediate exit and the ruin of Arlette's business evening.

"There are two here I daren't meet just now," I told her. "This has to do with Larry's disappearance. I'm leaving. I'll go straight back to Le Diplomate. You come when you're ready. I'm sorry."

"Don't be. I'd come with you, but I have to finish my business with Céline. I'll make your apologies. I'll most probably be late. Leave a key for me with the concierge."

"Do me one quick favor, please. Look outside and see if I can get to the door in a hurry."

She went out and back in a matter of seconds. She thrust a catalog into my hands.

"Go now! Bury your nose in this. Go!"

I went out at a fast walk, my face half hidden by the catalog. The moment I hit the street, I broke into a run, intent on grabbing a taxi and getting as far away as I could from the menacing presence of a young woman who—God help me!—did nothing more menacing than peddle travel services and occasionally peddle herself as part of the deal.

And yet, and yet . . . there was more to it than paranoia and panic. Read upside down or sideways, the script said the same thing. Claudine Parmentier had launched herself head first into a love affair with Liliane Prévost. There was no way to guess at her relations with her partner, Anne-Louise, but it would be folly to depend on her loyalties to Strassberger or to Larry Lucas. As for myself, I had to be her last and worst enemy—unless she were disposed to pay me as the matchmaker!

I flagged a cruising taxi and had him drive me straight back to Le Diplomate. From there I called Vianney at his home. He was not overly happy to hear from me. He was even less happy when I told him the love story of Claudine and Liliane from morning to evening of its first day.

"And what in God's name do you expect me to do about it? We gave her an executive contract at the beginning of the year. So far as I can see, she hasn't breached it in any particular. Her sexual preferences are no business of ours. How can we know what secrets are exchanged in pillow talk? One wrong move on our part and we'd have the lawyers and the press crawling all over us. And we'd have the Lucas affair in big black headlines. You did the right thing tonight. You walked away without fuss."

"I'm glad you approve, Vianney."

"I myself am going to do the same thing: sit quietly and observe, and judge our people by their performance for us."

"You'll be pleased to know my father agrees with you."

"You mean you've discussed this—this incident with him?"

"This incident, no. I have talked to him about your declared policy of noninvolvement in the Lucas affair."

"And what did your father say?"

"I'll give it to you verbatim. 'Vianney is running our business in Paris and running it well. Let him do that.' I think I've done what I should in reporting on Claudine Parmentier. You feel no action is needed. That's your decision. I remind you, however, that tomorrow there'll be two lives on the line, Larry's and mine. I'd hate to think we were put at risk by indiscretion or lack of vigilance—or simply pillow talk between lovers."

"You've made your point, Carl. I've taken it under advisement. If I sounded rude, I apologize."

"Please! Just keep the lines open for me. Tomorrow I'll be over the hills and gone, but I'm still going to need a support system. Just don't let the termites eat the stairs! Sleep well!"

For me sleep would be long a-coming. I put on pajamas and

dressing gown, poured myself a drink, and tried to watch an old Belmondo film on television.

I was quickly bored, so I switched off the program and sat in silence trying to make sense of the swift madcap affair between Claudine Parmentier and Liliane Prévost. I had to assume that Claudine had revealed, or would soon reveal, her connections with Strassberger and that my own cover was seriously compromised, if not totally blown. How could I know what damage had been done? How could I mend it unless I reasoned with the worst possible situation?

We had a lovesick, reckless woman in the office. We had a director blind to her defects and heedless of the caution he had been given. We had, behind them all, a shadowy but sinister character named Francesco Falco who had been in the luxury end of the warm-body business for a long time and would strongly resist any intrusion into his domain.

It was a dark picture and I could find few patches of light in it. Maybe, just maybe, Claudine was still playing her role of mystery woman, with a restless heart and money to burn. Maybe, just maybe, she could continue the fiction, because she did not wish to compromise her career at Strassberger. Maybe she would not resent me enough to betray my connection with Larry Lucas. There were too many maybes to gamble on. My whole mission was at risk, because of my own poor judgment.

I wished Arlette were there but I knew she would be late. She is a night owl with scant respect for time. I wanted to be awake when she came in. There were words to say and love to spend before we went our separate ways, she to her gallery in Nice, I to Milan clothed in my illusory armor: a set of spurious documents and a ramshackle personal history that I had not yet found time to memorize properly.

There was a knock on my door. A bellboy presented me with a sealed envelope on a silver tray. He told me it had been delivered a few moments ago, by a lady. He waited resolutely on the threshold while I found my wallet and delivered his tip.

The note was from Claudine. It was couched in the same mocking tone as her talk.

114

Dear Carl,

I behaved very badly today—and you, considering the provocation, behaved reasonably well. I'm still behaving badly, because I'm ignoring your good advice and diving headfirst into this little *folie à deux* with Liliane. I'm sure it won't last very long. I'll probably burn out before she does. However, I do owe you something for bringing us together. So here is my gift.

I have not given away any secrets, either corporate or personal. Liliane believes what I have told her: that I have independent means, a private practice as a computer consultant, and a lover I'm not prepared to leave just yet. That seems to suit her too. She's sensitive about her own affairs of the heart and she needs a lot of room to move. We're a crazy lot, aren't we?

Anyway, I raised again the subject of her American protégé. I played out the jealousy game. What was so special about this male client? Finally, she told me the little she knew. His file is held in Milan by Falco. He is seriously rich. He does have mental problems and is keeping his head down. He carries a Dominican passport in the name of Lorenzo Lehmann. Clearly it was Larry Lucas! At this moment, as far as she knows, he's still in Milan.

You'd better believe all this. I'm not going to repeat it and I'm not going to be cross-examined on it. I was fond of Larry. I wouldn't do anything to harm him. I like you too, but it takes longer to wash the starch out of your collar. Besides all this, I like my job and I want to keep it.

Bonne chance!

Claudine

P. S. It may surprise you to know that Anne-Louise is very calm about what she calls my excursion. She tells me she's become bored with my adolescent games and is disposed to take an excursion of her own!

I read and reread the note until my head was spinning. I had an impulse to call Vianney and recant my earlier conversation. Then I remembered I wasn't the Defender of the Faithful; that was Vianney's chosen role. I called Andrescu at Corsec. Again they routed me round the mulberry bush until they found him. When I gave him Larry Lucas's new identity, he was jubilant.

"Great! Now we're in business—provided your lady friend's telling the truth."

It was a wise caveat, but it was one item too many for a very crowded day. I gave up on Arlette and made ready for bed. I was asleep almost before I hit the pillow and I didn't stir, even when she crept in beside me in the small hours of the morning.

Next day, over the breakfast table, Arlette and I staged our own small melodrama. I was the triggerman. In an hour or so she would be on her way home to Nice. I was jealous and, let me confess it, suddenly afraid of losing her. The words came out of nowhere.

"Will you marry me, Arlette?"

She stared at me in disbelief.

"Now where did that come from? Why now? Why here? What does marriage offer us that we haven't got already? What are we now but a slightly shopworn Pierrot and Pierrette? What's got into you?"

"I don't know. I just needed to say it."

"Since when?"

"I don't know that either. I'm asking you a simple question. Will you marry me, please?"

"And you'd like yes or no before the coffee runs out?"

"Look! I know I'm doing this the wrong way. But it's the best I can say here and now."

"Why do you want to marry me? You know there's no need."

"I have a need, Arlette! Suddenly, I have a need to say: This is my woman! This is the center of my world! This is the one person I'm prepared to live and die for!"

"You can have any woman you want. Why me, whom you have already? I told you a long time ago we fit well together, but the notion of a permanent arrangement does not appeal to me. I see no reason to change. If you have one, you should explain it to me."

Which landed the hot potato straight back in my lap, and the discomfort made me nervous as a schoolboy.

"I'm not sure I can explain it. I'll try. Down there in Cagnes, in the studio, painting and studying, I knew exactly who I was. I knew exactly who we were: Pierrot, Pierrette, circling around the top of the music box, never quite together, never quite apart, with the happy music tinkling all the time."

"Is that such a bad thing?"

"I'm not saying it's good or bad. I'm just trying to explain it!"

"Go on, please."

"This next part isn't so easy. My father calls me to New York. My brother-in-law has taken off. He's sick, a threat to himself and the family. Suddenly I'm back where I never wanted to be: son of the house, the heir who doesn't want the patrimony but is sent out to find the prodigal and bring him home to enjoy the fatted calf."

"And you resented that?"

"I did. I do; but it goes deeper than that. I discover there are risks—life-and-death risks possibly—for him and for me. I assume those risks, because that's what it means to be the only son in our family. We take a certain pride in it too, and the working conditions are better than most; but that's not the point."

"What is the point, Carl?"

"For my family this is what it's always been: duty, the debt of honor. I don't grudge it and I'm paying it. But there's something else—"

I broke off because I had no words to name it.

"What else?"

"Please don't mock me. Promise you won't mock me."

"I promise."

"If anything happened to me on this search, I'd like to feel that there was someone other than my family to shed a tear for me and raise a toast to me and maybe say, 'God rest the man I loved.' I know I have no right to it, I've been selfish all my life; but I'd like to have it and I'd like you to be the one to raise the glass and say the prayer."

"But when you come back, and if you bring Larry back with

you and all your fear now turns out to be a bad dream, what then?"

"Then I'd still know what I know now: I love you, Arlette. I'd be happy to spend the rest of my life loving you."

She did not answer me immediately. She sat, elbows on the table, chin cupped in her hands, reading my eyes and my face. Then, very gently, she spoke.

"I believe what you tell me. I feel the truth of it. I've seen the change you describe in yourself, though I can't explain it—and you don't explain it very well either. But I'm a skeptic about love, Carl. I don't know how it begins or why it ends. What you offer me is wonderful. You're kind. You're intelligent. You're rich, too. I know that if I asked for the moon you'd look for a ladder long enough to reach it and hand it to me. It's tempting. God knows it's tempting. But if I accepted now, I'd never forgive myself—and in the end I'm afraid you'd hate me for the bad bargain I'd offered you. You see, I love you too, Carl, but in my fashion, on my terms. You're a Strassberger, an old-line absolutist. With you it has to be all or nothing. That's what you're really telling me, isn't it?"

"If that's what it sounds like, *chérie*, I've made an awful botch of my first proposal!"

Abruptly she pushed herself up from the table, walked to the window, and stood looking out at the lowering sky and the wheeling pigeons. When she spoke finally, there were tears in her voice and a flush of anger too.

"I wish to God this hadn't happened, Carl. I hate you for putting me through it when I wasn't ready. Here's what we'll do. You go away, fight your family battle. When it's over, come back and ask me the same question again. I'll give you a straight answer, yes or no. Meantime"—she turned to face me arms outstretched—"meantime, let's be what we are, enjoy what we have." She tagged it with the old refrain, *En ce bordeau ou tenons nostre estat*—In this brothel where we ply our trade.

Villon's "Ballade of Fat Margot" was the subject of a running joke between us. This time we still managed to get a small laugh out of it. The Strassberger suite at Le Diplomate was a very expensive brothel indeed.

An hour later she was gone, perched behind the wheel of her old blue van, which was stacked with her summer stock of canvases and my two suitcases, which she would hold for my return. I stood on the pavement and watched until she was lost in the traffic. Then I went inside to wait for Oskar Kallman, who was going to change Carl Emil Strassberger into Edgar Francis Benson.

7

FORTY-EIGHT HOURS LATER, when the Air France flight from Paris to Milan lifted off at seven-forty on a misty spring morning, I found myself, quite abruptly, in a state of psychic shock. The physical separation from earth was simultaneous with my psychic separation from my former identity. From this moment on there was no public act that could be attributed to Carl Emil Strassberger, whose former persona and all the evidence of its existence were sealed in an envelope and on their way to New York by bonded messenger.

Every document I carried, even the tags on the new clothes I wore, affirmed that I was Edgar Francis Benson, born in Toronto, Canada, unmarried, a footloose amateur artist, of independent means with a small private coterie of buyers for his works. The odd thing was that I had no experience of being this person, no history of virtues or guilts, loves, hates, or even sexual appetites. It was as though I were in free fall, waiting for the first impact of reality.

It came in the rush and bustle of Milan Airport, where I was met by Sergio Carlino, director-general of Corsec Italia S.p.A. I found him waiting by the luggage carousel with a large card inscribed with the name E. F. Benson. It was only when the crowd around the carousel had thinned out that I connected myself with the card. Sergio Carlino grinned at my discomfiture.

"I've seen it happen many times. The most embarrassing moment is when you're paged in a hotel lobby and you don't recognize the name you signed in the register! In any case, welcome to Italy."

"Thank you."

"My name is Sergio. How do you prefer to be called?"

"My given name is Carl. My *nom de guerre* is Edgar."

"Better we call you that from the start."

As he hefted my bags and led the way out to the parking lot, I had time to take stock of him. He was somewhere in his mid-thirties, tall, blond, and trim as an athlete—a throwback, perhaps, to one of the Lombards who swarmed through the Alpine passes in the sixth century and took possession of the river flats and marshes of the Po Valley.

He had a firm handshake, a ready smile, innocent blue eyes, and an air of indolent arrogance, as if fourteen centuries of bloody history had purged him of all illusions about Anglo-Saxons and Americans, any Italians south of Florence, and most Europeans north of the Gothard tunnel. It was not that he uttered a single derogatory word. On the contrary, he could not have been more courteous, but his courtesy itself was an expression of tolerance, which in itself conveyed a genial contempt.

While we worked our way out of the airport traffic and toward the autostrada, he explained a little of his background. Schooled by the Jesuits, he had been for several years an investigating officer with the carabinieri, the military force which is concerned with the internal security of the Republic. He had resigned in mid-career, because Corsec was offering a sack of money and because, he confessed, it was easier to maintain a mercenary loyalty to Corsec and its clients than to cope with plots and counterplots and double standards within the service.

"However," he assured me amiably, "I still maintain my friendships and my access to valuable information—which is why Corsec bought me in the first place."

They seemed to be paying him with reasonable generosity.

His vehicle was a chauffeur-driven Mercedes, with a glass screen to separate driver and passengers and some sophisticated communication equipment in front and rear. Carlino explained this too.

"In Italy today, big business, politics, and the law are dangerous occupations. Once upon a time, most problems were negotiable on a live-and-let-live basis. Now civic virtue is the catchword, but endemic violence is the popular remedy. Even among the clients we serve there are conflicts of interest. I have to navigate with a certain care. So I have a bullet-proof vehicle and a former police driver trained in evasive action. I also have a bodyguard for my wife and child."

This seemed an appropriate moment to ask him about Simonetta Travel and its director, Francesco Falco. His reaction was an exclamation of contempt.

"Boh! He was investigated years ago when I was still in the service. He began as a small-time smuggler running cigarettes and whiskey out of North Africa. Then he got into the expensive body business—illegal immigrants, some terrorists, some women. They were never able to able to nail him for anything, though they sweated him hard on more than one occasion. Now he's legitimate, and nobody can prove he isn't. This special service he advertises, this disappearing act, is a confidence trick in itself. There's nothing illegal about dropping out of society, walking out on your family, starting a new life under a new name. There may be some illegal aspects to it but they're very minor. For instance, you're illegal now. You're carrying a passport not issued by a government authority, but you're not an absconding debtor, you're not a fugitive criminal. So, on that side of things Falco is clean enough to get by.

"The other side of his business is hard to document and very hard to prove. I know they were never able to assemble enough evidence to file charges. Besides, his clients, like your brother-in-law, are paying for precisely the services he offers: a new identity, a break in the money trail. As far as money is concerned, he offers no more than an introduction to trustee services. He doesn't intrude—visibly, at least—into the money transactions. If you're fool enough to put your resources in someone else's hands, you do it at your own risk."

We were approaching the entrance to the autostrada, and I noticed we were heading not for Milan but eastward toward Brescia. I asked the reason. Carlino waved a conjurer's hand.

"We have to work together. We should get to know each other. I thought a lunch in the country might be a pleasant way to begin."

"Thank you."

"Also we can take a passing look at the Villa Estense, where Mr. Lucas was said to be in residence for a few days. I regret to tell you he is no longer there."

"Are you sure of that?"

"I called a friend who called a friend. The local police made a routine check of all hotel registers in the area. The name Lorenzo Lehmann and the number of his Dominican passport were on record."

"When did he leave?"

"Four days ago."

"Any forwarding address?"

"Care of Francesco Falco of Simonetta Travel, Milan."

"Who, I am told, owns the place."

"Now that's an interesting point," said Sergio Carlino with obvious satisfaction. "My information is a little more detailed and, I believe, more accurate. The principal shareholder is Simonetta Travel, which owns fifty-one percent. The other shareholders are all represented by a common nominee. His name is Dr. Hubert Rubens. He lives in Geneva."

"So Falco has a beautiful operation. He books his clients into establishments which he owns but which have been financed by their money, channeled through Dr. Rubens."

"Pretty, isn't it?" Carlino added his own footnote. "You want to disappear, you can even own a slice of the paradise you are living in—vicariously, of course—through Dr. Rubens!"

"How many such places does he have?"

"No way to know until one sees what he offers to you, but one thing is certain: There is a very large investment here and

Falco will be very anxious to protect it. This is what I want to talk to you about. From this moment on, I am responsible for you. I have to be sure that you are properly prepared before you tangle yourself in the spider's web."

He leaned forward and spoke rapidly into the microphone. The chauffeur raised his hand in acknowledgment, and a couple of kilometers later we swung off the autostrada and wound down to the network of secondary roads which crisscross the triangle between Brescia, Verona, and Mantua.

"We have time to kill," Carlino announced in his languid, lordly fashion. "Let's forget Larry Lucas and commune with the spirits of this place. They come in all shapes and sizes."

For a man whose profession was the protection of the rich and powerful from the criminalities of their peers, Sergio Carlino was surprisingly well-educated and affectionately versed in the history of his homeland.

"This is poets' country. This"—he pointed to the vineyards, where the tender vines were draped like garlands from tree to tree—"this is what Virgil called 'the marriage of vine and elm.' That little town over there is called Peschiera. Tradition says that's where Pope Leo the First confronted Attila the Hun, the Scourge of God, and turned him back from his march on Rome. The armies of Attila were camped along the banks of the Mincio, which runs between those hills. Their horses grazed the meadows along the river."

It took me a little while to understand what he was doing—talking me down from the state of high tension and defensive caution in which I had arrived. I was grateful to him. I felt myself relaxing and warming toward a trust in him. The Jesuits had schooled him well. He chanted some verses of Catullus and described how and by what waterways the poet brought his sailing boat from Greece to the Adriatic and thence to Lake Garda. He talked about the Scaligeri, who built their great castle to dominate the lake and shout defiance at invaders from the Alpine passes.

After a while, the lake itself opened out before us, ruffled by a stiff breeze from the Alps, which set the wavelets slapping against the long tongue of land on which Sirmione and its attendant estates were built.

The Villa Estense was sited under the shoulder of the hill which is the extremity of the peninsula. Its terraces and gardens looked southward toward the sun while the northern walls of the villa and the garden warded off the winds and hailstorms and the snow flurries from the high distant peaks of the Austrian Alps.

The principal building was a conversion of an old *casale,* a country farmhouse built around a courtyard, with an arched entrance. Down by the lake there was a modern complex of tennis courts, spa, indoor swimming pool, exercise rooms, solarium, and a dock for the small flotilla of runabouts owned by the hotel. The terrace gardens were in full spring flower and the orchard trees had not yet shed their blossoms.

We did not go into the villa itself but simply made the circuit of the drive in and out again. Carlino underlined the point he had made earlier.

"You see what I mean about money? This place would cost a large fortune to buy and God knows how much to maintain. If Falco is acquiring this kind of property, it follows that he is either a very rich man or is stretched very tight for money. Either way, he is a dangerous adversary." Abruptly, he changed the subject. "There's a pleasant place about halfway to Mantua. It's called the Locanda Velaggio. I thought we'd lunch there."

The Locanda Velaggio was a riverside retreat with a garden sheltered from the wind by lime and lemon trees. The food was simple but excellent: a country soup, a pasta in a rich cream sauce, river trout cooked on an open grill, fresh fruit, and a crisp Pinot Grigio to match it all.

Pierino, the driver, proved an agreeable table companion, who regaled us with tales of his service in the more outlandish regions of the Republic: the Barbagia on Sardinia; the Basilicata on Lipari, the island of exile. He was a natural storyteller, and when I had difficulty with his dramatic narrations, Sergio translated for me. When the meal was over, Pierino left us to our private talk. Immediately Sergio was the professional, crisp and clearheaded.

"So! Now we have to decide your next moves and ours in the Lucas affair. Let us be frank. Neither you nor we are yet prepared for what we hope to do. Let's talk about you first. You have new identity documents and a curriculum vitae which you have not adequately studied and on which you could be very easily tripped up. You are like a man wearing someone else's clothes. Do you not agree?"

"I agree."

"So you have to rehearse your new self in the role until you are absolutely familiar with it. That means a daily exercise in repetition, like a student walking up and down, memorizing his Latin tenses. You have to establish reactions to unexpected situations, to questions for which you have no ready answer. Another example: You are identified as an artist. Clearly your new mode will have to be different from the old one. Have you worked up any sketches or studies?"

"No, I haven't."

"So the moment you set up your easel you will either be working in your customary mode or fumbling with a new approach. You see where I am leading?"

"I do, very clearly."

"Now let's talk about us at Corsec. We in Milan are not the same people as Giorgiu Andrescu and his team in New York. The scope of our activities is different. We protect people and payrolls and premises. We are concerned with economic espionage and the theft of sensitive documents. We do not produce instant miracles of electronic intrusion. We are well equipped with hardware, but we do not have a large team of junior geniuses playing little games on their computers.

"Again, let me give you an example. We have established that Larry Lucas left the Villa Estense and drove himself to Rome. That is where he surrendered his hired car. We do not know the hotel in which he lodged, how long he lodged there, or what is his next destination. We know that Francesco Falco is out of town. The phrase his secretary used was 'out of town with a client.' He is not expected back for several days. It is a reasonable guess that he may be escorting Larry Lucas to his final destination,

126

but we have no proof of that. We are endeavoring to fill the gaps by various means which it is better you know nothing about.

"So, we need time—more time perhaps than Giorgiu Andrescu seemed to promise. I hope you're not angry at my telling you this, but this is what happens in international corporations. Each department works to a different rhythm, and the same brain does not control them all. I am not making excuses; I am giving you cold facts."

"I'd rather have facts than foul-ups, Sergio. I'm paying you for service and advice. What do you suggest I do?"

"Three things. Trust me, first. Everything depends on our mutual confidence. Second, go into retreat and study your résumé so that you can answer in a reasonable fashion any question that may be put to you about your life. Third, start working on your new image as an artist. You must have work to show. I am not talking of an exhibition but of sketchbooks, studies, and the like. These will constitute your response to the first and most obvious question: What sort of work do you do? Finally, I should like you to stay out of Milan."

"May I ask why?"

"Milan is an airport city, a busy commercial center. The risk of your case being blown by a chance meeting is real and quite high."

"How long do I have to stay out?"

"Until I'm ready to move you on."

"Which will be when?"

"As soon as I have enough pieces to fit into the puzzle. I know it's asking for a large act of faith in a man you've met for the first time."

"It is, but I guess I have to make it."

"One more question. What exactly is the brief from your family?"

"I'm not sure I understand what you're asking."

"Your family has sent you to search for Larry Lucas. What do they expect you to do?"

"Find him; talk to him; persuade him, if I can, to return to his family, pick up his career, and resume medical treatment."

"All the things he has just abdicated."

"Yes."

"Doesn't it seem a rather excessive demand?"

"I'm not in a position to demand anything. I can only try to reason with him."

"But the nature of his illness puts him often beyond reason."

"That's true."

"So, taking the worst case. You find Larry Lucas. You talk with him. He refuses to listen. What then?"

It seemed a pointless question. I said as much to Carlino.

"I turn around and come home, for God's sake!"

"You miss the point," said Sergio Carlino mildly. "You may well find yourself, a man with a false name and a false passport, isolated in hostile territory. You think I am exaggerating perhaps?"

Clearly he wasn't. He himself lived in hostile territory all the time. He had a bulletproof car and a driver trained in evasion. He had a bodyguard for his wife and child. I'd be a fool if I didn't listen to the advice for which I was paying him. I mused over it for a few moments and then told him, "Very well, I accept your advice. Where do you suggest I stay?"

"Why not here in the Veneto, a paradise of painters? You can paint up and down the centuries across the countryside—Verona, Vicenza, Padua, Venice, Ferrara. Your baggage is in the car. I can drop you anywhere you choose, and you're still only a phone call and a two-or-three-hour drive from my office."

"What's the nearest town?"

"Verona."

"Very well. Verona it is."

"Splendid choice." He was quietly triumphant. "I'll install you in state at the Due Torri, hire you some wheels, and commend you to San Zeno, who watches over the place. You can even write love letters to Juliet and have them answered by the municipality. Let's be on our way, shall we?"

Indeed, Sergio Carlino was a very clever fellow. At the cost of a lunch at a rustic inn he had bought himself time to set his own house in order, collect the intelligence he lacked, and penetrate the careful defenses of Francesco Falco. On the other hand, he

128

had impressed on me my own inadequacy and my need to work hard at being an effective client.

By the time he delivered me to the Due Torri I was beginning to see the humor of the situation. There was also something charming in the notion that the municipality of Verona would indeed answer a letter to Juliet, who quite possibly had never lived there, if indeed she was anything but legend.

My arrival in Verona was marked by good omens. The hotel offered me an elegant chamber that looked down on the Piazza Sant' Anastasia. A rented automobile was delivered within the hour and parked in the hotel garage. Sergio Carlino saw me settled, briefed me on his office communications, and gave me a final word of advice.

"Be patient, my friend. Nothing dramatic will happen overnight. Enjoy yourself. This is a charming city, and the women are civilized and chic. For the rest, be a good actor! Study your role and trust your director. I truly do know what needs to be done."

When he had left, I strolled out to join the crowds in the Piazza dell' Erbe, with its forest of bright umbrellas and clutter of vendors' stalls. From there I passed into the Lordly Square where Dante is perched, sour and somber upon his pedestal, and thence into the narrow alley crowded with the tombs of the Scaligeri, who were the lords of Verona in olden times.

I paused awhile before the tomb of Francesco Scaliger, who was called Can Grande, the great dog, because he wore a helmet with a hound's head on it. His sarcophagus is surmounted by his effigy in marble and carried on the backs of two great stone mastiffs. I fingered the ancient iron mesh, made of tiny ladders light and supple as a coat of mail, which surrounds the tombs and promised myself that I would come here tomorrow with a sketchbook.

I shivered a little as I made my leisurely way back to the hotel. It was not only the evening wind that chilled me. I was stricken with that commonest of ills, the loneliness of the traveler. I was in reaction now. I needed talk and laughter about me. I wanted to be open and merry with my peers. I needed the

129

company of a happy woman. These needs were simple enough, God knows, but they were not easy to fill on one's first night in an Italian provincial city—or any provincial city, for that matter.

However, I disposed myself, at least, for society. I showered, shaved, dressed with a certain casual care, fortified myself with a very expensive Scotch from the minibar in my room, and went downstairs to consult with the concierge. He was busy with a formidable dowager who might have stepped out of a Veronese canvas. His deputy, a fellow of my own age, was directed to take care of me.

I was, I explained to him, an artist on tour, recording *la vita caratteristica* of each town and region. I needed, therefore, a friendly place to dine, preferably one with music where it would not be too hard to fall into talk with one's fellow guests. I thought I did a fairly discreet job of expressing the needs of any red-blooded male, suffering from the solitudes of a traveler and anxious to divert himself with wine, women, and song.

The young man attending me was understanding and helpful. He recommended a place called Pantalone where the food was good, the wines honest, and the company a useful mix of students, tourist groups, visiting conventions, and local artists of one kind or another. The configuration of the place was helpful too. It was set like a German beer hall with long tables and benches so that a trio of musicians could work their way up and down the rows between the diners.

They did not take reservations, but he would tell them of my arrival and ask them to place me with congenial company. I thanked him. I shook his hand. Money passed discreetly between us. He summoned a bellboy to escort me to the door and point me in the right direction. It was a short walk only. I should go on foot.

I strolled under a new moon and a wind-scoured sky full of stars. By the time I reached the restaurant, a cavernous place in an antique alley in the old city, I felt elated and enlarged. I was out of the sickroom and back in the normal world, ready, open, and eager for any encounter.

130

Inside the restaurant, I found my concierge had kept his word. I was expected. I was saluted with the honorific title *"dottore,"* though I suspected this was due more to the status of the hotel that had recommended me than to any appearance of scholarship on my part.

The room was not yet full, so the headwaiter offered me a discreet choice of company on the benches: a walking club of males and females from Austria; a gaggle of local students, sparse groups of local businessmen, voluble or conspiratorial over their drinking; and three men and six women, touring scholars, he told me, from the American Academy in Rome.

They seemed the most promising group. The men were youngish; they looked neither hostile nor possessive. The women were well-groomed, cheerful, and animated—and they were in surplus! I opted to be seated next to them. As I followed the headwaiter across the floor, I remembered with a start that I was traveling under an alias and that I would inevitably be forced into some explanation of myself and my activities. The risk gave me a new surge of adrenaline and added an extra spice to the taste of liberty.

The group was absorbed in an animated conversation. As I sat down they gave me an offhand acknowledgment and continued with their talk. I busied myself with the menu and the wine list and with a covert inspection of the three women in the company who were seated diagonally across from me. The others I could glimpse only in profile unless I made a deliberate attempt at appraisal.

From their talk I gathered that they were graduates from various disciplines in the humanities who came from southern and western U.S. campuses. They had been attending a seminar convened by the Academy in Rome and now were traveling to the major centers of art and culture in the northern provinces of the Republic. They had arrived late in the day, were staying at a modest hotel called the San Luca, and were trying to plan their next day's tour. They were a lively bunch, eager and disputatious. They drank freely and aired their knowledge in a variety of regional accents without restraint. It was not long before they adopted me into their group. They were young enough to be centered on themselves and their own interests, so I was spared any too intense inquisition. I was an artist; fine!—I had no pretensions to fame; that was fine too. My name was Edgar and the woman next to me, whose name was Ellie, was as eager for my attention as I was grateful for hers.

We ate, we drank, we talked—God, how long and how confidently we talked! We sang or hummed or clapped or made la-la noises when the musicians strutted their numbers before and behind us. Then, somewhere near midnight, we decanted ourselves into the street and began what Ellie called the midnight tour of Verona.

I was drunk and floating happily on an ocean of Veronese wine. Don't ask me what any of the academics said. I don't remember. All I remember is that Ellie was lively and agreeable and her lips were willing and she smelled good, and all through our nighttime promenade we were as close as Siamese twins.

We stood together under Juliet's balcony and recited snatches of the balcony scene, and what we couldn't remember we improvised. We embraced in the shadows of old archways and threw pebbles into the Adige River. We straggled after the others, caught up with them, lost them again, and were finally reunited under the timeworn portico of the Hotel San Luca.

That was where it ended, at three in the morning, because the steam had gone out of the evening, the liquor had worn off, the women were sharing rooms, and—though nobody said it, everybody accepted it—lovemaking between strangers in a foreign place was not a recommended diversion. We all agreed it had been a great night. We made wafer-cake promises to meet again. Ellie and I had a lingering good-night embrace under the basilisk eye of the night porter. I made my solitary way back to the Due Torri, where I slept in celibate splendor until midday and woke with the worst hangover in the recorded history of Carl Emil Strassberger.

The hangover taught me a lesson. I was getting too old for drinking bouts and sessions of unsatisfied lust. In terms of simple survival, in my new uncertain world they were a risk I could no longer afford.

I looked with disgust at my image in the mirror: bloodshot eyes, dull skin, stubbled jowls, unsteady hands. I needed as much restoration as any ancient ruin. I rang room service with an urgent order for coffee and orange juice and fresh rolls. I requested politely that the rolls be crisp from the oven; otherwise I might be tempted to use them as missiles against the staff. It was suggested with a certain good humor that as it was already past noon I might care to consider a light luncheon instead. That prospect pleased me not at all. Please! Please! The client does know what he wants, if not always what he needs.

Then I had another saving thought. The best restorative in the world is a session with an old-fashioned Italian barber—hot towels, a razor honed like the scimitar of Saladin, lotions, frictions, a hair trim, a massage of face, neck, and shoulders, a manicure, the drowsy drone of conversation, the click of scissors, the buzz of clippers, the slap of steel upon the honing leather. When one steps into the street after a session like that it is like Resurrection Day for Lazarus.

Problem: where to find such a master barber at the butt end of the twentieth century? Once again my friend, the junior concierge, was instant to help. He knew exactly the place, a stone's throw from the hotel: old management, spotless hygiene, instruments sterilized in a modern autoclave—and, yes, they offered manicures and pedicures. He would be happy to make an appointment for me. Say in one hour? And how had my evening at Pantalone turned out? More than a success, I told him, a riot of pleasure for which I was now paying dearly! While I had him on the line, could he recommend a good store for art supplies? In half a minute I had the address and the directions. My day, if not my destiny, was beginning to make sense—provided I wore sunglasses to take the glare off it.

The sunglasses prompted another thought. Instead of shedding my stubble, why not have the barber shape it and begin, at least, to nurse it into a beard? Beard and sunglasses together would provide a minimal shield against casual recognition, though it might raise a

133

query or two at immigration barriers because my image would not match the photograph in my passport.

I was at least beginning to take Sergio Carlino seriously. So I opted for the beard and resigned myself to some uncomfortable days as the stubble grew into facial hair. With luck and enough time, it would be fully grown before Carlino picked up Larry's trail and set me again on my pursuit of him.

The session with the barber was everything I had hoped. He charged mightily and I tipped generously, but I walked out a new-minted man with the shape of a handsome beard dark against my smoothly barbered skin. I made early morning appointments for the following days so that the master could nurture his creation. It was an expensive indulgence but our meetings would represent a break in my solitude, a small affirmation that I still held some control over my own destiny.

The purchase of the art materials was another agreeable diversion. The woman who served me was obliging and attractive. As we worked comfortably through my list, she told me she held down an evening job as a teacher of drawing. She understood my dilemma. I wanted to travel as lightly as possible but I had no idea where or how long I might decide to sojourn. I needed well-packaged, easily transportable materials, a collapsible easel and stool, papers for gouache and watercolor, canvases in manageable sizes, acrylics and oils and acquarelles, and an array of brushes for them all. It was a brief but pleasant rediscovery of that other self—egoist though he might be—whom I found much more pleasant to live with than the wary hunter I had become. I paid for the goods, which would be delivered before nightfall to my hotel. Then with sketchbook and crayons only, I set out to walk the city.

Once again, the need for change impressed itself upon me. I was an architectural artist trained in the long tradition of Piranesi, Vanvitelli, and Canaletto. I was anchored to the visible form. I had accepted what Andrea del Sarto had deplored in Browning's version of him: "All is silver gray, placid and perfect in my art—the worse!"

Now, not for art but for a shabby trick of concealment, I had to wrench myself out of that frame of reference into another. I would have to quit the city and go out into the countryside, to the crags and torrents and the light on restless waters and the shifting patterns of cloud and shadow—but not yet. I needed this late afternoon under the fishtail battlements and ancient chimney pots of Verona and the time-worn Gothic symbols of the tomb of the Scaligeri. The mere exercise of architectural and sculptural drawing soothed and relaxed me. I felt that part of myself was restored to me even as I was going through the exercise of shedding it.

As I worked over the drawings, one part of my brain was rehearsing the details of the life of Edgar Francis Benson—a man I had never known, a life invented for me. Another part of my brain busied itself with translating the facts into French, so that hopefully I would not react too suddenly to questions addressed to me in English.

It sounds like a foolish and confusing exercise, but Oskar Kallman had taught me that up to a point it would work. It slowed down my instinctive reactions. It introduced elements of confusion into the memory process which might prove useful under a normal social interrogation. Kallman had impressed on me that, because we are all victims of information overload, one can with reasonable conviction plead in conversation a defective memory of people and events.

When one is working on open-air studies, people stop and stare. Some will attempt to engage you in conversation, which can sometimes turn into a pleasant encounter. This afternoon, however, I was trying to cultivate a deliberate inattention, a certain grumpiness, a refusal of eye contact so that I would not raise my face from the sketchbook except to glance at the object in front of me.

There were moments when I felt very foolish, a gullible fellow conditioned by fear and ignorance to cringe at shadow shows upon the wall of his prison. However, there was a harsh logic in the drama which was unfolding itself in my life. Larry Lucas, by turns acutely rational and destructively psychotic, was the agent of disorder in our family life. We were playing by his rules and not our own. At the same time, he was the pawn and the victim in a more sinister money game, whose outlines were clear enough but of whose rules and players we knew very little.

Sergio Carlino, on the other hand, had played many such games with similar characters. Therefore, I had no ground on which to challenge his advice. I simply had to follow where he led me, knowing all the time that I was leaping from a high place into deep darkness.

I was working now on a sketch of the equestrian statue of Can Grande, Great-dog Scaliger, trying to catch his famous sinister smile and the way his dog-headed helmet was thrown back to lie between his shoulders. Out of nowhere a woman's familiar voice hailed me: "Edgar!"

I kept my head down and continued laying in the shadows of Can Grande's time-frozen face. Then a hand was laid on my shoulder and I was slewed around to face Ellie, my companion of the previous evening.

She bent and kissed me and then leaned close to me to make a critical appraisal of the sketch.

"Well! We were all flying so high last night I felt we'd never see each other again, but here you are! And that's a very nice piece of drawing!"

"Thank you. It's coming along. Where are your colleagues?"

She shrugged indifferently.

"Here and there, all doing their own things. Academics in full cry give me a pain in the butt. I needed a break and I half hoped I'd run into you again. You talked about this place. I took a chance and came. . . . Please don't stop. I'll shut up and watch. This is too good to spoil."

Last night she had been talkative and cheerfully rowdy. Now she was silent, standing a pace away, leaning against a stone buttress watching the sketch develop. Came a moment when I paused and held it at arm's length to survey what I had done. Then, seeing me hesitate over the next strokes, she said quietly, "With great respect, maestro, enough. Leave it just as it is!"

It was a bolder act than it seems now as I record it. Try taking a bone from a puppy and you'll get your fingers nipped. Pass judgment on a work while the maker is still uncertain of it and you risk a dusty answer. This time, however, a second glance convinced me she was right. Her eye was true and her tone too tactful to deserve a reproach. I took one more look at the sketch and closed the pad over it.

"You've got a good eye," I told her.

She dismissed the compliment with an offhand statement.

"I teach art history. I design jewelry."

"May I offer you some coffee—a drink perhaps?"

"Coffee, please. After last night I feel like a candidate for Alcoholics Anonymous."

"That makes two of us."

She took my arm and we walked together toward the forest of umbrellas and awnings in the Piazza dell' Erbe. It was an intimate little promenade. We were comfortable together, but—how shall I say it? —close as we were, I was still not conscious of anything but her presence. I had taken no lasting note of her face, the contours of her body, the color of her hair, the texture of her skin. It was only when I faced her over the coffee cups that my mind began to assemble her into a physical image and I reached for the sketchbook and pencil to record it.

With her casque of jet-black hair and her honey-colored skin she looked like Isabella d'Este, whom Titian painted as a young girl and da Vinci as an older woman. There was the same sweep of the neck column, the same bone structure in the face, the same hint of mischief—and of temper, too—in the dark eyes. She was a good sitter, placid and patient in the pose I had asked her to take: chin cupped in her hands, looking past me toward the passage of folk in the square.

When the sketch was done, I pushed it across the table for her approval. She was obviously pleased.

"May I keep this?"

"Of course."

"Will you sign it for me, please? And write a line or two on it?"

I had the pencil already poised to dash off the serpentine symbol which was my normal signature when suddenly I remembered my lesson with Oskar Kallman. I sat there, pencil poised, caught in a small heart-stopping moment of understanding. This was how easy it was to betray oneself, to surrender without a fight to the executioners.

"Something wrong?" Ellie asked. "Suddenly you weren't with us!"

"I'm O K. I was just trying to think of a suitable inscription."

I wrote it very carefully in that slow Gothic script which somehow contradicted the swift confident lines of the sketch: *For Ellie, a reminder that we laughed a night away in Verona. E. F. Benson.*

I passed the sketch back to her. She studied it carefully. She looked up, nodded, and smiled. She touched her fingers to her lips, reached across the table, and laid them on mine.

"Thank you. I'll treasure this."

"And I'll remember the sitter."

"I wanted you to have a richer memory. I hated to let you go last night."

"I hated to leave."

"Tomorrow we're leaving for Venice. We're booked for three days there. I wish I could get out of it."

"First visit?"

"Yes."

"Then you shouldn't pass it up. There's still a special magic that clings about the place."

"How long will you be staying here in Verona?"

"I'm not sure. It may be only a few days. It may be longer."

"You wouldn't think of coming to Venice with us?"

"I can't, I'm afraid. I'm waiting on word from my agent. He is discussing a commission for me. I have to be ready to meet the client at short notice."

Again there was the uncomfortable reminder: every moment in the life of Edgar Francis Benson demanded its own little lie.

"So how will you spend your time?" Ellie asked again.

"As you saw today. I'll probably fill a couple of sketchbooks. I'm trying to loosen up my style. Right now it's too formal and tight. I have a car in the garage at the hotel. I can get out into the countryside and do some landscapes."

I hoped Sergio Carlino and Oskar Kallman were listening to

my performance. It wasn't great theater but I was trying. Ellie gave me a slow, sidelong smile.

"If you've got a car, that changes things. You could take me along for the ride and drop me off at the nearest ferry station for Venice. Also you'd have a model on call."

"It's an interesting thought."

"Is that all it is—interesting? What if I offered nude sittings as well?"

It was interesting and tempting. I had dropped out of my own world into another, which the Japanese call most aptly the world of flowers and willows, the floating world where nothing is permanent, where everything is permissible provided you can pay the score. If your mind changes there is no blame. If your inclinations change, no guilts accrue. That is why it is always a reckless world and sometimes dangerous. I was aware of the change in myself, though I could not yet put a name to it. I had proposed marriage to Arlette. She, wiser than I, perhaps, had deferred her answer. I was still free to roam among the flowers and the willows. Ellie was waiting for my response. She was posed now as I had sketched her, chin cupped in her hands; but her eyes were fixed on my face, challenging me. I had to tell her at least a fraction of the truth.

"It's an attractive idea. It presents no problems for me, except that once I'm summoned I have to leave. That's the way my life works. On the other hand, I don't want to be responsible for separating you from your colleagues and leaving you adrift in the lagoons!"

Her head lifted defiantly and there was fire in her dark eyes, even though her lips still smiled.

"Understand something, Mr. Benson! I am responsible for me. I offered the invitation. All you have to do is say yes or no. We enjoyed ourselves last night. I'd like to think we could have a few more laughs together. The day the laughter stops, we kiss good-bye. What do you say?"

"I say we have dinner tonight. Eight-thirty at the Due Torri. In case you like the place, I'll get you a room for the night, so bring your passport and toothbrush and a change of clothes."

"And if I don't like it?"

"You return to your friends. Deal?"

139

"Don't push your luck, Edgar Benson."

"I'm not pushing it, believe me; but I'm damned if I'm staging another version of Rodin's kiss for the doorman at the Due Torri—which, I have to tell you, is one very ritzy hotel."

"You're praying I won't disgrace you, is that it?"

"I know you won't."

"Are you married?"

"You asked me that last night."

"I know, but we're both sober now."

"I'm not married. Are you?"

"I used to be. I'm divorced."

"Do you have any more questions?"

"Hundreds."

"I think you should save them."

"For what?"

"Until you really need the answers. Otherwise they're just a load to carry."

"What's my last name?"

"I don't know. You didn't tell me. We seem to be doing quite well without it."

"I find it strange that you didn't bother to ask."

"So how do you think we'll survive as traveling companions with all these questions asked and unasked?"

"I'm not sure. I'll think about it and let you know at dinner tonight."

"I promise you it will be a good dinner."

"I never doubted that." She gave me a long speculative look and a small crooked grin. "I know you're playing some kind of game with me—or with yourself perhaps. I can't quite figure what the rules are."

"There are no rules. I don't have the right to make them, for you or for anyone else. I accept what is at face value until it's necessary to know more."

"When you were drawing the Can Grande sculpture, when you were sketching me a moment ago, you were questioning every stroke before you made it."

"I look at a watch to know the time. Unless I'm a watchmaker, I don't have to count the pieces and put them together. Right now, Ellie, my love, I have a great need to be very simple. I don't want to waste time raking over the past or predicting the future. Enough that you are an agreeable and beautiful woman, sitting at this table with me. I see you, feel you, smell you. God damn it, I've just made an image of you which you can pass on to your children. But I do need to know your last name after all, because I have to make a reservation at the hotel and it has to match the name on your passport."

"I thought you'd never ask. It's Milland. Eight-thirty at the Due Torri, check?"

"Check."

She got up, came swiftly around the table, kissed me, and left without another word. I knew I was committing myself to a folly, but in the floating world follies are like petals scattered on the water. The moment they fall, the current carries them away.

When I got back to the hotel I went immediately to reception. I told them an old friend, a lady, had just come into town. She was staying at a quite unsuitable hotel. I had invited her to transfer to the Due Torri. Could they offer her a room, preferably on my floor? After a brief interval, they decided that, yes, it would be possible. I took the room and asked them to put the charges on my account. With that good news in hand they were able to tell me what I knew already, that the room adjoining my suite was vacant and that housekeeping would prepare it for immediate occupancy.

I asked them to send up flowers and champagne in time for an eight-thirty arrival; then I rode upstairs to prepare myself for the happy event.

8

AS USUAL, WHEN I MADE my evening calls, I spoke to my father first. He sounded weary and indifferent. He asked where I was. I told him. Without waiting for the rest of my story, he said, "It's over, Carl. It's not worth spending any more time or money. To hell with Larry. Go back to France and get on with your life."

"What's happened, for God's sake?"

"I've got two letters in front of me. One is addressed to me, the other is a photocopy of what Madi received this morning. Both were sent by courier from Rome. Both are in Larry's handwriting. There is no doubt about their authenticity. This is his letter to me:

"Dear Mr. Strassberger,

"This is a farewell letter. It is written with much respect. I trust you will believe that. Tonight I begin what I know will be a very different life and, I pray vainly, a happier one. I know that my abrupt departure from New York has caused everybody a great deal of concern. I was insulted when you decided, as a very first step, to audit my dealings in Paris. With hindsight I recognize that it was completely in character. You were always a faithful custodian of your clients' interests. I hope you will now concede that I was a faithful custodian of yours and that I have left Strassberger somewhat richer than before.

142

For this you owe me nothing. There are no debts outstanding between us.

"I have, however, one request. I have written today to Madi asking her to divorce me. She has ample cause. There will be no dispute on my part over property or the custody of the children. I love them but I know they will be safer and better off in Strassberger care than in mine. My only hope is that no bitterness will be injected into their memory of their father. I desire— indeed, I beg you, to advise Madi to start divorce proceedings as soon as possible. It is better for everyone to cut clean. This is what I failed to do in the first place.

"My sincere respects to you and to your wife,
Larry

"P. S. It has been suggested that you might send Carl to pick up my tracks and coax me home. Don't bother. He'd be wasting his time. I like him but I've got more street smarts than he has and my finger is always on the quick-release button."

My father did not pause after the reading. I heard the rustle of paper as he picked up the next page and continued with a monotone recitation of Larry's letter to Madi.

"My dear Madi,

"I started this letter full of bitterness and anger, but now the bitterness has all boiled away and the stew of emotions in which I have lived for too long lies dry and burnt at the bottom of the pot.

"Our marriage is a mess because I'm a mess. I have to live with me, but you don't and our children don't. Whatever love you have left for me—and there can't be much after all this— spend it on them. Let them have good memories of their father, who in his own crazy fashion loved them and still loves them. Just don't encourage them to believe that I'm coming back. I'm not. I'm leaving here tonight for a place where I propose to live as merrily as I can and die when I get too bored to bear it.

"I only wish I could have made a better exit from your life. That's the sort of thing I've always fouled up. I can't help it

143

when the black devils take over. You Strassbergers are different. You've all been trained—quite ruthlessly trained, I may add—to exhibit grace under pressure. I'm the opposite: no training, no grace. The moment the pressure's on I explode or deflate. Either way, I'm no fit company for civilized folk. All I can say is that my life from now on has to be a private experience. I can't risk the agonies of trying to share it. I tried to write to Alma Levy but I couldn't do it. Just show her this letter and ask her to try to make sense of it for you.

"I wish I could say I love you but I know it would sound like a mockery and it isn't. It's just that I don't feel anything anymore. I'm like the man who lost his shadow. Until it happens to you there's no way to understand it, no way to describe it. Just file the papers, Madi. Get me out of your lives. Make it fast. The sooner and the cleaner it's done, the better for us all. You know I've always hated long good-byes.

Larry."

My father's voice broke a little as he read the last words. He recovered enough to add a terse postscript of his own.

"I've seen Madi. I've told her she should do exactly what Larry asks. She told me she wanted to talk to Dr. Levy first."

"Before you hand out any further advice, Father, I want you to do something for me. Fax a copy of each letter, together with the name of the courier and the time of collection in Rome, to Sergio Carlino at the Corsec office in Milan. Please do that as soon as you get off the line."

"I'll do it, of course. However, my view is that you should back out now."

"I'm not at all sure of that."

"Why not?"

"I don't like the idea that we take our sailing directions from a sick man. Look at it another way: We've got a lot of money out on our deal with Corsec, on all the arrangements I've made and you've made for me. Nobody's going to hand that back to us. I'd like to see some results—I'd like at least to know where Larry is headed and what he's going to do when he gets there. Remember

144

he knows everything there is to know about Strassberger, its organization and its activities. He holds a substantial parcel of voting stock. We have to keep tabs on him. As far as Madi is concerned, she'll have to make her own decisions and she has Alma Levy to help her. The family, you especially, shouldn't intrude. Just listen and offer comfort."

"Meantime, what will you do?"

"I'm here in Verona, painting and amusing myself until Sergio Carlino can point me to Larry's destination."

"Well, I've told you what I think."

"You have, Father. I've taken it under advisement."

"Will you talk to Madi?"

"In due course, yes."

"You know, Carl, I feel very angry about this man. He's caused us all so much grief."

"I know. You should step back now from the whole affair and let me deal with the rest of it. Give my love to Mother, and remember I love you too."

"It helps to know that, son. Keep in touch."

My next call was to Alma Levy. Madi had just left her office. She had read Larry's letters. Somewhat to my surprise she had advised Madi to begin divorce proceedings. Her reasoning was simple and practical. Larry was out of contact. The action would take time. It would, however, serve to define Madi's own position and affirm her liberty to act. For me, Alma Levy had other counsel.

"The letters are mirror writing, Carl. Everything is the reverse of what it seems. The letters are a cry for help but he puts himself beyond help. He is desperately afraid yet he becomes destructive and burns the bridges he needs for his return. He affects to despise you because you are not smart enough to find him, but he hopes against hope that you will not abandon the search even when he makes it more difficult—as he will."

"Frankly, my dear Alma, I'd like to break his damn neck."

"That's exactly what he wants, Carl." There was real humor in her laugh. "He wants to know that you are strong enough to subdue not Larry Lucas but the demons who plague him. He's challenging you to combat. If you don't answer the challenge, he is left a battered clown, flailing in an empty ring. The moment that happens he'll kill himself."

"Why has he written to Madi and my father and not to you?"

"The mirror writing again. It is precisely because he knows that I can treat him, because he knows he cannot bluff me, because I am the last anchor to his self-respect. Therefore—this is the mad logic of his life—therefore he will not face me."

"If you were prepared to travel, Doctor, once I know where he is I could arrange—"

"Impossible, I'm afraid." She was very firm. "I have many others who depend on me. I cannot leave the many for the one."

"I understand. I shouldn't have asked."

"Try to understand something else, too. If I were talking to Larry at this moment I would be giving him the same message: 'If you need me you must walk toward me.'"

"But you're telling me exactly the opposite. You're urging me to keep up the search."

"Because that's your role, Carl. You are the messenger. You carry the news of available salvation."

"Don't they sometimes shoot the messenger?"

"Sometimes they do," said Alma Levy somberly. "It's a thankless job at best."

I had two more calls to make. The first was to Carlino in Milan to tell him to expect faxed copies of Larry's farewell letters. The date of their writing and Larry's small slip of the pen— *I leave tonight*—might help to narrow the area of our final search. Flight schedules from Fiumicino Airport for the night in question would at least define the range of destinations. Carlino, condescending as ever, gave me a qualified approval. "You're a clever fellow, my friend. If you were a little younger I'd recruit you into the company. Now tell me, what are you doing with yourself?"

"I'm entertaining a lady."

"A Veronese lady?" I could almost see his eyebrows lift as he asked the question.

"No, an American. An academic."

"Always an interesting choice. Study is an isolating occupation. We all chafe under the discipline and welcome a lover's soothing hands. I wish you luck. What are your movements in case we want to get in touch with you?"

"I'll keep this hotel as my base. During the day I'm going to be out and about in the countryside between here and Venice."

"With the lady?"

"Possibly."

"If you decide to change location, don't fail to let me know. Meantime, enjoy yourself. Let me worry about our wandering friend."

I told him I would take his advice and I meant it. Like my father, I found no joy in the thought of Larry leading me around the world like the Pied Piper. My motives for continuing the search were very mixed. Some indeed were trivial. I hated the jibe that I didn't have enough street smarts to find the bastard. We had spent an unconscionable amount of effort and money on him; I wanted to see some return, however illusory. Added to that, I had to admit a sneaking sympathy for his plight—a fragile psyche chained to the millstone of money and commerce as I had once been. I had escaped without scars. He was harried by other demons as well.

I called Vianney in Paris. I wanted to get his reading on another phrase of Larry's in his letter to my father: *It has been suggested that you might get Carl to pick up my tracks and coax me home.*

"We know that Larry was in Paris just before my arrival," I said. "We know that he was staying with Liliane Prévost from the Simonetta Agency. We know that he had at least one contact with Claudine Parmentier during the same period. Claudine is now the acknowledged lover of Liliane Prévost. Question one: Did she tell Larry of my impending arrival? Question two, much more important: Has Claudine fed any more information to Liliane Prévost since my departure? I have a note in which she swears that she has not given away any company secrets; however, she has lied before. Is she lying now? If she is, I could be in deep trouble."

"I see that." Vianney was his usual reluctant self. "I don't see how I can approach the question at all. If Claudine is lying, she'll lie again. If she's telling the truth, then she's insulted and we lose a very good member of the staff. However, let me give it some thought. How are things with you?"

"Well enough. I'm waiting on the results of some current investigations."

"Then you musn't tell me what they are. I would not wish to fall under suspicion of leaking information."

"Vianney, you're a good banker, but really you are a horse's ass! Good night."

And that, it seemed to me, was enough for one day. I had been nursing the thought that I should call Arlette. Then I had a second thought. I didn't want to lie to her, but I most certainly did not want to account to her for my nights and days with another woman in the Veneto.

That decision, I told myself, was a liberating act. I was not required to hang suspended between dome and pavement like the prophet in his coffin while Arlette made up her mind about marrying me. As far as Larry was concerned, the family had released me from my obligations. My continued acceptance of them was the free act of a free man. I had paid out money and effort. I had appointed a competent delegate in the person of Sergio Carlino. Until he summoned me why not enjoy myself? When I looked into the bathroom mirror, I saw the clear eyes of a just man—and a stubbled face that almost, but not quite, made me lose courage over the project to grow a beard. Once again, my liberated conscience assured me that it was *my* face, *my* beard. I could manage them any way I chose. A wave of elation took hold of me and lifted me high. I was surprised to find myself in quite tolerable voice singing in the shower the triumphant finale of *Nessun dorma*: At dawn I shall triumph.

In point of fact, I did not have to wait until dawn for my triumph. Punctually at eight-thirty Ellie Milland arrived, with a suitcase and hand luggage and the clear intention of installing herself with me at the Due Torri. She was dressed with understated art: a black cocktail dress with an old-fashioned cameo brooch pinned to the breast, a gold bracelet, and a bezel ring, both in the old Florentine style. Her dark hair was bound by a narrow filet of black velvet from the center of which a small gold ornament gleamed in the light. She looked good and she knew it. She made me feel good and she knew that too. This was no longer the boisterous hoyden from Pantalone. This was a very assured woman who was prepared to ritz it with the best at the ritziest hotel Verona offered.

She signed in at the desk. We had the luggage sent up to the room and went straight into the bar to drink champagne before dinner. There was no hurry now. This was only the prelude to the mating ritual, the slow pavane to let the lovers display themselves before they sat together at table, long, long before they retired to their bedchamber.

We were partway through the champagne when Ellie remarked, "You were right about this place. It does impose itself upon you; but I feel we fit, don't you, Mr. Benson?"

"We most certainly do, Ms. Milland."

"It must cost the earth to stay here."

"It does—and a slice of the moon as well."

"Well, I'm prepared to enjoy it as long as your money holds out."

"I assure you it will, but if it doesn't we can always take to the road."

"That's fine with me too." She reached out to touch my cheek in a caress, then withdrew her hand swiftly. "You haven't shaved."

"I've decided to grow a beard. My barber gave it the first shaping this morning. He tells me it will be very handsome—like a Venetian doge. He also told me that in the old days Verona signed on as a vassal with the Venetian Republic and thus guaranteed herself prosperity and protection."

"What's that got to do with growing a beard?"

"Nothing, I guess. The history's recorded fact. The beard is still my whim."

"Won't it be uncomfortable?"

"For me, a little in the beginning. For you, I hope not. There's an old saying: 'A kiss without a beard is like an egg without salt.' In any case, I thought it would make a more interesting self-portrait."

"Come to think of it"—she drew back a little to study me—"come to think of it, yes, it might. I'll suspend judgment for a few days and see how the growth turns out."

I raised my glass to offer the toast.

"Let's drink to the next few days."

"Let them be happy ones," said Ellie Milland.

"They will be. I promise."

Which was, of course, a foolish and presumptuous thing to say. The old Romans had a couple of warnings on the subject. The milder one was simply that the gods might have something else in mind. The more fearful was that when the gods wanted to destroy someone, they first sent him mad. Of course, when you're drinking champagne with a lively and willing companion, such warnings sound faint and far away, if indeed you hear them at all.

I floated through that evening on a white fluffy cloud of well-being. I was happy with Ellie Milland. I was even happier with Edgar Francis Benson, in whose cardboard identity I was masquerading. I admired his skill in fielding awkward questions about his family history and his career. He managed to turn Ellie Milland's shrewd inquisitions into a kind of chess game. There were, however, a couple of questions which even so smart a fellow as Edgar Francis Benson could not avoid answering.

"Where do you exhibit, Edgar?"

"I don't. I have a number of people in Canada and the United States and France who commission works from me."

"And that's enough to pay for this kind of lifestyle?"

"Hell, no! I have a private income."

"Lucky Edgar!"

"And how do you market your designs for jewelry?"

"Pretty much as you do, I guess. I have two big-name houses, one in New York, one in LA, who contract with me for design work. I do a circuit of lectures each year on jewelry design, and that with my academic work keeps me eating. I'd love to find a way into one of the big Italian houses, like Bulgari or Buccellati."

"At a glance I'd say that ring you're wearing is a Buccellati."

She smiled and shook her head.

"It's a Buccellati design. I modified it for myself. I even did the casting and setting. I was very proud when I had finished it."

"You should be. May I take a close look at it?"

And that, of course, was followed by a short interlude of hand-holding across the table while we waited for the next course to be served and studied the new arrivals in the dining room. They were watching us too. Lovers' games are a very public matter in this city of Romeo and Juliet. This one was going well because we were both familiar with the rituals and played them happily like well-schooled actors. Ellie made a sidelong comment on that too.

"How come you never married? You've obviously been around the traps more than once."

"They've all been women traps, if that's what you're worrying about."

"It's something women have to worry about these days. You still haven't answered my question."

"My mother used to quote Thomas Moore, who was a friend of Byron and no mean poet himself. 'The more you have known o' the many, the less you can settle to one!' I've always had women in my life. I've managed to make friends with most of 'em. So marriage was never an urgent question."

"You've had it too easy, Edgar Benson. I hope you haven't given up looking."

"Hell, no! Why else do you think we're here?"

I remember that little indiscretion very well. I remember the swift glance she gave me and how I was happy to see the waiter advancing with our next course. I remember also that it made me realize I was floating very high indeed on my fluffy cloud and that I'd better not have too much more to drink. This Edgar Francis Benson with his scruffy beard and his reckless talk was a very risky game player.

When the meal was over we declined the coffee and liqueurs and rode upstairs clasped in a silent embrace. When she saw the configuration of the rooms and the flowers and the dressing gown laid on her bed, Ellie stood, hands on hips, and gave a small whistle of approval.

"Well, you have to hand it to him! The man has style!"

She gave me a long passionate kiss and then thrust me away.

"Now get the hell out of here and give me a chance to get ready. You know the rule. Safe sex or no sex! After that, anything goes."

By now the fluffy white cloud was riding high in a sea of moonlight and starshine, but the sea was wild and we were tempest tossed to exhaustion. When I woke it was seven in the morning and Ellie Milland was singing in the shower.

By nine we were out on the road and heading toward Vicenza, which is the city of the architect Palladio and the gateway to the lush country between the Adige River and the Brenner Pass. Even the barbarian developers of the twentieth century have not managed to spoil it utterly. Between the windbreaks of acacia trees there are still the spreading acres of sugar beet and corn and orchard trees and the garlands of vines strung between the elms.

We took the back roads, stopping from time to time so that Ellie could photograph and I could sketch. We were timing ourselves to arrive in Vicenza before the Olympic Theater and Civic Museum closed at lunchtime. The open-air work was good for me. I needed to break the crust of architecture and let my drawing flow freely and my colors run wild. Even so I found myself working to method: formal sketch, color notes, and abstraction afterward.

After watching me for a while, Ellie remarked, "You've had good academic training."

"I had, yes. I know all the old adages: You have to put in before you take out . . . construct before you demolish. . . . It's not always an advantage."

"That shows too. Not that you can't free yourself, but in a way you're wedded to the first ceremony. You're like a conjurer. You have to make the passes over the hat before you let the pigeons flutter out."

I was laying down a swift gouache abstract of a drawing I

had just completed: a foreground of cornfields with the roll of foothills toward the distant purple of the Alpine ridges. Four broad brushstrokes and it made a sudden sense. I turned it to Ellie for inspection. She nodded a curt approval.

"Good! Why didn't you let it come straight out like that, without the sketch?"

"I want the sketch for future reference. Anyway, what's the problem? It comes more comfortably this way."

"Perhaps it would come better and more quickly if you were less comfortable."

"That, my dear Ellie, is pure academic gobbledegook! Your jewelry doesn't take shape with a random bashing of metal. You work through the process—"

"It's not the same thing!"

"Why don't you kiss me instead of trying to prove a point?"

She hesitated a moment; then, with a reluctant grin, she surrendered. We climbed back into the car and headed for Vicenza.

As we drove, Ellie lectured me on Palladio, his special contribution to architecture, and in particular the famous trompe-l'oeil stage set which is the glory of the Olympic Theater: archways which seem to open onto the streets and alleys of a whole city and which are, in fact, only a few feet deep. Ellie's information was accurate and extensive. She talked with genuine enthusiasm. I listened in silence, distracted all the time by the irony of the situation.

Her bailiwick was art history, and she was walking me up and down all its paths and byways. Mine was architectural art. I had chosen it as a lifetime study, but I couldn't say a word because it was an integral part of the very identity I was trying to shed.

Another, more subtle, irony insinuated itself slowly. Ellie Milland was herself a divided soul. In bed she was a passionate and practiced lover. Outside it, she was something of a bluestocking, eager to affirm what she knew and careful to conceal the gaps in her knowledge. More, she had been once around the matrimonial traps and was sedulous to establish that any future mating games would be played by her rules.

Not all of this was immediately evident. I wanted to enjoy

myself with her, so I pushed the vagrant thoughts far back in my head and hoped they would stay there. One thought did linger a little longer than the others. My relationship with Arlette had honed itself down to a considerable comfort. We had learned to converse in shorthand—we no longer had to spell the words or analyze the arguments. If she declined to marry me, what then? Was I ready for a new clipping and shaping to fit myself to another woman? And if I weren't ready? Then, good solid Strassberger sense told me, I shouldn't get too addicted to bed play with Ellie and I shouldn't let her get addicted to the company of the fictional Edgar Francis Benson.

The Olympic Theater provided a cheerful little interlude. We trod the stage, we tried our voices in a short duet. I did a swift sketch of Ellie emerging from the classical gateway with the foreshortened streets behind her. Then we left, with an apology to the guardian for keeping him late for his lunch and a tip to add savor to his meal.

We had just time enough to pay a visit to the dwarfs at the Villa dei Nani. A sad little legend says that they were set on the walls of the garden by a doting father whose daughter was herself a dwarf. He wanted to persuade the child that the world was inhabited by little creatures just like herself. When she discovered the sad truth—that the world was full of monsters—she killed herself.

The story was sad, but inside the villa the frescoes by Tiepolo and his son created another world of fantasy, secure against any intrusion of reality. Once again, Ellie delivered her cheerful little lecture, but this time I surrendered myself with every appearance of pleasure to the steady flow of her eloquence. I have never been happy with verbal expositions of the visual arts, so I still claim a certain merit in my smiling patience.

After the dwarfs and Tiepolos, we turned off the main road into a country lane, where we ate our picnic lunch on the grassy verge of a cornfield under a pale blue sky. Afterward we made love on the grass—a quiet playful love this time, which for both of us, I think, pushed the haunting questions further and further into the darkness of the unconscious.

In the quiet of the afterglow, while a speckled thrush cocked an inquisitive eye at us, Ellie made an ingenuous confession.

"This is the best part. Desire's satisfied. There's no more passion to spend. You're full of each other. You're empty of yourself. There's nobody to compete with, nothing to prove. I can even believe I may come to like myself one day. Then I tell myself not to ask too much and to enjoy this single moment." Before I had time to answer, she closed my lips with her fingertips. "You don't have to say anything. You're a good lover and you make me feel good too, but there's another you, living in another room. I know he's there. I hope he'll invite me in one day."

When finally she let me speak, I told her gently, "You've just shown me another Ellie Milland."

"I'm glad I have some mystery for you. That's what frightens me, I think. What's left when the mystery is gone?"

"Don't ask to know. Just lie there. Don't move!"

I hurried back to the car for my sketchbook. When I returned she was lying just as I had left her, sprawled on one side on the grassy verge, her breasts exposed under the open shirt, one hand under her cheek, the other extended along her flank, holding the unzipped Levi's down from the curve of her belly. . . . I took time over it and it turned into a very sensual little study about which there hung the exhalation of relief and abandon after a coupling of lovers.

I showed it to Ellie. She said simply, "It's good. It's a pretty compliment too. Keep it for me. Show it to me when I need a morale booster. Now help me up and let's get on the road."

It was still only midafternoon and Padua was a bare twenty kilometers away, so we decided to push on and give ourselves at least a taste of the town and perhaps touch the tomb of its most famous citizen, Sant' Antonio. One of his specialties is the discovery of lost objects, so I had a faint hope, which, regrettably, I could not reveal to Ellie, that the saint might point me on my way to Larry Lucas.

Ellie flinched from the sight of the great rectangular tomb and the steady stream of devotees sidling along it, touching it with their hands, trailing scarves and handkerchiefs against the stones, to draw into them some of the virtue of the long-dead wonder-worker. I persuaded her to join me in the little pilgrim rite, just so she could say she had done it. She was still reluctant but she did it with me, shivering with some revulsion from a primal dread.

After that we were ready for another kind of pilgrimage, to the fabulous Giotto frescoes in the Scrovegni chapel, which are a picturebook of the life of Christ and the Blessed Virgin. Ellie was stunned into silence by the simple splendor of the frescoes and the awesome miracle of their preservation in World War II while the nearby Augustinian church was hit by British bombers and every one of the Mantegnas was destroyed.

We drank coffee in the Caffè Pedrocchi, where once the heroes of the Risorgimento had gathered. We paused briefly to salute the great Erasmo da Narni, whom the Padovani call Gattamelata, arrogant and triumphant as the day Donatello created him. There was no time left to tour the university, sacred in the history of European medicine since the thirteenth century. I promised Ellie that when I delivered her to Venice to rejoin her friends we would make that our special visit. For now we had to fight our way out of the city and find ourselves the least traveled roads back to Verona.

Ellie was drowsy with fatigue, and somewhere near Vicenza she fell asleep, her dark head pillowed against my shoulder. It was a pleasant end to a companionable day, which I hoped might well end with a long hot tub and supper in our suite.

Arrived back at the Due Torri, I left my gear locked in the trunk and paid the doorman to have one of his boys refill the tank and hose down the country dust in preparation for the next day's excursion, which we thought might take us down to Ferrara and on to Ravenna.

When I stopped by the concierge's desk to collect our keys, I was handed two messages. The first was from Sergio Carlino; it said simply; *Call me most urgently, Sergio.* The second had come a couple of hours later: *Mr. Benson senior called from New York. He would like you to call him at his office.* I shoved them in my pocket. Ellie gave me an inquiring look.

"Your agent?"

"Yes. He wants me to call him back."

"There were two messages."

"The other was from New York. Personal business. I'll deal with them both when we get upstairs."

"I hope this isn't going to foul up our plans."

"I hope so too. It was a good day, wasn't it?"

"It was a friendly day, a loving sort of day. Thank you, Edgar Benson."

"Thank you, Ellie Milland."

"If this isn't private business, you can make your calls while we're in the spa together."

"We'd probably scandalize the people at the other end. You get in first. I'll join you when I've made the calls."

"That's the other man talking now, the one I don't know."

"Run along, woman, and stop teasing me. You slept on the way home. I drove. You can be the bathhouse girl and scrub my back tonight."

She padded through my room on her way to the tub, while I was punching out Sergio Carlino's number. When she turned on the taps, I called to her to shut the door. She slammed it hard. After the usual interval for rerouting, Sergio came on the line. He was excited.

"We've flushed our fox! On the date his letters were written, he was staying at the Flora Hotel on the Via Veneto. In the evening he checked out, to fly from Rome to Zurich. He was in a wheelchair and was accompanied by a Swiss doctor. At Zurich airport a wheelchair was again ordered, and an ambulance was in attendance. The ambulance was sent from the Burgholzli Clinic, which is the most famous place in Switzerland for mental cases. And that, my friend, is a piece of investigative work of which my colleagues and I are very proud, even though we could be arrested for some of it. You may now express your appreciation by prolonged applause."

"My compliments, Sergio. My thanks to your diligent staff. Now can you give me any idea of what this means and what led to it?"

"The information is sparse. The Flora's hotel register showed a Dr. Alois Langer, Swiss nationality, who arrived and departed with him. We checked back to the Villa Estense in Sirmione and found that Dr. Langer had been there too. Same arrival, same departure."

"So, he's sick and in custodial care."

"More precisely, he is now in institutional care."

"That means, or may mean, that his trustee is empowered to act in his name. I don't like the smell of that at all."

"Neither do I. You'll like this next part even less. Your father called our New York office today to institute a market watch on worldwide transactions in Strassberger shares."

"That sounds ominous. I have a message to call him. I'll do it after we've finished here. What suggestions do you have about our patient?"

"None that I want to discuss now. You and I should talk face-to-face as early as possible tomorrow. I'll be in my office at eight. Check out of the Due Torri and drive into Milan. We'll have your car delivered back to the rental agency."

"I'll leave at six in the morning."

"Allowing for traffic, I'll expect you between eight and nine. . . . I hope you can handle the lady."

"So do I. It's not going to be easy. Until tomorrow, then."

I called my father in New York. Before I had time to tell him what I had just learned, he was launched on his own list of complaints.

"The sharks are circling round us, Carl. This morning there was a line of bidders in the Paris Bourse, in London, and in New York. There are also a few bids from the West Coast. It's too early to say yet what the backwash is going to be. I've already had a call from the SEC, asking whether I have any explanation for the stock movements. I told them I didn't. I don't, either, but I'll swear that somehow Larry is connected with what's happening. You'll remember I told you from the very first, you might raise a wolf instead of a fox."

"I remember, but it so happens our wolf is hospitalized in Switzerland in the Burgholzli Clinic."

"God almighty! When did you hear this?"

"Just now from Sergio Carlino. I'm checking out of here first thing in the morning to confer with him in Milan."

"This has to mean a radical change in your plans—in all our plans, perhaps."

"I know that, but it's too soon to make decisions, and we can't do our planning on open telephone lines. I'll call you as soon as I've heard more from Carlino. Meantime, you beat off the sharks in New York."

"I've put out buying orders on all available stock. The company will top any bid."

"That's a very risky game, Father."

"I know, but for the moment we can play it. We're cash rich. If the game gets too tough, we'll think again."

"I wish you luck."

"We need some good intelligence, too. There's another aspect to this, Carl. It calls in question not only Larry's loyalties but the attitudes of all our regional offices: France, London, Singapore, even as far as Sydney. Your reports on Vianney take on a new color in this light."

"I know. I know, too, that we musn't rush judgment. Your own words: 'Hasty judgment means a long repentance.' At least you have me here on this side of the Atlantic. Is Madi home tonight?"

"I believe so. It's the nanny's night off."

"I'll talk to her and then I'll call Dr. Levy. We need her advice very badly now."

"Recruit the devil if you can use him," said my father grimly.

When I put down the phone, I was startled to see Ellie, wrapped in her dressing gown, leaning against the jamb of the bathroom door.

"That was a quick bath."

"I haven't had it yet. The tub's full and hot. I'm waiting to scrub your back as you asked."

"Meantime, you've been eavesdropping on a private conversation."

"No. I've been asking myself how much should be private

159

between two people who share each other's bodies and make love talk together and even create images to be passed on to the children they may have. Primitive people say that's a magical act, don't they? You make the image, you possess the person's soul. Well, right now, Edgar Benson, you possess my soul and I'm damned and double-damned if I know what to do about it!"

She stood there, propped against the doorframe, her face crumpled, weeping quietly like a child who had experienced her first random cruelty. I went to her and took her in my arms. She did not struggle. She did not respond, but simply leaned into me for support while I groped for words of comfort or explanation. They were hard to come by. Ellie's own plaintive plea filled the silence.

"I know you told me that you might be called away. You didn't lie—at least I don't think you did; so I can't be angry with you. I'm just surprised that I feel so bad after so short a time."

"I feel badly, too. Something has happened which I didn't expect. I'll try to explain a little of what it's about, but I can't tell all of it. That's hard for you, and it's hard for me too. I have a secret which isn't mine to share and a responsibility I can't delegate either. All the other things we shared yesterday and today are real . . . Nobody can take them away from us."

"But they'll wear away, won't they? The finest gold is soft and wears away even when you wear it between your breasts. I don't blame you. I wish it could be different, that's all. Now I'll go and take my tub while you finish your calls." She gave me a small uncertain smile. "Then, if you're not too long, I'll either scrub your back or strangle you!"

She slipped from my arms and went into the bathroom, closing the door behind her. A moment later I heard the whirring of the pumps and the bubble of the water. I turned back to the phone to call Madi and Alma Levy.

Madi was shocked at the news that Larry had been hospitalized. Her immediate conclusion was that he had gone off the drug dosages prescribed by Dr. Levy and thereby precipitated a major episode which had required hospitalization. There was a fundamental objection to that idea: the continued presence of

Dr. Langer. A more likely scenario was that Larry had traveled with the doctor, who had deliberately treated him with psychotropic drugs to procure his collapse and a prearranged committal in Switzerland.

I told Madi I would be back to her as soon as I had finished my discussions with Sergio Carlino. Meantime, she should be ready to leave for Switzerland at short notice, bringing with her Larry's original passport and their marriage certificate and any other relevant documents. I encouraged her to believe that it would not be too difficult to secure Larry's release from he hospital. I did not tell her that I was less sure about getting him to rescind any power of attorney he might have vested in Dr. Rubens.

For the rest, I told her to sit tight and trust brother Carl to sort out the mess. I did not tell her that brother Carl had a mess of his own to tidy: a sad and angry companion, waiting either to scrub him or kill him in a bubbling bathtub. My conversation with Alma Levy produced a firestorm of anger.

"This is outrageous! I have never heard of your Doctor Alois Langer; but if what you tell me is true, he has taken a criminal risk! With some of these compounds the effects are irreversible. They were used in Soviet mental institutions on political prisoners forcibly confined. Fortunately, the Burgholzli is a legitimate institution with a long history of excellence. Great names worked there, Jung, Bleuler, Ferenczi, the pioneers. One may hope that today's staff will be observant enough and careful enough to diagnose Larry's condition. In any case, I have changed my mind. I shall come to Europe whenever you call me. I cannot bear to think of this—this criminal tyranny against a patient of mine! Meanwhile, I'll see if I can rake up a contact with the Burgholzli itself. It shouldn't be too difficult. The problem is that one has to be very formal with the Swiss, very respectful of their protocols. Leave it to me. I'll see what I can do."

"But please, Doctor, please consult with me before you act. There is more than medicine involved here."

"I know, Carl. Trust me."

"One more question—which I shouldn't ask: How's Madi holding up?"

161

"She's fine. She's bruised and angry; but she's liberated from her own dependence on her partner's infirmity. How are you?"

"Put it this way: Right now I'd rather be feeding the ducks with you in Central Park."

"That's nice to hear. Shalom, Carl Emil. I wish peace on your house."

I breathed a long and fervent amen to that; then I stripped hurriedly and climbed into the tub with Ellie. She made no move toward me, but watched as I let the churning water engulf me and the jets pound my tense muscles.

Finally, she asked calmly, "Any more phone calls?"

"No, that's all."

"So what's next?"

"I have to check out at six in the morning."

"Where does that leave me?"

"I'll order a limousine to take you on to Venice so you can rejoin your friends. You don't have to get up early. The room will be paid for. Check out when you choose."

"And that's the only choice?"

"No. You may stay here for a couple of days if you like. I'll be happy to arrange it."

"And what will I do, write letters to Juliet? Mourn my lost love at her tomb?"

"Alternately, you can get up early, ride into Milan with me and go on your way from there."

"And that's the end of the story for Ellie Milland?"

"Not quite. You did promise either to strangle me, or scrub my back. Strangling might be the more welcome fate at this moment."

"When you were talking on the phone, you looked troubled. You sounded troubled."

"I was. I am."

"But you won't talk about it."

"I can't. Too many other people's lives are involved. Some of them are at real risk."

"Then so you won't be any more troubled, I'll tell you now. I accept your offer of a limousine to Venice in the morning. So while I'm scrubbing your back and you don't have to look at me, talk to me about you, talk about you and me. Tell me nice things that will be pleasant to remember and make me feel a little more confident than I do at this moment. Will you try to do that, Mr. Benson?"

"I'll try, Ms. Milland. God knows you deserve it."

I slewed myself around in the tub, so that I sat between her legs, and she began soaping and scrubbing me while the tension between us drained away slowly into a kind of confession.

"You guessed right. I'm not the crazy fellow you met at Pantalone. I am, most of me anyway, the fellow you were with last night and all today. Tonight is still open, but that's entirely up to you, Ellie Milland, and you'll hear no sour words from me if you refuse.

"The name I travel under isn't my real name. The signature on your drawing isn't the real signature. One day, when this is all over, I'll send you an authentic signed piece. The problem is, I can't tell you why. All I can say is that I'm not a criminal. I'm not running away from anyone. Before I came here, I asked a woman to marry me. We've been close friends for a long time, though we've never lived together under the same roof because she's very independent and I'm a selfish fellow and this has been a very satisfactory arrangement for both of us. I was the one who was feeling lonely, so I asked her to marry me. She wasn't at all sure it was a good idea. So, I came down here, and the night before last I was still lonely and I went out cruising—in Verona of all places!—and here we are. I know you're lonely too, and lonely people shouldn't hurt each other, though sometimes they do.

"If you ask me where we go from here, I have to say I don't know, because there's a lot of unfinished business I have to deal with and I won't be thinking straight until it's done. I can't even give you my card and say call me, because the one I carry is a stage prop. If you give me yours, I'll promise to call when all this is over, but only if you'll promise not to sit around waiting and wondering and feeling diminished by yet another son of a bitch who didn't know the treasure he'd lost. Have you finished my back yet, Ms. Milland?"

163

"Just this very minute, Mr. Benson. Now if you'll turn around we'll deal with the front of you."

And the rest? As the ancient chroniclers used to say, the rest is silence. I carried her to her own bed in the very small hours of the morning and drew the covers over her, kissed her good-bye, and returned to my own bed, where I lay wakeful until the night porter called at cockcrow to tell me it was time to rise and hit the road.

9

THE HEADQUARTERS OF CORSEC Italia S.p.A. were a surprise. They lay outside the city itself on a stretch of reclaimed swampland, surrounded by a double row of chain-link fence topped with barbed wire. There were exit gates on four sides, each with its own guardhouse, and private roads led from them onto separate arteries, so that it would be difficult if not impossible to blockade the compound.

Company vehicles, armored vans, and various automobiles were housed in bunkered shelters around the central block, which was an eight-story concrete building crowned with a steel tower and a whole array of antennae. The place was a witness to money and power, a defensive alliance of giant companies against outside enemies and traitors inside their corporate walls. I guessed, though I had no evidence to support it, that this fortresslike place was financed by a consortium of Italian and European businesses, held in uneasy alliance by the patrician hand of Sergio Carlino.

I was whirled up to his office in a high-speed elevator and ushered through an anteroom, where an aloof young woman received me and conducted me into the presence of the master himself, enthroned behind a huge desk with a battery of computer screens on the right and a modern intercom board on the left. A single folder lay mathematically centered in front of him. He stood to greet me, shook my hand, waved me regally into a chair, ordered coffee, and made courteous inquiries about my sojourn in the Veneto. He offered condolences on my all too brief acquaintance with my "academic friend." He commented on my short beginnings of a beard. He thought that it made me look younger—scruffiness being the badge of youth. Then the tongue-in-cheek talk was over. He opened the folder and plunged straight into business.

"Your brother-in-law is now in Switzerland. He is obviously sick enough to be confined in a reputable institution. You and your family can arrange access to him at any time—though what success you will have in the encounter is still a question mark. To arrange the access, you will need to reveal your true identity to the medical authorities—and possibly to the police. This means that your change of identity will have no point or purpose any-more, unless. . . ."

He hesitated long enough to prompt my question.

"Unless what?"

"Unless you are prepared to play out the charade a little longer."

"For what purpose?"

"The original one: to see what it might reveal about the activities of Falco and Dr. Rubens, who, at least on the face of it, are manipulating a sick man and engineering a stock-market operation against Strassberger."

"If it will produce anything of course I'll do it, but it could leave Larry out on a limb."

"Not so far out," said Carlino amiably. "He is in the care of a most reputable clinic. He is safer there than on the streets of any city."

"So what do you propose I do?"

"What you planned from the beginning: Present yourself at Simonetta Travel, quote their own publicity back to Falco, ask them if he can arrange a disappearance for you. See what sort of response you get. I'll send you in wired so we can pick up the

166

talk in one of our surveillance vans. We'll analyze it together afterward."

"There's no guarantee he'll see me."

"A phone call will prove it, one way or the other."

"When would I do this?"

"Today, if possible. We can call the agency this minute."

"Does Falco speak English?"

"Quite well. Can you remember enough of your briefing to pass his questionnaire?"

"I won't know until I face it, will I?"

"No, you won't." Carlino was suddenly grave. "Think about this when you go in. Falco's a practiced rogue. He's pulled himself up to a position where—if our reasoning is correct—he is now able to bid for control of an important merchant banking enterprise. He lives, like every feral animal, on his instincts. If things go wrong, if he finds flaws in your story, don't back off. Attack, accuse! The worst that can happen is that he will refuse you as a client or you decline to become one."

"Do you think that will worry him?"

"It will disturb him, at least. He's got a lot riding on this game. He will be doubly careful of his image, as you must be of yours when you confront him."

"Let's get on with it, then."

He picked up the phone and gave rapid directions to his secretary. A few moments later she had Falco on the line. Carlino threw a switch so that the conversation was audible to him as well. I began in a tentative, halting style.

"I hope you speak English, Mr. Falco. My Italian isn't very good."

"I speak English, yes." He was cautious and curt. "Who is this?"

"You won't know me. My name is Edgar Benson. I'm a Canadian. I've been holidaying at the Due Torri in Verona. I've just arrived in Milan. I'd like to see you urgently about some travel arrangements."

"Who recommended you to us, Mr. Benson?"

"No one. I found you myself."

"How did you do that?"

"There was an article about you and your agency in a hotel magazine. It spoke about the special services you offer. You know the piece I refer to?"

"Oh, that! Yes. Like most journalistic efforts it was a little overdone, but yes, we can make special arrangements. They are, however, quite expensive."

Now it was my turn to be curt.

"I assure you, Mr. Falco, I have excellent credit references. On my part, I should need to be assured that your performance as travel agents matches your publicity."

That set him back on his heels, but only for a moment. His tone changed in an instant, to warm and ingratiating.

"Of course. Our very existence depends on client service. May I suggest eleven this morning, in my office?"

"Eleven would be convenient, yes."

"You know where we are?"

"I'll find you."

"Would you care to give me a preliminary idea of your requirements, so we may have some material ready for you? We have offices in Paris, New York, and Los Angeles and worldwide affiliation in the hospitality industry."

"Requirements? Let me give you a short list. I don't enjoy discomfort. I don't want undue health hazards. I need reasonable access to medical care. My tastes are for the exotic, preferably for places where there are indigenous local arts and an agreeable local support system in terms of household service. Above all, I require privacy and safe communications."

"That's a challenging list, but I'm sure we can find what you need. May I ask what kind of work you do?"

"It's not work, Mr. Falco. It's a life which I have been lucky enough to enjoy. I'm an artist, a designer, and I draw much on indigenous art and craft work. I have a very select clientele. So: eleven o'clock, then."

"I look forward to our meeting, Mr. Benson."

Sergio Carlino leaned back in his chair and surveyed me with lordly approval.

"Well! Now we have the other face of art. An actor indeed! A great comedian!"

He might well be pleased. He might well shower me with praise. His fine Italian hand had just moved me into play against the adversary who had so far eluded him and his former colleagues in law enforcement. He asked me what I was grinning at. I told him he was a very clever fellow. I was paying the money; he was using me as the instrument of his own vendetta against Francesco Falco.

He seemed flattered by the accusation. He gave me very good reasons for it. Actors had always been rated as rogues and vagabonds. Even the Church, not so long ago, had held them excommunicated de facto and—saving a deathbed repentance—damned to hell. Conclusion? They were usable and expendable and if they footed the bill, as I was doing, so much the better.

That seemed to have carried the joke far enough. There was never enough humor in it anyway—and a slight hint of malice. I suggested that Sergio brief me for my eleven o'clock performance opposite Francesco Falco. He thought about it for a few moments and then set down his answer.

"What I give you now is a wish list, not a prescription. In the end, you will have to improvise anyway. This is how I see the direction of the meeting. You offer yourself to Falco as a bona fide client. He will present you with a whole list of questions, not only to ascertain your tastes and needs but to give himself a profile of you. You will answer freely but always with a certain reserve. You will remind him—as you have just reminded me—that you are the man who pays the money. You want a pleasant, possibly a permanent, change of lifestyle. You also want a safe channel for your funds and protection against tax gatherers. This leads, if not immediately, then certainly before the end of the discussion, to Dr. Rubens. You lean on the financial aspects of your situation. Your references will be impeccable, but be sure Falco will check them all. Once he has done that, the hook will be in his mouth and you can begin tugging on the line."

"Alternately, he may decide he doesn't like me at all and decline to have me as a client."

"Believe me, he will do that with great reluctance. So let's work on the interview itself. Hand me your passport and the copy of your life story. Let's see how good you are at telling lies. After that, we'll get you wired up."

Simonetta Travel maintained an expensive storefront and offices in one of the most expensive locations in Milan, the Galleria. It was designed to catch the eye of the shoppers and the promenaders and all the other actors in the daily drama of the glass palace.

Inside there were three young women in well-tailored suits, each with the Simonetta monogram embroidered on the breast pocket: an *S* imposed on a *V*, for Simonetta Viaggi. They were not only pleasant to look at; they were well trained. I was greeted cordially, and when I stated my business my welcome was effusive. Signor Falco was, indeed, waiting for me. If I would come this way, please.

The man who greeted me was a surprise. The mind-picture I made of him was a stereotype from film fiction: a swarthy, sinisterlooking gangster with a hoarse and threatening voice. Instead, I found myself shaking hands with a tall white-haired gentleman with classic aquiline features who carried himself with all the dignity of a Noble Guard. His voice was soft, his gestures restrained, his handshake firm and dry. He sat me down, offered me coffee and mineral water, and began the interview.

"I have to tell you, Mr. Benson, that silly little magazine piece has brought us more inquiries than any single piece of paid advertising. It's quite extraordinary how many people read the magazines in hotel rooms. Where, for example, did you see it?"

"If memory serves—and my memory is never the best—it was in Switzerland at the Baur au Lac."

"What was it in particular that interested you?"

"I can tell you that exactly. It was the idea of a carefully organized retreat from the unpleasant realities of normal existence: things that can't be cured but which one is unwilling to endure. Then, of course, I was impressed that you yourself seemed to be

170

doing research on the locations. You were not simply selling travel packages, sight unseen."

"This is very interesting. Please go on."

"Well, it seems to me that everyone comes to a moment of crisis from which one needs a place of retreat and the means to maintain oneself there. I find myself at such a moment now."

"My English is not perfect. I am not sure that I understand what you mean by *maintain*."

"Forgive me. I'm expressing myself rather badly. I am thinking of two separate issues. The first, I could not contemplate living in a hotel for any extended period. I should need a house and a well-trained staff to run it."

"That, generally speaking, can be arranged. The standard of residence and staff depends, of course, on what you are prepared to pay."

"I am prepared to pay for the best, Mr. Falco—which is not necessarily the most extravagant."

"Your point is well taken. Your second requirement?"

"It's the matter of money management. The comfortable existence I desire depends on a regular and safe transmission of funds across national borders with a minimal tax obligation, either in my home place, Canada, or the place of my new residence."

He rose to the bait, as I had hoped he would. Yet he did it with considerable caution.

"Surely your present bankers can provide all the services you need?"

"My present bankers—that is to say my bankers in Europe—are Morgan Guaranty in Paris. I maintain funds in Canada but I use them only when I am at home in that country. So far, I have been able to introduce an acceptable hiatus into the money trail."

Falco said nothing. He smiled and nodded approval of my cleverness. I went on with my explanation.

"However, there are problems for any client of any bank who lives in an exotic location. You must be aware of them. Indeed, if I remember the article rightly, it suggested you had developed a means of dealing with such problems."

"What problems, Mr. Benson?"

171

"My bankers, Morgan Guaranty, transmit funds to me wherever I require them by bank-to-bank electronic transfer."

"We use the same system."

"However, in certain places, even in Europe, it takes a week or more to verify that the funds have arrived. That suits the receiving bank, which is using them for overnight transactions. Meanwhile, the client is embarrassed. I do not wish to be embarrassed in any circumstances! Suppose I fall sick and need immediate medical attention. I don't want to die because I can't touch my own funds to charter an aircraft. Do I make myself clear?"

"Very clear, Mr. Benson, and you are right; these are situations against which we provide very carefully for our special clients. We find that, as far as major institutions are concerned, they are inclined to fail in small but important matters of detail."

"And how do you address such details?"

"We run our own banking system. It is private. It is small but financially secure, founded, chartered, and directed from the home of banking, Switzerland. If you should wish to use the system, Mr. Benson, we can certainly assist you with the necessary introductions."

"Before making any such arrangements, I should require to meet the principal."

"Nothing could be simpler. He is in Geneva, which is only a short flight from Milan."

"Good! Now let's see what kind of new world you can offer me."

Falco smiled tolerantly and held up a hand in admonition.

"Please, let's do this properly. We have a method which we use with all our special clients. I'll call in one of our young ladies, who will take you through a questionnaire. With that information we can save you and ourselves a great deal of unnecessary labor. It's called client profiling. We find it works very well. Do you agree?"

"It sounds like a good idea."

"Now, before the young lady comes in, there are certain questions I have to ask you personally. It may be less embarrassing if we do it here and now."

"Go ahead."

"You mentioned, in our telephone conversation, 'domestic arrangements.' Are you married, Mr. Benson?"

"No."

"So, when you refer to domestic arrangements . . ."

"It means that I have a taste for exotic women. I am not promiscuous. The dangers are too great these days. I would accept no woman into my household unless she were thoroughly examined by a competent physician. So far as domestic staff is concerned, I need a majordomo to run the household and maintain good relations with local merchants."

"The woman should not be hard to find, Mr. Benson. The majordomo may be more difficult. Still, so far we have been successful with other clients. Next question. Do you have any chronic illnesses requiring medical supervision?"

"None. I'm an A-grade insurance risk."

"Do you have any venereal diseases?"

"No."

"Will you carry your own health and accident insurance, or will you ask us to find an insurer?"

"I'll provide my own."

"Are you an absconding debtor?"

"No."

"Do you have a police record in any country?"

"No."

"Are you subject to any court orders for the payment of alimony or child support?"

"No."

"How long would you wish to maintain a secluded lifestyle?"

"If I found the right place, I might be tempted to maintain it forever."

"You understand, Mr. Benson, that in the case of an extended stay, we should require an adequate credit reference."

"What would you call adequate?"

"That would depend on the location and the lifestyle you chose. From our point of view, we should look to a sum that could maintain you in your chosen style for not less than three years."

"A question, Mr. Falco."

"Please!"

"Once having established me in paradise, why should you care whether I live or die, whether I am rich as Croesus or a beggar on the beach?"

"Because we are not just a travel agency, though we function very well doing just that. Our special clients are, in effect, asking us to provide them with their own private paradise. To do that effectively, we send them to places which we ourselves own or which we lease and manage. We provide them with the best that is available in their style of living. We have to be sure that they can pay the bills. You asked a few moments ago about transmission of money. I told you we had a private banking system. We do. Under that system we are able to supply local credit to our clients, saving them a great deal of tax while we collect the money from an approved source—in your case, from Morgan Guaranty. There is another advantage. Our people in Geneva will accept to act under powers of attorney while the client maintains what he or she sought in the first place: a secret existence with no intrusion from outside."

"You have still to tell me the name of your banking principal in Geneva."

"Do you wish to meet him?"

"Not at the moment. I'd like to run his name past Morgan Guaranty, who, after all, would be the people instructed to deal with him."

"A wise precaution, Mr. Benson. It's a pleasure to deal with someone who knows his own mind. The name of the person is Dr. Hubert Rubens. When you leave here, I'll give you his card attached to your other papers. One more point: When we have finished our conversation and explored the possibilities, you will take whatever time you need to consider them. However, any further work we do on your project will be subject to contract and, of course, a deposit of working funds."

"I'm not sure I understand."

"Mr. Benson." His tone was very patient. "You are not asking us to arrange a vacation. You are not even asking us to build you a house. You are asking us to build you a new life. That takes time, money, and travel—on your part and on the part of our personnel. I did warn you this could be costly."

"You did. And I shall pay willingly if you come up with an attractive proposal. I assume you'll give me a copy of your contract, so that I can study it along with your suggestions?"

"Certainly! That's a normal part of our paperwork. It is, however, a confidential document, and we ask you to treat it as such. Now, why don't I call in our young lady and complete the rest of the questionnaire. We'd like your passport, driver's license, credit cards, and the name of your contact at Morgan Guaranty."

He pressed a buzzer on his desk, and a few moments later Liliane Prévost walked into the room with a notepad and clipboard under her arm. For one instant I was panic-stricken. My polite smile of welcome seemed frozen into a rictus of fear. Then I remembered. I had seen her at Céline's gallery, but she had never seen me. There was no way in the world she could identify me. Francesco Falco introduced us calmly.

"Mr. Benson, this is Mlle. Prévost. Mr. Benson is a candidate for our special client list, Liliane."

"Welcome to Simonetta, Mr. Benson."

"Thank you."

"Mlle. Prévost has just joined us from our Paris office, where she dealt with several special clients. I leave you with her to complete the questionnaire. After that, we can take a first look at possible destinations for you."

He got up from his desk and Liliane took his place behind it. He gave her an approving smile.

"We encourage ambition here, Mr. Benson. Our senior personnel move from country to country. Who knows? One day Mlle. Prévost may well be occupying my place. By the way, Liliane, Mr. Benson is Canadian, so if your English lapses at any moment, you should be able to get along in French."

"I'm sure we shall arrange ourselves very well," said Liliane Prévost primly. "Now, Mr. Benson, I need first your passport."

From documents we passed to interrogation. The questions she put to me were less intimate than Falco's but they covered a

175

lot of private ground: religious affiliation, dietary needs, next of kin, diplomatic connections if any, the kind of guests I might wish to welcome, my blood group.

I could afford to be good-humored about what was, in effect, a pack of lies but I felt some token protest should be made about such an intrusive document. She acknowledged my protest serenely.

"Yes, it is intrusive, Mr. Benson. It is also intended to protect you and to protect us. We are, after all, considering a very intimate relationship with you. We are assuming a large responsibility for your well-being. Let me show you what I mean. The religious question, for instance. If you are Christian or Jewish, you may be disinclined to reside in a predominantly Muslim area, say in Indonesia or in certain Philippine islands where we have established accommodation. You may be totally against surgical intervention, even in emergency. We have to know that. Visitors? You may decline any contact with relatives. You may wish to be protected from reporters and photographers. To serve you properly, we must be aware of these things. We cannot construct a life overnight and without a plan. Quite recently, I was appointed to travel with a client—a very important client—whom we were about to settle in the Seychelles. I looked after him in Paris and then set him on his way to Rome. Unfortunately, he became ill and had to be flown to Switzerland for hospitalization. He wanted no contact with his family, so our people managed the whole operation. We flew in a doctor to treat him and take him to the hospital."

"What was the matter with him?"

"Oh, he had mental problems. He was a nice man, quite young, quite brilliant. I enjoyed his company."

"I am sure he enjoyed yours. Where is he now?"

"In the best clinic in Switzerland."

"That's comforting to know. It says much for your care of your clients."

"Thank you. Now let's get back to our list."

"What happens to this list?"

"First, your name is changed to a case name. The information is then coded and stored in our computer system. The original paperwork, which I am doing now, is destroyed immediately after encoding. If you decide not to go ahead with your plans, your file is erased from the computer."

"Do you circulate the file to your other offices?"

"Of course. Each office is asked to offer its own suggestions for this particular client. The resources of each one are different. Vacancies occur in one area. New developments occur in another. As I pointed out, the process is time-consuming. It took us several months to find a satisfactory proposal for the client I mentioned. With some, it has taken even longer. People are very—what is the word? —inconstant?"

"Fickle, changeable?"

"Thank you. Now the next question." She gave a small laugh. "Mr. Falco usually asks this himself."

"What does he ask?"

"Sexual orientation, health, pattern of domestic life—"

"He has asked me. I wondered why he placed so much emphasis on them."

"The health question is very important. Not all our resorts are able to offer a full range of medical services."

"And the sexual questions?"

"Some places are permissive. Others are very strict—for example, in matters of sex with children."

"Why is all this information filed in each of your offices?"

"Because each office is asked to discuss the client's dossier and make recommendations on it. Of course, that occurs only after the information has been checked."

"Especially the financial information."

"That, yes, but the rest of it also."

"And if it doesn't check out?"

"Mr. Falco himself contacts the client to discuss the situation. He's very good with people, very sympathetic to their problems. Now, we really should finish this. . . ."

When the interrogation was finished, she pressed the buzzer and got up. Falco came back and resumed his seat at the desk; Liliane Prévost left, carrying her papers. I offered a comment and a compliment.

"That's a very intelligent young woman."

"Intelligent, efficient, and quite beautiful, yes?"

"Yes indeed."

"I had the impression when she came in that you recognized her from some other occasion."

"I thought so too. I couldn't place her. I still can't."

"And she had no memory of such an occasion?"

"I didn't ask. Quite frankly, I'm too busy simplifying my life to risk complicating it with any other woman, however beautiful or interesting."

"Which brings me," said Francesco Falco in his quiet fashion, "to the very last question, the one which is not on the list. It comes in two parts. What are you running away from and what are you hoping to find?"

"I should have thought that was my business, Mr. Falco."

"It was. It is no longer." He pointed across the room to a large display screen suspended on the wall. "In a moment, I shall switch on an illustration, a map of the world. It will show you the locations we can offer you. Following that, we will show you in simple graphic form the attractions of each one, its merits and its demerits, and what it will cost you to establish yourself there and, as you put it, maintain yourself. A problem will then arise. The moment you step outside the door, you will forget what you have seen. Then you will have to refer to the large folder of illustrated material which we shall give you to take away and study. After all that, you will still find yourself faced with the two-part question I have just put to you: What are you running from and what do you hope to find?"

It was a moment of unexpected danger. I found myself so angered by his air of disdainful power that I was tempted to abort the whole event and challenge him to tell me about Larry Lucas. Somehow, I managed to act myself through the moment. I closed my eyes and palmed them with my hands in a simulation of weariness. Finally, I answered him.

"Mr. Falco, I am not good enough with words. I am not clear enough in mind to answer those questions immediately. Let me see the picture show; let me read the material. I'll be back to you in a couple of days."

"Where are you staying in Milan, Mr. Benson?"

"With an Italian friend of mine."

"Address?"

"It's his address, not mine. Occasionally he entertains a lady there."

"I understand. One has to protect one's friends. Talking of friends, I shouldn't give up too easily on Liliane. She's a very interesting young woman. She's new in this city and feeling quite lonely. She might appreciate a telephone call, and it might be useful if, in the future, you find yourselves working together on your new life project."

"And you don't object to your staff associating with clients?"

"On the contrary. The members of our staff are trained as essential elements in our client support system."

And there, behind the gentleman with the white hair and the patrician face and the bland good manners, was the image that had lurked for a long time in my head: the gangster, the trader in warm bodies, the perennial pimp.

I acknowledged his offer with a smile and a word of thanks. I told him I would think about it. What I was really smiling at was the fact that I had just loaded a heap of garbage into his information system. What I was thinking about was a sudden villainous inspiration. What would happen if I brought Liliane Prévost and Sergio Carlino together for a demonstration of his skills as an interrogator?

With that happy thought in mind, I settled down with Francesco Falco while he displayed the wealth and beauty of his travel empire.

"That's really what they're doing." Sergio Carlino made the emphatic announcement. "They're building a tourist empire. Rubens is at its financial core. Falco is what he has always been, the hustler, drumming up business. This"—he tapped the brightly colored map which was spread out on his desk—"this is a big enterprise with a hell of a risk factor, but a huge potential. Cheap land and cheap labor in third world and marginal countries.

Low-cost resort development for a high-income clientele. Backing from trustee funds of long standing run by Rubens and, subject to minimal scrutiny, big potential profits at sell-off time. It's a fast, high-rolling game. So their bid for Strassberger, or any similar institution, is a normal element in the pattern. Rubens himself is another such element. Their special clients, like Larry Lucas, are subsidizing the enterprise by a system of double and triple mulcting."

He tapped the Simonetta contract which lay beside the map. "This is basically a slave contract. Once you sign it, once you appoint Rubens as trustee with power of attorney, you're set in concrete. You can't get out without a huge financial penalty. If your brother-in-law has signed that—as he probably has—then everything he owns is in trusteeship with Rubens. If he ever recovers, he'll find himself impoverished. If the bid for Strassberger shares is even halfway successful, your father—your whole family, for that matter—will be partners with a bunch of scoundrels."

"So how do we break the chain?"

"At its weakest link: the young woman with the ambivalent love life, Liliane Prévost. Certainly you should call her. Invite her out tomorrow night. Promise her a special evening. Your Italian friends are arranging a mystery party for you—talented people, very chic."

"And where will this party be held?"

"At a country villa between here and Como. It's a thirty-minute drive, no more. Tell her you'll meet her at the party. You'll send a car and driver to pick her up and deliver her safely home."

"What time?"

"Pickup at seven-thirty. Get the address and telephone number of her apartment. Go ahead, do it now!"

I made the call. Sergio switched on the recorder and listened attentively to every word of the conversation. Liliane Prévost was surprised but interested. She asked me to hold the line a moment. It was a courtesy to check with the Director to see if he had any social assignments for that evening. She was back inside a minute.

She would be happy to join me. Where? I told her this was a mystery party; even I didn't know where it would be held. She would be picked up at seven-thirty. Dress? I guessed that it would be informal-smart. She gave me her address and telephone number. I asked if I had embarrassed her with Mr. Falco. On the contrary, he had urged her to accept. He had found me—why should he not? —an interesting man. Also, parties with the chic and talented were an excellent recruiting ground for Simonetta clients.

Sergio was pleased. He thought I was a very good liar. I asked him how he proposed to stage the evening. He smiled and shook his head.

"Better you don't ask. You act better in ignorance. Now, I should like you to call your Paris office and see if you can get some information from Mlle. Parmentier."

"On what?"

"The circumstances of Liliane Prévost's transfer from Paris to Milan."

"Dammit, Sergio, that's too dangerous. One phone call from Claudine to Milan and all we've done is down the drain!"

"Not necessarily. You told me, did you not, that she had written you a letter before you left Paris? She wanted you to know she had not broken faith with the company?"

"That's right."

"Did you ever answer the letter?"

"No."

"Then you're calling now to respond to it. You've been feeling very guilty. You inquire tactfully about how the job's going and, in the most natural way, how her love life is proceeding. As I remember, that too was mentioned in the letter. Do it now, please. I'm arranging a party. I need your help."

As a precautionary courtesy, I called Vianney first. He was out of the office. I asked to be transferred to Claudine Parmentier. She, fortunately, was at her desk and, to my surprise, sounded glad to hear from me.

"Carl! What a pleasure! I thought you had written me off altogether. M. Vianney gave me to understand he would be reporting directly to you."

"That's true. But this isn't a business call. It's an apology."

"For what?"

"Before I left Paris, you wrote me a note, assuring me that you had never leaked any company secrets."

"That was true."

"I believe you. That's the reason for this call. I didn't acknowledge the note. I've been traveling and I've been very busy, but that's no excuse. I'm calling now to thank you for writing and to ask you to pardon me."

"Please! This is very touching. I never felt badly toward you. Considering my last performance, you let me down very lightly. Where are you now, by the way?"

"I'm just about to leave Verona. This is a very romantic town. Last night I stood under Juliet's balcony. Would you believe I was reminded of you and Liliane? How is that big love story?"

"Deader than Romeo and Juliet! Liliane was transferred to Milan almost overnight. She hated to leave, but she was told she'd lose her job if she didn't accept the transfer."

"What brought that on?"

"I suppose you could say I brought it on myself. We were at dinner one night with one of the seniors from the Simonetta staff who is also one of the sisterhood. I got a little drunk and Larry's name slipped out. There was a silence; then I was peppered with questions. Finally it came out that I worked for Strassberger. Either the senior made the report or forced Liliane to make it herself, but next day—*whoosh!*—the fire was under the pot. I had a very short phone call from Liliane, who was obviously frightened for her job and for herself. Now I'm back with my former partner and doing a daily penance for my sins. I'm not sure how long I can stand that; but we'll see. Have you anyone with you?"

"Not at the moment. Tomorrow, who knows? Look after yourself."

"Do you want me to tell Vianney you called?"

"It doesn't matter. I'll be calling him tomorrow."

"Carl, what's the meaning of all this activity in Strassberger shares?"

"There are various opinions. It certainly looks like a raid, but we're prepared for it. What does Vianney say?"

"What he always says: 'On the one hand and on the other.' He's a *funambule*, that one! A real tightrope walker. Does it have anything to do with Larry's disappearance?"

"Indirectly, I suppose it does."

"Do you know where he is now?"

"We think we know, but his wife and my father are coming to the view that probably we should call off the pursuit and let him go his own way."

"That's what Vianney thinks too. He says, 'Let the poor bastard go! Let him be happy in his misery.'"

"And what do you think, Claudine?"

"I try not to think about it at all now. I don't understand it. I can't do anything about it, but I find the whole affair quite frightening. Liliane's last words to me were, 'Keep your head down and your mouth shut, Claudine. Falco lives up to his name. He's a predator with a sharp beak and claws that never let go.' I must go now. My client has just arrived. Travel safely, Carl."

Sergio was as near to jubilant as I had seen him.

"That was splendid. That gives me exactly what I want for tomorrow's party pieces, a clear complicity between Liliane and her employer."

"Complicity in what?"

"Oh, there's no problem finding a name for the charge. Our problem is to find hard evidence to prove it. That little conversation will be very useful in dialogues with the young lady."

"What sort of dialogues?"

"Well, they'll be more in the nature of conversation pieces."

"Let's be clear on something, Sergio. I won't be party to any violence!"

"Violence? My dear man, you mustn't fret. This will be as pleasant for her as a massage. Trust me! Now, a few more phone calls and you are free."

"Who's next?"

"It's your choice, really. I confess I would feel much more

183

comfortable if we could arrange some adequate cover for Larry Lucas at the Burgholzli."

"You said he was safe for the moment."

"I did; but I like to cover all contingencies."

"What sort of contingencies?"

"Lucas was admitted to the Burgholzli on the recommendation of a Swiss physician, Dr. Langer, and obviously with the consent not of his family, as would be usual, but of the person who holds his power of attorney, Dr. Hubert Rubens. That's guesswork, but I believe it's right. So, in effect, Lucas is a voluntary patient who may be moved elsewhere by the same people who committed him. I'd hate to find he'd been discharged from the Burgholzli and whisked off to a private clinic in Germany or Hungary. So you'd better work out with Lucas's wife and your father what family intervention is possible with the Swiss medical authorities and possibly the police."

I glanced at my watch. It was four in the afternoon. My father would be in his office, watching the opening market in New York. Alma Levy would be working with her morning patients. I was undecided which one to call first, the doctor or the money man. I decided on the money man because of a little story he had told me in my salad days. The burden of the story was very simple: 'Switzerland,' said my father, 'is run by the Swiss Army!' I was immediately embroiled in an argument— which was exactly what he had intended. I was less than well versed in the workings of Swiss democracy. In the end my father forced me to listen to his thesis. "Every able-bodied male in Switzerland is trained to bear arms and, while he is of service age, is required to do a period of service at stated intervals. Result, every Swiss executive in the state or in civilian life carries a military rank. So," urged my father with a grin of triumph, "the senior bankers and the senior company officials are generally of high field rank in the reserves. That creates a kind of relationship—of comrades in arms—very hard for the outsider to penetrate. On the other hand, it lends a special power to those special friendships, which certain outsiders are privileged to enjoy."

I now decided to see what kind of special friendships he could invoke in the case of his own son-in-law.

I caught him at a bad moment, when a buyer was scouting the market for a block of ten thousand Strassberger shares and our broker's man on the floor seemed less than vigilant. However, I managed to command his attention, to explain Larry's situation, and, with Carlino prompting me, to outline a plan of immediate action.

All of it depended on securing immediate legal advice in Switzerland and then bringing enough power and patronage to bear on the Burgholzli institute itself that they would refuse to release Larry Lucas without a court decision. However, any such action would require the presence of the next of kin, his wife. It would call for the production of authentic documents of identity: Larry's U.S. passport, social security card, certificates of birth and marriage. It would also help enormously if Dr. Levy could present herself in Zurich with her patient's medical history. I impressed on my father that I had to depend on him to organize all this and, as a final requirement, to send with Madi my own real passport and credit cards.

I suggested that they all stay at the Dolder Grand and I would meet them there as soon as I was free. My argument made him even more stubborn. Larry's letters to him and to Madi were still a bad taste in his mouth. He hated the idea of asking favors from overseas colleagues. Any legal action would produce publicity. Larry's flight and disappearance would make new headlines. We had spent all this time and money to avoid just that. If Madi came to Europe, who would look after the children? My mother was in no condition to do it. He had never met this Dr. Levy. She could refuse to talk with him at all.

It was ten minutes before I could get a grumbling consent—and then only because I told him he should take a close personal look at his overseas offices, especially Paris, which, we knew, was where the trouble had started. It was time he began inspecting the house of Strassberger for wood rot and verminous infestation.

As always, once he took a grip on an idea, he worried it like a terrier. He made me rehearse my suggestions. He talked through his possible contacts in Switzerland. He thought Madi should take the children and the nanny with her.

He himself might consider accompanying her and then make his own visits to company offices. Finally, yes! He had all the briefing he needed. Now, what was my contribution to this part of the operation?

I was tired and edgy and I snapped at him. I told him that Carlino and myself were trying to find conclusive evidence of criminal conspiracy on the part of Falco and Rubens. If we found it, we had a chance to hold off the share raid and limit the peripheral damage the publicity would cause. It might also show Larry in a different light from that in which we were now viewing him. My father did not for one moment accept that idea. He did, however, buy the rest of it and promised to make immediate phone calls to Madi and to Alma Levy. I reminded him that Dr. Levy might well provide her own medical contacts in Zurich, but I gave him a firm warning that she was just as tough as he was and he should not—repeat not—start an arm-wrestling contest with her. His answer was typical.

"Thank you, Carl! A wise son makes a glad father!"

Since it was he who had taught me the old game of capping one aphorism with another, I gave him one to taste with his morning coffee.

"The problem with fathers is that they want their sons to be a credit to them."

"You stole that from Bertrand Russell," said my father cheerfully. "He was a brilliant mathematician but he would have made a very poor banker—just like you, my son!"

Carlino was vastly amused by this piece of family dialogue. He told me it reminded him of his talks with his own father. I wanted to drop the subject. I had a more mundane problem. I had left Verona very early in the morning. I had a car full of gear. Where was I going to sleep tonight?

Sergio Carlino had everything planned. My car, as he had promised, was on its way back to the rental agency. My gear was already stowed in a Corsec vehicle. The driver was standing by to take me to my destination. And where, pray, might that be?

"The Villa Calpurnia, scene of tomorrow night's revels. You will be safe from intrusion. You will have a good night's rest, and tomorrow you can spend a relaxing day with your sketchbook and canvases. Michele will drive you wherever you want to go."

"And who is Michele?"

"He and his wife, Elena, are custodians of the place. She's a very good cook, and he is driver, gardener, and butler."

"How many guests are you expecting?"

"We'll be eight at table, including you and Liliane Prévost."

"Will your wife be there?"

"No. We keep our married life quite separate from business. I'll have another companion at dinner."

"And all I have to do is be there?"

"That's all. Of course, you'll be witty and charming and perhaps even show some sketches to keep the talk rolling. And for God's sake get rid of that beard. It makes you look like a vagabond!"

10

WHEN I LEFT CORSEC headquarters that afternoon, I felt weary, dispirited, and uneasy. I had been on the road since daylight. I had lost Ellie Milland, who deserved better than I had offered her. I had been through a series of critical encounters, with no clear idea where any of them might lead. Now, at day's end, events were out of my control. I was sidelined from the game—to rusticate for twenty-four hours in a villa in the flatlands of the Lombardy plain—while my father brusquely assumed command in New York and Sergio Carlino played his own secretive drama in Milan.

There was nothing I could do about it. There was nothing I wanted to do about it. My meager psychic resources were running out, and I saw no prospect of renewing them in a strange house and in an ambience where I had fewer affinities than in any other place in Italy.

My driver was a taciturn fellow, so I allowed myself to drowse into reverie. For me, there was a hint of Gothic melancholy about this region—I have always associated it with long fogbound waits at the airport or diversions to Nice or Rome. The mists of sadness still trailed about its history too. Mussolini and his mistress, Claretta Petacci, were murdered near the village of Azzano by an official assassin from the Committee of National

Liberation. Now, at the tag end of the twentieth century, old rivalries and old hates were being called up again by a new Lombard league and new divisive propaganda by modern dukedoms of money and influence. Once, on a walking tour, I had been shown the Iron Crown of Lombardy—that strange relic which is kept in a chapel of the cathedral in Monza. Forty-four emperors are said to have been crowned with it. The curious thing about it is that it is too small for the head of any man, or woman, or child, yet its magic was potent enough for Barbarossa and Charles V and Napoleon to demand to be invested with it. It was on the same day, I remembered, that I was shown the Index of Oils: the list, written by an antique hand, of the vials of oil from the lamps on tombs of saints in Rome. A monk named John had brought them in the sixth century as gifts to the Empress Theodolinda. Theodolinda, I had never known any girl called by that name . . . or had I?

My head was still fogged with these irrelevant snippets of memory when we stopped outside a big gateway of wrought iron whose elaborate scrollwork carried the legend *Villa Calpurnia*. The driver sounded his horn; a few moments later, a small wizened fellow who looked like an elderly jockey came trotting down the gravel path to open the gate and close it behind us.

I had time to note that the garden walls were high and topped with slivers of bottle glass and that the trees and shrubberies, though carefully tended, were thick and reclusive. The villa itself was set square and uncompromising on a small rise overlooking a formal garden, screened from view by the border trees and bushes of the perimeter.

It had three stories. The windows of the first and the topmost levels were all shuttered. Those on the middle level were open to the late sun. The small fellow came hurrying up the path to usher me into the house and present me to his wife, a good-looking matron in her early fifties. She led me to my bedroom, a large chamber with a bathroom and dressing room attached, whose windows opened onto the fall of the terraced garden and a tumble of evening clouds blown up by the wind from the south.

Michele and the driver arrived with my luggage. Elena bowed

herself out. The driver followed her. Michele demonstrated the old-fashioned bellpull which would summon any help I needed. He offered to unpack my clothes and deal with any pressing or laundry. I was happy to let him do it, while I laid out my toilet gear in a bathroom large enough to harbor a warship. He asked me whether I would like him to draw a bath. I told him I would draw the bath if he could find me a drink. Immediately, Signore! He opened one side of the wardrobe to reveal a minibar, a bucket of ice, and a bottle of mineral water. I asked him whether he could find me a small carafe and a couple of old saucers for watercolors and gouache. His eyes sparkled with pleasure. He asked whether he might see something of my work. I showed him the sketches from Verona and Padua. He nodded approval and, I thought, looked at me with a more respectful eye. Every Italian is a critic in his own right.

This prompted me to ask what sort of visitors were usually entertained at the Villa Calpurnia. A sudden cloud of unknowing enveloped the lively little man.

"Visitors? This is not a hotel. This is a private property of the Carlino family. It used to be part of a much larger estate, which the family has sold off over the years. Only Signor Sergio uses it now, for business conferences and seminars. Sometimes he lectures here to small groups."

"What sort of groups?"

"We are not usually told who they are. It is a good policy. What we do not know, we cannot tell."

"You mean you could be threatened?"

"We know that Signor Carlino's work carries certain risks. He does not wish us involved in those risks. We are, therefore, very careful. We do not gossip. We do most of our shopping in Como itself. . . . Do you take water with your whiskey, Signore?"

"Only a little. No ice."

"I am told you may want to go painting tomorrow. I am at your disposal with the car."

"I'll let you know. I may decide to work in the garden—perhaps in the woods."

"If I may suggest, we take a little drive after breakfast and then you decide where you want to work. I will leave you with a mobile phone. You can call me when you are ready to return. I have to help Elena prepare for tomorrow evening. Now I shall leave you to take your bath. Afterward, there is a library in the *salone*, and music and a television—if you can bear the garbage!"

He mixed my drink and handed it to me. Then he left, with my suit draped over his arm and my laundry bundle in his small fist. He strode out jauntily as if he were walking into the saddling paddock.

Before I turned on the bath, I examined the room more closely. At first glance, the furniture and the draperies, ornaments, and pictures looked like heirlooms. On closer inspection, they looked more like auction-room items, bought cheaply and assembled with reasonable taste and skill. The linens and the towels were spotless, but of ordinary quality. The few bedside books were vintage fare from the early seventies.

The telephone installation, however, was modern, and a printed direction indicated a direct-dial service without any prefix. The minibar was another utilitarian feature. Michele's description of the villa as a place of business seemed, so far, accurate. It was certainly a good place to keep someone like myself on ice while other, more competent folk went about their business.

My feelings of isolation and unease persisted. I decided to test the phone service with a call to Arlette in Nice. The phone was working, but the gallery was not; Arlette's recorded voice asked me to leave a message and number and she would return my call as soon as possible. I thought of calling Ellie Milland in Venice. Then I remembered there was nothing I could say to her, because I had hidden myself behind my own shabby grab bag of secrets. I looked at my watch. It was coming up to six o'clock. Even with a long soak in the tub and another generous whiskey, it was a long time to dinner, and it would be a long, solitary evening. I was just about to climb into the bath when the telephone rang. I was surprised to hear my father's voice on the line.

"How the devil did you find me?"

"Simple! I called your friend—what's his name? Carlino—at

191

the Corsec office in Milan. We had an interesting chat. He told me where to find you."

"It's only a few hours since we spoke."

"I know. But while you're disporting yourself in the country, I've been busy. I found us a good attorney in Switzerland, recommended again by my banker friend. I outlined our situation for him."

"And . . . ?"

"The news is not promising. He has dealt with a similar situation in which a young woman joined one of the more extreme sects which practice peer pressure and virtual brainwashing. She had executed a deed of trusteeship in their favor. The property involved was considerable. Her parents sought to have the deed overturned. The court action and all appeals failed. The girl was deemed sane and responsible at all relevant times. The indoctrination procedures were not deemed to be force majeure."

"So where does that leave us with Larry?"

"On very doubtful ground. First, and most important, we have to begin a civil action. The police will not involve themselves unless there is clear evidence of criminality somewhere along the line. Second, the best we can hope for in the first instance is an interim injunction to keep Larry in the care of the Burgholzli until the case is heard. Even the application for such an injunction is bound to fail if Larry is deemed to be rational and responsible when depositions are taken."

"So what does the lawyer suggest?"

"Basically what you propose. Madi and I will fly to Zurich tomorrow with the children and their nanny. We will bring all the documents, including your papers."

"And Dr. Levy?"

"She will take another flight, but she has agreed to stay with us at the Dolder. We are picking up all her expenses and indemnifying her for lost fees and the expenses of a doctor to cover for her."

"What does she think about the lawyer's opinion?"

"She agrees in general with his judgment. She points out that prima facie Larry's letters to Madi and to me are a lucid expression

192

of a clear and rational desire on his part to break the family ties. However, she has managed to get in touch with a Swiss psychiatrist who does voluntary work at the clinic. He has agreed to make discreet inquiries about Larry. At least it's another contact in the medical community."

"Will you need me for the first depositions?"

"No. What you are doing with Carlino may be even more important. Make you way here in your own time."

"You said you spoke with Carlino. How did he impress you?"

"Very well. He's lucid. He's decisive. He has police and military training. He is determined to ferret out some evidence of criminality on the part of Falco and his associates. If he could, that would enable us to involve the police. This session he has arranged tomorrow night sounds like an interesting exercise."

"He has explained it to you?"

"In general terms, yes. What do you think of it?"

"Like you, I think it's a very interesting idea."

Of course, the irony was lost on him. Whatever Carlino had told him was much more than he had confided to me. However, my father was the last man in the world to whom I would confess my ignorance.

By ten in the morning, with Michele's guidance, I had found myself an agreeable subject for a painting: the white temple in the public gardens of Como, which is dedicated not to ancient gods but to a physicist, Alessandro Guiseppe Antonio Anastasio Volta, who invented the electric battery.

The scene made a pleasant plein-air study: the reflections in the lake water; the formal gardens with their flush of spring blooms, the hills beyond, which marked the run of ancient glaciers. The passage of people gave movement and color to the scene, and I found myself painting freely and boldly in a manner which for a long time had eluded me. The architecture of the temple was no longer a constraint. It seemed somehow fluid, flexible, accommodating itself to me, rather than confining me to its own classical form.

The tension inside me relaxed too. I was able to free part of my mind to contemplate Larry's problems. On this sunny morning, I was able to face the questions that we, his family, had so far sidestepped. How was Larry himself feeling? How had he felt as a conspirator planning his own disappearance? How had he judged the rogues with whom he was consorting as a client? How was he feeling at this moment, confined within the walls and perimeters of the Burgholzli in Zurich?

We, his family, had judged him, each in the light of our own interest. Only Dr. Levy had seen him and empathized with him as a patient in need, lost in a wasteland of whirling confusion because the chemistries of his brain were out of kilter.

What would he do, how would he feel, if the court judged him incompetent and made his wife his legal guardian? How would he feel if, judged sane and competent, he had no place to go but back to the company of rogues? Having taken possession of his estate, what would Falco and Rubens offer him beyond arm's-length maintenance and effective exile? How would my father deal with him? How would Madi receive him, now that, as Alma Levy expressed it, she had liberated herself from the tyranny of his infirmity? How would he feel toward his children? How would they react to him? Come to think of it, how would he feel toward me, the hunter who had dogged him around the compass but still wasn't street-smart enough to find and confront him face-to-face?

While all these questions were buzzing like bees inside my skull, there was still a quiet alcove where the small elusive soul of Carl Strassberger the artist played happily with lights and shadows and forms and watched the hand that made the brush strokes, bolder and bolder on the canvas.

It was, I had to confess, a very little soul, and not too bold a wanderer, for all the freedom it claimed for itself. It was too firmly anchored in family and tradition, too well cosseted by wealth and generous parenting. It would never take to the dusty caravan roads, never arrive at the cold and lonely peaks where the giants lived and made their masterworks.

Arlette knew this and was wise enough not to commit herself

to a marriage vow. Ellie had grasped it, swiftly and painfully. I clung to my cozy little soul because I could not risk it half so far as the wild follies of Larry Lucas or the stubborn, shrewd, but fearless forays of my father.

He was the one who was flying across the Atlantic to stage the last act of the drama, while I sat here at the placid lakeside, dabbling on a canvas while a group of children, women, and idle old men stood watching. Last night I had told myself that the race was over for me. I had run my sector of the relay, and I could now be a spectator.

In the cold light of morning, I understood that there was one more person I had to confront: the man about whom I knew least, Dr. Hubert Rubens of Geneva. He was the one who held the money box and all the magical spells required to open it. Before I left the villa with Michele, I had telephoned Falco in Milan and told him that I was almost ready to make a decision but that I wanted an early meeting with Rubens. I asked him to fax the good doctor, telling him that I would be in Geneva in three days' time and asking him to make time to see me. I also asked him to send with Liliane a copy of his fax and any reply.

Falco was delighted that I had come so close to a decision. He asked me where I was calling from. I told him I was on my way to Lake Como for a day of painting. Would he please remind Liliane that the mystery party was still a mystery but she would be picked up promptly at seven-thirty? I had one more question for him. Did he happen to have a copy of the standard trustee agreement with Dr. Rubens? No, he did not. Each agreement was tailored to the needs of the client. Dr. Rubens was skilled and flexible, and a tower of strength to his clients.

It was curious how the thought of this man inserted itself into the painting. Like the mountain peaks in the background, he and others like him were fixtures in the landscape of twentieth-century Europe. Their financial roots were plunged deep into the burial grounds of the dead and the dispossessed, victims of the concentration camps and the mass migrations and the legalized looting of the horror years. They were scot-free now

195

because old money has no smell and people have short memories for the misery of others.

But you and I will meet soon, Dr. Rubens, and I hope, I pray, I may be able to remind you where and how your future was founded.

As I began working on the mid-ground of the picture with a palette knife, an elderly man standing just to my right said to the woman next to him, "This is no amateur. He knows what he's doing."

I affected not to hear or understand the words and frowned in concentration over the palette, trying to tone down a blob of cadmium orange. Then a tiny dark-haired girl tugged at my sleeve, pointed at the canvas, and let out a babble of words whose meaning escaped me altogether. The old man was quick to see my puzzlement.

"*Lei e' Americano?*"

"*Canadese.*" I had learned to be cautious.

The old man switched to English.

"She wants to know whether you'll let her paint with you."

"I'm working in oils. She'll get paint on her dress."

The old man shrugged.

"If she gets stars in her eyes, what does a dab of paint matter?"

I put down the palette and knife, hoisted the child on my knee, picked up a small filbert brush, and, holding her hand, helped her to drag some of the fresh chrome into the color masses of the flower beds. My audience was delighted. There were murmurs of approval. I was good and kind and gentle. When I set the child down, she scampered off happily while I worked on with the canvas, hoping to make it at least the conversation piece which Sergio Carlino had recommended for dinner that evening. Watching an artist at work is a little like watching grass grow. After a while the crowd drifted away, and I was left in peace to contemplate my handiwork.

It wasn't bad, I decided. There was a certain vitality about it which was absent—perhaps necessarily absent—from my normal work.

I called Michele on the mobile phone and asked him to pick

me up. It had been a pleasant, meditative morning. I liked the world and myself a little better. I wondered what surprises Sergio Carlino would produce that evening from his box of tricks.

Sergio Carlino arrived at the Villa Calpurnia at five in the evening. He was accompanied by one of the most striking women I had ever seen. She was somewhere in her late thirties. Her hair was jet black, her skin the color of dark honey, her eyes as black as her hair. Her features were soft in repose, yet expressive of every momentary shift in emotion, surprise, pleasure, amusement. She was dressed in a light cotton confection which molded, as she moved, to the contours of a body shapely as that of a Renaissance madonna. There was an extraordinary aura about her: of authority, of calm, of sex, of a huge reserve of passion. Her name, Sergio told me, was Sibilla, and, in true Italian style, he swallowed the rest of it so I was never sure whether I had heard it or not.

To me she extended a gracious hand, which I knew I was expected to kiss. There was a spark even in the touch of it.

She smiled approval of the greeting and told me in English, "I know everything about you. I am here early to rehearse you in your role and to make sure that you remain in control of it at all times."

"I hope you are going to explain it to me first. To this moment, Sergio has left me in complete ignorance of what is to happen here this evening."

"Only because Sibilla prefers to direct the whole performance herself." Sergio was unrepentant. "Everybody is wholly under her direction, including the two observers from the police who will be asked to certify the legality of the proceedings and the authenticity of the record, if a denunciation is made and a criminal complaint is filed."

That left me as much in the dark as before. Sergio led us into the *salone,* served us drinks, and then left me alone with my Sibilline instructor. She began with a long preamble.

"What will take place here tonight will be a psychodrama,

which, we hope, may end in some act of revelation or purgation. It is, in fact, a modern version of a very old ritual, which, even in ancient times, had many variations. It begins always with a meeting of friends—and of strangers who are invited to join the magic circle. Greetings are exchanged and introductions are made, intimate introductions in which only first names are used. Alcohol is served, music is played, relaxation and intimacy are encouraged. Then the meal is served. It will be a buffet dinner from which the servants are excluded. Everything, therefore, is private. There are no prying eyes to see what happens later. That is, if you like, the mise-en-scène, the location and mood setting for the action which follows."

"Are you sure it will follow? Or is this just a tryout performance?"

She gave me a tolerant smile.

"Oh, yes! It will happen," she assured me. "Everybody, even the spectators, will be involved in one fashion or another. Only the climax may be different from what we expect."

"So who are the actors and who are the spectators? And what roles do the actors play?"

"Let's take the spectators first. There will be two officers of the police, one male, one female. Both are Sergio's friends; both have been trained in what is, in Italy at least, a new investigative discipline. They may elect to ask questions or to intervene in an emergency situation. It is unlikely that they will have to do so. They will, however, participate as guests in all the preliminary activities. Apart from the police, there will be another couple, again male and female. They are the ones who will pick up Prévost at her apartment and return her there afterward. They will also prepare her for the informality of the occasion."

"But the occasion will have no value if it is not recorded."

"It will be recorded on sound and film. The tapes will be held until it is decided to release them."

"And who will make that decision?"

"You will, unless the police make a recommendation to the contrary. Whether you release them or not, you are the producer of this drama. You're the man who's paying the bills."

"You mean I'm paying the police too?"

She threw back her dark head and laughed, a deep, velvet sound.

"You'll have to put that question to Sergio. Now, let's talk about the actors. Sergio is the host, the *compere*. He is staging this special performance for you, his friend. You have an understanding of the theater of history and of ritual."

"And what part am I expected to play?"

"You are a minor character. You are the one who does not understand the full import of the happening. You delight in the new experience. You express the excitement of it. You applaud and you incite the cast."

"Am I drunk or sober?"

"At least sober enough to hear and understand and judge the dialogue between the two principals."

"Who are?"

"Liliane Prévost and myself."

"And your roles?"

"You will see them develop, slowly, from the very beginning of the evening to the end. Some of what you see may shock you, but you must not, under any circumstances, step out of your role or intrude in the play between Liliane and myself."

"Who controls that?"

"I do. I alone. Even Sergio will not dare to interrupt the flow of the drama. Do you understand clearly what I have told you?"

"What you have told me, yes. I don't understand what you are proposing or why."

"Good! That's exactly what we need: the innocent and the ignorant helping to elicit the truth. But even you, my friend, will not escape what the ancient Greeks called 'the experience of the god.'"

"What will happen to Liliane?'

"No harm will come to her, I promise. Now, would you be kind enough to get me another drink? Every sybil requires a small libation to keep her eloquent."

I was just pouring the drinks when Sergio came back. I asked whether he would join us. He signaled yes and looked from me to Sibilla.

199

"Where are we?"

Sibilla answered with that half-mocking smile.

"Ed, here, is a quick study. He knows everything he needs to know at this moment—though he claims he doesn't understand it."

I handed them their glasses. Sergio made the old Hispanic toast: "Health, money, and love," to which Sibilla responded: "And time to enjoy them all."

We drank.

"Shouldn't we look at the set, Sergio?" Sibilla asked.

"Certainly. One question before we go down. Would our artist here be prepared to do some life sketches of our cast?"

"If you like, sure."

"Are you any good?" Sibilla asked.

"I'm told I am. What do you want them for?"

"It's another party piece," said Sergio cheerfully. "It's like a television show. We need warmups and happy, happy moments to keep everyone loose."

"Let's look at the set," said Sibilla firmly.

"*Subito*," said Sergio, and led us downstairs to the lowest level of the villa.

The shutters were still closed but the lights were burning. We were in a large chamber with stone walls and a marble pavement, in the center of which was a tiled swimming pool, set about with canvas lounges and chairs. Each lounge and chair had a fresh dressing gown and a beach towel laid across it.

Along one wall of the chamber was a refectory table set with dishes, glassware, and napkins. In the corner near it was a bar with liquors and wines. At the far end of the room were toilets and showers and clothes lockers. Sergio demonstrated that the light could be raised and lowered at will. Sibilla surveyed the place with a critical eye.

"Good! It will work, Sergio, I promise. Now, let me give you the routine. Cassio and Candida will be the last to arrive, bringing with them Liliane Prévost. Michele will receive them and bring them down here to us."

"When they enter, we'll be five." Sergio picked up the narration. "Sibilla and I, Ferdy and Isabella, and you in the role of Edgar Benson. We are all lounging around the pool, in dressing gowns, sipping champagne, very relaxed and intimate, all friends together."

"We are decorously draped." Sibilla smiled. "But we are naked under our robes."

"What is this, an orgy?" I had to ask the question. Sibilla delivered the answer very concisely.

"It is the prelude to an experiment in hypnosis, aided by sexual stimulation of the subject. As I understand it, this woman is lesbian by inclination, as I am myself; but she is, for professional or other reasons, bisexual in practice."

"I have that only on hearsay."

"It doesn't matter. For me it is a hypothetical beginning. The truth I shall discover for myself. You, Sergio, and the rest of the company will be witnesses to what occurs."

I was about to interrupt, but she held up a warning hand. "No comment, please. Let me instruct you first. When Liliane Prévost arrives, you, Edgar, will greet her warmly. You will be delighted that she has come, et cetera, et cetera. I shall be at your elbow. You will introduce her to me. I shall take her around to meet the rest of the company. I shall be the one who conducts her to the changing rooms and instructs her in the ritual of our little parties. I shall feed her drinks and be close to her during our playtime in the pool."

"In other words, you're going to seduce her."

"Not quite; in any case, not here and not yet. By the end of the evening she will be wanting me to do just that, and I may be interested enough to do it. In that case, I shall go home with her. However, before she leaves, you will have all the information she can give us about her work at the agency and her personal connection with the man you are seeking: Larry Lucas."

"And you propose to film and record the whole procedure?"

"Do you have problems with that?" The question came from Sergio Carlino.

"I have questions about it."

"Ask them, please."

"Will Liliane Prévost be coerced in any way to take part in the hypnotic procedure?"

"No, she will not. I shall ask for volunteers. Candida will agree and Ferdy will offer. Both are good subjects for a simple demonstration. I shall invite Prévost to take part. I'm sure she will agree. There will be no coercion."

"Next question, then. You realize, I hope, that very little of her evidence—if indeed we get any—will be admissible in an American court. Most of it will be hearsay and the rest tainted by the method of obtaining it."

"You forget." Sergio reproved me quietly. "We are not in America. We are in Europe, where American and British rules of evidence do not apply. Here in Italy, and in France, a charge is made upon denunciation. An inquiry—an inquisition is made. It continues until the truth—if truth exists—is fished up from the bottom of a deep well. In America, you still have trial by adversarial debate, which is just another form of trial by combat. Sometimes the combat is rigged. Here we are seeking grounds to make the first denunciation. If we find them, we may either file the denunciation or remedy the situation by other means. Any more questions?"

"One more. What happens to the video and the sound tapes?"

"That's up to you." Sergio gave me his most winning smile. "You're paying for them. You're paying for everything and everybody here tonight—including Sibilla. I just want to make sure you get value for money!"

"He'll get it!" Sibilla made the affirmation with superb conviction. "The only time I ever lost an audience was years ago in Bali. I was entertaining some wealthy Germans when one of the servants ran amok with a kris. But that won't happen tonight, I promise you!"

She laughed, cupped my face in her hands, and kissed me full on the lips. The energy that went out from her was like fire in the blood.

* * *

Even as I write now, I cringe at the memory of that evening at the Villa Calpurnia. The images are banal enough—a small group of affluent and cynical people, disporting themselves naked in a private pool, drinking, eating, exchanging gossip, building about themselves a hothouse atmosphere of privileged indulgence. Caresses were exchanged, and brief bodily contacts made and broken, under the vigilant stage management of Sibilla.

My own contribution was a series of sketches of male and female bodies in action and in brief moments of repose; but the figure of Sibilla dominated them all. It leapt from every page of the sketchbook, dynamic and demonic.

She hovered over us all like a guardian spirit, but she seemed literally to envelop Liliane Prévost, to draw her into a whirlpool of desire from which, even had she wished it, there was no possibility of escape. In and around the pool, sharing food, sipping each other's drinks, exchanging caresses, the pair of them gave a performance of such balletic intricacy and sexual intensity that we were like spectators at an exquisite piece of erotic theater.

There was no question but that Liliane Prévost was the happy and willing victim of this extended seduction. But victim she was, just as the rest of us were collaborators, in a drama of oppression of the weak by the strong. When the meal was over and Sibilla called for volunteers to play her game of hypnosis, Liliane Prévost was the first to offer herself.

Sibilla accepted her immediately and made her lie down, with her dressing gown drawn about her, on one of the chaise longues directly in line with the camera and the microphone housed on one of the roof beams. Then Sibilla seated herself beside her and began the opening ritual: the concentration of vision, the monotone incantation to induce hypnotic sleep, the continual assurance. "Trust me, let go. Nothing but good will come to you. When I call, you will wake and you will remember nothing but good. . . ."

Then, as she had promised, it happened. Liliane Prévost seemed to lapse into a deep hypnotic trance, oblivious of her audience and her surroundings. Sibilla gently parted the dressing gown, so that the girl's body was exposed to us all and to Sibilla's own caressing hands.

There was a rhythm to what happened next, but it took a little while before the rhythm established itself in our minds. First Sibilla asked a question, softly and persuasively; then, when the answer came, she rewarded it with a brief erotic caress. If Liliane hesitated, or seemed to be groping for an answer, the caress was withheld or merely suggested by the touch of a fingertip. As the interrogation went on, their rhythm and the rhythm of the responses became faster, as Liliane's desire for stimulation became more urgent.

However, it was not the sensual quality of the scene which came to dominate my memory, it was the unquestioning ruthlessness with which Sergio Carlino and Sibilla had embarked upon it—and most of all my own readiness to come to terms with what they were doing, in my interest and with Strassberger money. It was the old old story, worthy ends vitiated by unworthy means. It was the argument of all tyrants: If you want omelets, you have to break eggs, and the bigger the omelet, the more eggs you crack.

You ask, as I ask still: What did we get at the end of it that was worth the ceremony of mutual debasement? The most important pieces of information were the organization plan of Simonetta and the relationship of Simonetta and Dr. Hubert Rubens of Geneva. Liliane Prévost had a sharp, gamine intelligence and she had been trained to collect and interpret snippets of information from client prospects and sources of information like Delaunay, the concierge. The working model of the travel agency had been put together by Francesco Falco. It was he who had conceived the idea of a press gang of attractive young women, hustling travel business through expensive hotels and, in the same operation, sweeping up the lost, stolen, or strayed men and women of substantial means, whose lives had been disrupted by domestic tragedy of one kind or another and who dreamed of a fresh start in a faraway place. Liliane's comment, while still under hypnosis, had a certain pathos: "I never knew there were so many sad ones with so much money."

There was a fringe business, too, from certain criminal elements who needed money washed or documents provided or couriers moved on the safest possible routes. This business, however, was handled exclusively by Francesco Falco with a select team of girls of whom Liliane had been one but was no longer. It was too risky, she said, and Dr. Rubens did not approve. Falco was forced to be careful to keep this sector and its revenues under wraps.

However, the core of the organization was Dr. Hubert Rubens. He saw it not only as a money earner but as a route into foreign real estate and a source of information on mining and related enterprises, where he did not have to risk either capital or reputation until his information was complete.

According to Liliane, the staff was more in awe of the mysterious doctor than of the ever-present Falco. Falco could be rough and dangerous, but he was a type with whom they were familiar. Rubens was a more legendary threat whose power reached across frontiers, who could arrange your death as easily in Rio as in Rome.

Larry Lucas? He was everyone's favorite. He was rich, amusing, generous, but—come down to the facts of a girl's life—he expected too much of women. When the dark moods were on him, he needed to be coaxed, soothed, mothered, and what kind of role was that, even for a professional companion? When he came back to Paris, after he had left his family and the company, he was in a high manic mode. Liliane called it *"une excitation hors raison."* He was obsessed with the idea of going to some distant place in the Indian Ocean, Mauritius or the Seychelles. The Simonetta staff did a lot of research work. Dr. Rubens laid out an elaborate financial system. Everything seemed to be under way when Dr. Rubens became alarmed at the rambling quality of Larry's phone calls. He advised Falco to hold Lucas in Europe as long as possible. Meanwhile, he sent Dr. Langer to meet him at Sirmione and accompany him wherever else he wanted to go. In Rome, the mania reached its peak. Lucas disappeared. He was picked up by the police, talking and raving incessantly in a bar in the Via Margutta. Dr. Langer administered medication and took him back to Zurich for hospitalization. For Falco, all this was a great bore. According to him, "This kind we should push quietly off a train."

For her own part, Liliane Prévost asked little enough out of life: a well-paid job, which she still had, a passionate lover, "Like you my dear Sibilla, just like you," and some way of escape from the sinister currents in which she found herself swimming. "But you don't really know how dirty the water is until you're swimming in it. Then it's too late, isn't it?"

Sergio and Sibilla looked at me. Each asked the same question.

"Enough?"

"Enough. Bring her out of it."

"She deserves her reward," said Sibilla firmly. "It would be a cruelty to refuse it."

In full view of us all, she stimulated Liliane to climax. Her action was cool and detached as that of a professional masseuse. Then, when Liliane's body had subsided into calm, she covered her with the dressing gown and awakened her with a curiously peremptory phrase.

"Wake up, child!"

Liliane woke and stretched herself in comfortable languor. Sibilla held out a hand to draw her to her feet and then into an embrace. She was in possession now, and she wanted us all to know it.

"Get dressed now, my love. Candida and Cassio will drive us home to my place."

Liliane drew close, leaned her body against the older woman, and allowed herself to be led, lover and captive, toward the bathrooms.

It was after midnight. All the guests had gone. Sergio was staying overnight at the Villa Calpurnia to drive me to the airport in the morning. We were sitting in the *salone,* savoring the last brandy of the evening. Sergio grinned at me over the rim of his glass.

"I observed that Carl Emil Strassberger did not enjoy the evening's performance."

"You're right. I didn't enjoy my own, either. I feel like a god-dam pander! I was paying for that exhibition. Who is Sibilla anyway?"

"Formidable woman, isn't she?"

"She's a cannibal!"

"She's also very clever at what she does, which is sex—sex and show-business hypnosis. She's much in demand in certain wealthy circles from Turin to Venice. She helps, by her own account, to redress the imbalance of the sexes in noble families. You must admit that you got what you paid for. That cassette is a very usable document, against Falco and, to a lesser degree, Rubens."

"We can't use it at all."

"Why not?"

"It would be a death warrant for Liliane Prévost."

"Possibly." Sergio gave me a sharp sidelong look. "If, however, it were leaked over the right journalist's name, it could take a lot of market heat off Strassberger and company."

"No way, Sergio! Not for Strassberger, not for my father, not for anyone! Remember, I'm not coming back here. It is known that Liliane spent this evening with me. Therefore, she would be immediately identified as the source."

"You're the paymaster." Sergio spread his hands in surrender. "I admire your virtue, but don't think too badly of us. We've always been bloody-minded tribes in these parts: the Visconti, the Gonzaga, the Borgia. Even the artists were a hell-raising crew. We've always worked on the principle that it's quicker and cleaner to send in the assassins first and argue later. But don't worry too much about Liliane. Part of my deal with Sibilla was that she take the girl under her protection, give her a job, and move her out of the danger zone. She's a powerful woman, that one! I doubt even Falco would face up to her. She knows too many secrets, has too many high connections. What's your next move?"

"A meeting with Rubens in Geneva, to see what deal he offers me as a special client of Simonetta. Falco has faxed him about my arrival."

I handed him the copy of the Falco letter which Liliane had brought from Milan. He gave it a cursory glance and handed it back.

"That's nothing! In effect, all it says is: 'Talk to this man. See if he makes sense to you.' That is worse than nothing. There's no enthusiasm in it, no positive recommendation. Falco is obviously hedging his bets on you as a financial prospect. Maybe he does it with everybody; I don't know, but it troubles me. If it troubles Rubens too, it's an open invitation to spit in your eye and send you packing."

"Then we have the big transformation scene. The man who faces him is Carl Emil Strassberger."

"Who, with the rest of his family, has been rejected by Larry Lucas, who is Rubens's client. Where in God's name does that get you—unless you use the tapes?"

Abruptly he abandoned the argument, drained his glass, and stood up, a trifle unsteadily. "Why don't you go to bed, Carl? We have to be up at six in the morning. I don't know about you, but pointless arguments and vicarious sex before bedtime always give me nightmares!"

11

GENEVA, THE CITY OF CALVIN and Rousseau and Voltaire, the name place of the Geneva Convention, the birthplace of Swiss clockmaking, lay placid under a warm spring sun. The lake sparkled; the water jets spouted high in the still air; the park lawns were green, the flower beds bright with blooms. My eyes saw it all on the drive in from the airport. My brain registered little of it. I was too busy composing my opening address to Dr. Rubens.

I had called him from the Dolder in Zurich, where my family had not yet arrived. He told me he had received the fax from his colleague, Falco. He would be happy to meet me for what he was pleased to call "an exploratory conference." His mode of address was formal. His tone was studiously neutral. I felt like a student about to present a rather rickety thesis to an exacting professor.

Rubens's offices were in the Rue des Granges, that sector of the old town where the great bankers of the eighteenth century established their mansions. The atmosphere of old, discreet money still trailed about them. Inside the Rubens establishment, the same air of discretion prevailed.

I was met at the reception desk by a young male attendant who stood respectfully to greet me and then made a brief, low-voiced call on the intercom. A few moments later, a gray-haired, sober-suited woman appeared, led me up a flight of stairs, and ushered me into an interview room. It was austerely furnished with a mahogany boardroom table, straight-backed chairs, yellow notepads, freshly sharpened pencils, bottles of mineral water, and glasses. The walls were hung with eighteenth-century lithographs of life in the lakeside city. The lithographs belonged to the Age of Enlightenment; but the spirit of John Calvin, rigid and righteous, filled the room. My guide begged me to be seated, offered me a glass of mineral water, which I declined, and left me with my thesis still half prepared and a growing conviction that this "exploratory conference" was a disaster waiting to happen.

It was three minutes exactly before Dr. Rubens presented himself. He was tall, thin as a rake, with a long face that reminded me oddly of Don Quixote—except that the mouth was a hard, mirthless line and the eyes were dark and filmed over like those of a bird of prey. His skin was pale, his manicured hands thin as a bird's claws. His handshake was a brief silken contact, his greeting a simple acknowledgment of my presence and my name. His preamble was a terse exposition.

"My colleague, Falco, has sent me your personal details. I have studied them carefully. I have also made contact with the person who handles your affairs at Morgan Guaranty in Paris. Now I should like you to tell me what service you believe I can offer you."

"I understood, Doctor, that your service was an integral—indeed essential—part of any life plan designed by Simonetta Travel for special clients. I sought this meeting as a matter of common prudence. One does not entrust one's assets to unknown persons or organizations. Clearly, because of the information I filed with Falco, you know more about me than I do about you."

"How much do you know about me, Mr. Benson?"

"I asked for a banker's report. It came back to me in the usual form. You are a long-established trustee house. Your father has retired. You are now the principal shareholder and chief executive. Your dealings within the banking community have been punctual and correct. You are, to use the old-fashioned phrase, 'deemed good for engagements.'"

"You have the jargon right, Mr. Benson. Do you yourself have any experience in money matters?"

"Enough to have run a small specialized art and design business and to have accumulated enough capital to contemplate a complete change of lifestyle."

"That's what interests me, Mr. Benson. You are clearly a successful and prosperous professional. Why do you want to abdicate your present lifestyle for another, quite different? Why do you want to change your banker before you have determined what you want to do with your life?"

"I have certain clear reasons, Doctor, and certain others which are hard to express but which are, nonetheless, real to me."

He did not smile. He did not unbend by a fraction.

"Let us take the clear reasons first."

"I am stale. My work is stale. Fortunately, my clients haven't noticed it yet, but I have. I am, to be blunt, at a critical stage of my career. I need new input, new experience, a new viewpoint. I need change, Doctor."

"Permanent change?"

"Radical change, certainly. My professional life demands it."

"And your personal life?"

"That, too, needs rethinking, reconstruction. I have just been through two difficult love affairs and, though I could never admit it to the women concerned, the difficulties were largely my fault."

"Are you talking here of sexual problems?"

"No. My potency is not in question; rather, my need for a variety of relationships with a variety of women. One hopes that there are still places in the world where it is possible to achieve such variety without too many problems."

I saw, or thought I saw, a faint twitch of amusement at the corners of his thin traplike mouth.

"You have never thought of converting to Islam?"

"Quite often, in fact. The problem is that I should have to swear off alcohol, which I enjoy in moderation. Also, I am uncomfortable with rigid orthodoxies."

"Instruct me a little further, Mr. Benson. You are an artist, a designer. What precisely do you design?"

"Any and all of the decorative elements of interior living: fabrics, carpets, ceramics, glassware. I seek out and adapt to modern life the motifs of primitive and indigenous peoples."

"So—correct me if I am wrong—there are two elements in what you do, the creative synthesis and the adaptation to a social purpose?"

"Precisely."

He paused before asking the next question. This was a very skilled fencing master. He would probe for every weakness in my defense. His next move was a feint.

"For the creative process, I understand readily that you may need seclusion, space, privacy, even an eccentric personal lifestyle." He paused a moment before the next thrust. "But for the second, you need—indeed, you must maintain—social contacts: consultation with colleagues, an exchange of ideas, contractual discussions. How would you find those if you lived in permanent isolation?"

"I had hoped, Dr. Rubens, that the Simonetta Agency might help me toward an answer."

"On what did you base your hope, Mr. Benson?"

"On something that your colleague, Mr. Falco, called a 'silly little magazine piece,' in which the agency was represented as able to help people to drop out of their normal lives and begin new ones."

"I am familiar with the piece, Mr. Benson. I confess I have always found it something of an embarrassment."

"I understand, however, that it has brought many clients to the agency—and to you, Dr. Rubens."

"Do you know any of them?"

It was what fencers call a flèche, a running attack, aimed high inside the body; but it left him wide open for a direct low thrust, if I had nerve enough to make the move. The words

212

came out swiftly, as if they were spoken by another mouth than mine.

"I know one of them."

"Oh? Who is that?"

"A man called Laurence Lucas. An American."

"And how did you come to meet him, Mr. Benson?"

"He married my sister."

"And you are?"

"I am Carl Emil Strassberger. There is a situation we need to discuss."

He was made of iron, this one. He sat immobile, eyes blank, palms flat on the table, while he digested my statement. Finally, with singular calm, he spoke.

"There is no reason in the world why I should discuss anything with you. You present yourself in my office, using a false name. You ask me to discuss with you the confidential business of a client. If you really are Carl Emil Strassberger, you must know that you have no standing place in this matter at all. Your brother-in-law has renounced his family ties. He has asked his wife to divorce him. He is a sick man. He has placed himself and his affairs in my hands."

I expected him to rise and dismiss me instantly. He didn't. He sat there dead-eyed and still, waiting for me to argue my case. He had to find how much I knew, what action the family or I myself might be contemplating. There was more at stake here than the future of Larry Lucas, an ailing man, in flight from reality, and with only a modest fortune in trust to maintain him to the problematic end of his days. I decided that the best way to hold my ground with Rubens was by reason and not by combat.

"Your point is well taken, Doctor. Although I have not seen the documents, I have always assumed that Larry did appoint you his trustee with power of attorney."

"If you assumed that, why did you not refer directly to me on matters of concern?"

"Two reasons. First, your reputation was clouded by the association with Francesco Falco and the Simonetta Agency. The reason for my masquerade as Edgar Benson was to penetrate that company and find evidentiary proof of its very questionable activities."

"Which you believe you have?"

"Which I know I have, Doctor."

"And with which you now propose to threaten me."

"On the contrary. I should much prefer to bury it. But your Francesco Falco is a very unsavory fellow."

Rubens made a small gesture of dismissal.

"He runs a successful travel enterprise. That puts him already halfway to heaven. He works in many different jurisdictions. It would be expensive and probably futile to mount any legal action against him. Your family has been in the banking business a long time, Mr. Strassberger. You must know that money is the most widely acceptable proof of innocence. You must also know that a trustee is accountable only for the administration of the funds he holds. He is not asked to explain their origins. My company is quite separate from Simonetta. Mr. Falco is wholly responsible at law for that company."

"But as a trustee with power of attorney, you are directly and personally responsible for the well-being of Larry Lucas, who is presently confined in the Burgholzli psychiatric clinic in Zurich."

There was a faint flicker of surprise in the hooded eyes, but his cast-iron calm was unshaken.

"You are not suggesting, surely, that his confinement represents a delinquency on my part or an invasion of his civil rights?"

"No, I am not. I know from my own inquiries that when Larry was in Sirmione, he entered a manic phase and you promptly sent a certain Alois Langer to stay with him and, ultimately, bring him to Switzerland for treatment. We—all his family—are grateful for that."

"You are concerned, then, about my administration of his funds?"

"No, they are, after all, his funds and he can dispose of them in any way he chooses."

"So what, precisely, is troubling you, Mr. Strassberger?"

"His future."

Again he made that curt, dismissive gesture.

"Once he is stabilized in the hospital, he will be released. He will be free to go where he chooses, live as he likes."

"Subject to quite heavy charges against his funds if he rescinds your power of attorney or breaks his contract with the Simonetta Agency."

That was a guess, but it turned out a good one. Rubens was swift to state his position.

"Both contracts were executed in good faith, while Lucas was in full possession of his faculties. Those who witnessed the contracts can testify to that. It would take a long and expensive lawsuit even to call them in question, let alone overturn them. So what do you really want, Mr. Strassberger? What was the point of this whole cloak-and-dagger charade—which I find quite absurd?"

"It is absurd, Doctor, but as Dr. Langer must have explained to you, one of the problems of this illness is that the sufferer draws many others—family, friends, business associates—into his zones of unreality. He, or she, plays manipulative games. Larry's disappearance, his change of identity, the secrecy of his dealings with his own and his family's funds, were all designed to involve us in a melodrama in which he was, and still is, the central character. As a money man, you must have factored this into your original deal with him. For example, how much time and money did you have to spend to get Larry out of Italy and into safekeeping in Zurich?"

"Quite a lot. But, as you know, we recover out of the funds deposited with us."

"And how much would Simonetta factor in to get him safely to the Seychelles and maintain him there, at least without scandal?"

"Again, quite a lot."

"My charade, too, was a costly exercise which involved an international security organization; without it, I doubt we would have discovered so much in so short a time. I was warned, before I set out, that this illness is, in a very special sense, a communicable disease. The warning was not overstated."

"So tell me plainly what you want from me."

"Larry's wife and children, my father, and Larry's New York physician, Dr. Alma Levy, arrive in Zurich tomorrow morning. They want free and open access to Larry Lucas at the Burgholzli Clinic. For that, as things stand, they require the consent of the admitting physician and your permission as the legal custodian of Larry's interests."

"Failing which?"

"An attorney in Zurich has already been briefed to secure an access order from the District Court in Zurich."

"I would see no point in contesting such a case. My sole concern is the well-being of my client. If his family can help him, good! I am all in favor. If they can't, I am still bound to serve him to the best of my ability. This isn't a one-way street, Mr. Strassberger. My fees are high, but I do give service, even to the most difficult clients. Before you leave, I shall dictate a brief letter of authority to the clinic and I shall speak personally with Dr. Langer, who resides in Zurich."

"Thank you. I am grateful—my family will be grateful for your cooperation."

"My compliments on your handling of a difficult brief, Mr. Strassberger. I confess I was a little concerned before our meeting."

"About what?"

"My colleague, Falco, called me this morning. He told me that in your incarnation as Edgar Benson, you had invited one of his staff out to dinner last night. She didn't show up for work this morning. She had not returned to her apartment. You didn't, perhaps, bring her to Switzerland with you?"

"No. I sent her home at eleven-thirty in the company of three other guests, a man and two women. I was up at dawn to catch a flight to Zurich and come here."

"So you will not be seeing her again?"

"No."

"And, obviously, you will not be pursuing your inquiries as a potential client of Simonetta?"

"Obviously not. I'd be grateful if you'd inform Falco."

"I shall."

"You should also inform him that any action by way of

threat, intimidation, or harassment against the girl, because of her brief contact with me, would be met by immediate publication of very damaging material. Last night's dinner party was attended by two police officers and the Italian director of Corsec S.p.A. Liliane Prévost went home in their company and is substantially under their protection. One further point: Falco himself urged me to take an interest in the girl. He said she might well be my future guardian angel if I became a special client of the agency. He did not know that I knew she had acted in a similar role with Larry Lucas in Paris. Do you know why she was posted to Rome?"

"Suppose you tell me, Mr. Strassberger."

"Because she had embarked on a lesbian love affair with a senior employee at Strassberger and there was some indiscreet talk over a dinner table."

"You are better informed than I expected."

"The charade helped."

"You have helped me also, Mr. Strassberger. A review of our own security seems overdue. Now, if you'll excuse me, I'll have your letter prepared."

"Please, indulge me a little longer. Doctor. There are questions I need to ask."

"I'll take the questions. I may decline to answer."

"Your privilege, Doctor. First question. Are you in any fashion involved with the present market raids on Strassberger shares?"

"I am. The extent and nature of my involvement are confidential."

"Was Larry Lucas the initiator, or is he now a participant, in this market action?"

"No comment."

"He holds a substantial parcel of shares in the company. These presently lie under your power of attorney."

"They do, yes."

"Have you disposed of them?"

"No comment."

"Did you yourself plan the raid using information supplied by Larry Lucas?"

For the first time, his control cracked. There was a flash of anger in his eyes. He lifted his palms from the table and slammed them down against the polished surface.

"Enough, Mr. Strassberger! Let us have some reality here! Your company is a public corporation. It is subject to market strategies and the operation of market forces. This is end-of-century capitalism. This is how it works, like it or leave it. It's clear the company is defending itself by buying in its own shares. There's a limit to that game. Once the cash runs low, you have to start buying on margin. Then the real battle begins. You've made one big mistake, Mr. Strassberger.

"You've totally misread my interest in Larry Lucas. You've seen him only in the light of his affliction—a man haunted to despair by his own demons. I watched what he did with that takeover of the old Suez company properties—a five-billion-dollar deal put together like a first-class Swiss watch. The man is a genius! He's flawed, yes, but name me one genius who wasn't. He's repairable, he's usable, and I made up my mind to get him. I have him now. I'm taking care of him, not for the sake of his personal assets—which, in banking terms, are small—but for the talent which resides in him, talent which Strassberger recognized but seemed unable to protect and nurture."

"And how do you think Strassberger failed him?"

"They let him drive himself too hard and too fast. Finally, like an overheated mill saw, he exploded into fragments. No company should do that with a brilliant man. No family should ignore the danger signs."

"And will *you* recognize the danger signs, Dr. Rubens?"

"I have lived with it all my life, Mr. Strassberger. My father built this business out of the decaying fortunes of the Thousand-Year Reich. Out of the twilight of the fallen gods, all sorts of people, victims and villains alike, came to him to save the relics of their onetime wealth or the loot they had plundered. My father's creed was a very ancient one. *Pecunia non olet,* money carries no smell.

"I learned differently as I grew older, that the stink of the slaughterhouse hangs over every money market in the world. I don't quarrel with it anymore. I live with it as a fact of human existence. My problem is I have no children and therefore no one to whom I can even delegate the powers I exercise—or the acquisitions I may make in the empire my father left me. It's a very large empire, Mr. Strassberger. There are some very strange people in it."

"And you see Larry Lucas as your vice-regent?"

"For all his flaws—possibly because of them—he's the best I've seen so far. Dr. Langer tells me that once he is through this phase and stabilized again, the condition can be much better controlled."

"It's your own business, Dr. Rubens, but I'd say you were taking a hell of a gamble."

"Strassberger gambled on him and cleaned up fifty million dollars in fees and commissions. Then they lost control of the game. You know what the Strassberger problem is? I've analyzed it very carefully. You're a good, solid, respectable family company—too good, too solid, too respectable, too much family for a dog's world like this one or an erratic genius like Larry Lucas. You deserved to lose him. You deserve to lose the company too. You yourself, the son of the house, are not interested enough to fight for it. I'll say good-bye now, Mr. Strassberger. My secretary will bring your letter in a few moments."

I had an hour to kill before my flight left for Zurich. I spent it in the airport lounge, sipping whiskey and trying to make some sense of my talk with Dr. Rubens. There was a winter quality of despair about the man which made a stark contrast with the passionate contempt of his final outburst.

He did not strike me as an evil man, but as one who lived in defiance of a flawed universe and exploited it as an act of anger, rather than for a profit, which he was sure of making but incapable of enjoying. He would insist, as I was sure he was doing, on the last cent of his contract with Larry, yet he would nurture and protect and—more importantly—respect the erratic genius which he perceived in him.

219

The compassion and tolerance he expressed were genuine. I was sure of that, because I knew he could afford them. His strategy to acquire Larry's services was risk-free. He was the trustee of his estate. Larry, therefore, was paying for his own rehabilitation. If the funds ran out, he would reward Larry quite richly for services to be rendered. Either way, the donkey would trot toward the carrot in front of its nose.

That was my cynic's reading of a cynical bargain, but it was not the whole text. Dr. Rubens was a man who supped comfortably with the devil, not only because his spoon was long enough but because he was not hungry enough to fight over the food. Either he was served his rightful portion or he left the table. He had discovered, as a result of his father's education, that the devil, in many of his disguises, was a gentleman, and that it was possible to have a mannerly, and even pleasant conversation with him. I knew what he meant when he said success in business brought one halfway to heaven. He implied much more: that the road to riches ended at hell's gates, where the devil was no longer a gentleman.

I had been insulted and angered by his dismissive comments about my father and Strassberger & Company. I was less angered by his reference to me as the son who disdained to stand and fight for his own heritage. I had enough guilt about that already. I had reasoned with most of them, but now the linchpin of my logic had dropped out. Larry Lucas, who had been nominated as successor to my father, had abdicated. So unless Madi moved in—and I could not see her doing it—the house of Strassberger would be left without an heir and my father without family support in the years when he would need it most.

Which brought me to a moment of musing on Strassberger & Company itself. Rubens had described it aptly: "too good, too solid, too respectable, too much family." They were words of praise, yet he had turned them into insults. In my father's mind, they stood for enduring virtues: honesty, trust, the handshake as the bond of faith. Yet, to tell the truth, I had left the company because they seemed, to me at least, to impose unacceptable limitations on modes and manners and attitudes in a changing world—to be too inflexible, too judgmental, as though the mess of an evolving creation were simply an exercise in double-entry bookkeeping.

Larry Lucas had accepted the role I had rejected; but the effort to conform and, at the same time, to function in what Rubens had called "this dog's world" had cost him too much. The pressure plates in the fault zone of his mind had shifted and the foundations of his reason had rocked. My father made the proper Strassberger judgment. The family must hold together, the lost sheep must be found and brought back to the fold, the gates must be closed against intruders, gossip must be silenced.

The problem, as I saw it now, was that the proper Strassberger judgment wasn't a judgment at all. It was a law and a tradition, inscribed on tablets of stone. It dealt with tribe and family. It took little or no account of the individual, the strayed or maimed one. It ignored the secret war between reason and unreason which was being waged inside his brain-box. It recked nothing of the question which must even now be haunting him, as he huddled in the clinic like a fetus in the womb, waiting for the installment of reason: What happens tomorrow when I am expelled from this refuge into reality?

Rubens had an answer for him. It seemed more adequate than any his family could offer him, because, although it did not offer love, it predicated respect, a clear measure of his personal value, an acknowledgment that genius, with all its flaws, was genius still. We, caught in our own private crises, offered only an exasperated love, familial duty, a resumed career, but one always monitored and under surveillance. Why, I asked myself, did that death's-head fellow, Rubens, look like a better bet for Larry than the Strassbergers? Good question. I had better find the answer before we came face-to-face at the Burgholzli Clinic.

They were calling the Zurich flight. I dozed from takeoff to landing. When I finally reached the hotel, I found the roof had fallen in on the Strassberger family.

*   *   *

221

Madi had arrived with the children, both of whom were prostrate with an attack of gastroenteritis. The nanny was near tears. The house doctor had come and gone, leaving a prescription and a counsel to keep the patients rested amd hydrated. He also left a piece of sour comfort. The worst should be over within twenty-four hours; if it weren't, he would arrange hospitalization and intravenous feeding.

That, however, was only the hors d'oeuvre to a menu of disasters. My mother had fallen in the bathroom at home, fractured a hip, and broken a couple of ribs. She was now in the hospital for surgery. Because of her frail health, there were postoperative risks. My father could not, would not, leave New York. Communication might be difficult, as he was back and forth to the hospital. I had all the authority I needed to act for him and the company.

Then, by way of a dessert to disaster, Madi told me that our father himself was far from well. The stress of company business was taking its toll. He looked gray and old. His senior colleagues were worried. They had urged him to slow down, to have a full medical checkup. He had brushed them aside. I could almost hear him doing it: "Later! Later! We have problems here and abroad! Let's clean those up. Mine will cure themselves in short order!"

Finally, Alma Levy had come to Zurich as she had promised, but she had offered only a curt greeting and left immediately to meet her colleague from the Burgholzli. She had no idea when she would return to the hotel. She, too, had problems in New York. She was dubious about her New York replacement. A schizophrenic patient, apparently in a stage of remission, had run berserk with a kitchen knife and almost murdered his wife . . . and so forth and so on.

I listened with what I thought was admirable patience to the litany of lamentations. I helped Madi minister to the children while the nanny took tea in her bedroom. Then Madi and I went down together to the bar, which in the Dolder is so spacious and formal and old-fashioned that it is the worst place in the world to drown a load of sorrows.

Madi, herself, had a private list of complaints. She was not at all sure that this proposed meeting with Larry was a good idea. If he were bad enough to be hospitalized, he could be in no shape for rational discussion about their future as a family. Besides, she had already done what he had asked: She had briefed an attorney to prepare and file a divorce petition. She hoped Larry would be prepared to sign the consent documents she had brought. She was worried about his first contact with the children. She wondered whether he would have enough grace and control to spend some tenderness on them.

For herself, she had passed a crisis point. She was no longer prepared to be torn on the rack of conflicting emotions. She was ready to admit that she might still be in love with Larry, but she was no longer prepared to pay a high price for the painful experience. She was even less eager to hear of my adventures in search of Larry than I was to recount them.

Much more important, from her point of view, was what was going to happen to our parents: to Mother, if she deteriorated into chronic invalidism, to Father, if the stress of market battles proved too much for him. Had I thought of that? No, dear sister, I had not. It was scarcely an hour since you had delivered this sackful of bad news. Before that, I had been like an old-fashioned Pinkerton man, chasing one Laurence Lucas, husband and father, lost, stolen, or strayed. I had found him at last; now I was waiting for instructions on how to deal with him.

Madi and I were walking on eggshells. She was travel-weary, distressed about the children, disturbed about Larry, and near to tears. I was worried too, plagued by my own guilts, still smarting under the lash of Dr. Rubens's contempt.

I felt a sudden surge of relief when I saw Alma Levy enter the bar and look for us. I stood to greet and embrace her. I strung out the ceremony of settling her at the table and ordering her drink—which to my surprise was a very large neat vodka on ice.

"I need it," she affirmed emphatically. "I've earned it! I had a long briefing session with my Swiss colleague who has connections with the Burgholzli. You will remember that I spoke about him. I had hoped he might invite me out to the clinic to see Larry, but he thought that would be unwise until all the protocols were settled. However, he made a number of useful phone calls. He was able to assure me that Dr. Langer has an excellent reputation. He is a good clinician and a compassionate carer for his patients. In legal terms, the problems are not excessive. As a foreigner, Larry required a Swiss doctor to admit him to the clinic and the consent either of his next of kin, or a Swiss attorney representing his interests. If we want access to Larry now, we have to take the process in reverse order. The attorney agrees, the admitting physician accepts his direction, the clinic is happy. If there's a dispute, it can be resolved by a decision of the District Court of Zurich, which may be appealed in the High Court. I understand we are prepared for that."

"We're two steps ahead of the game. The attorney consents to access. The only condition is that Alma is to confer with Dr. Langer before any family contact is made with Larry."

I handed her the Rubens letter of authority, which also contained confirmation of his call to Langer and Langer's contact number. Alma read swiftly, then raised her glass in salute.

"Good! Very good! This saves us much time and heartbreak. I'll call Langer now. Then you can buy me another drink and take us all to dinner."

She got up hurriedly and walked out to the phone booths, which in the Dolder Grand are located behind the concierge's office. Madi reached out and laid a hand on mine.

"I'm sorry, Carl! I haven't even said thank you for all you've done. I've been snapping and snarling since we met."

"Forget it, love. That's family!"

"I love you. You know that."

"I love you too, little sister. But we'll talk later about the parents. One day at a time, yes?"

"One hour at a time is as much as I can manage. I'll see to the children and join you and Alma for dinner. If I'm not down in time, start without me."

I ordered a second drink for myself and another for Alma Levy. I asked the waiter to make our reservations for dinner and settled back to contemplate the comings and goings of the good Swiss burghers and the moneyed folk of Europe and the Middle

East who were still very happy to do business with these solid sober folk.

It was nearly half an hour before Alma came back to the table. She was grave and preoccupied. She reported with deliberate care.

"First, Dr. Langer himself. I am impressed with him. On the phone he was pleasant and helpful. His diagnosis is sound. His medication is on the conservative side, but it seems to be working. In psychiatry, he is a Jungian. He has taken advantage of his association with Larry, outside and inside the clinic, to embark on a series of exploratory analytic sessions with him. He claims some interesting insights which he is eager to discuss with me. He admits freely that Dr. Rubens is Larry's legal custodian. He sees it as a necessary situation made more imperative by the fact that Larry is traveling on a Dominican passport and is, therefore, deprived of any protection by his own embassy. It seemed a curious point to bring up in a medical discussion; but in fact it was a very ethical disclosure. He claims that Rubens has—and I quote—'an attitude of benevolent patronage in respect of Larry's future career after he is through this episode.'"

"I know about Rubens's patronage. I mistrust it greatly. What is Langer's prognosis for Larry?"

"Please, Carl!" She silenced me with a gesture. "Let me take my time with this. I am, I always have been, more deeply involved in Larry's problems than you may realize. From the beginning, he fixed on me as the substitute for the mother he lost. It's not the best role for a therapist. It makes me an object of both love, dependence, and resentment. Larry has similarly ambivalent feelings toward your father. He sponsored Larry's career. Later, he became his father-in-law. However, he was never able to demonstrate a personal, emotional support in Larry's life. You Strassbergers are such a tightly knit group, you find it hard to understand the loneliness you impose on the outsider. It has taken Madi herself a long time to understand this. Her love for Larry has always been modified—and in some sense diluted—by her family ties. Even their children became

225

mixed up in this psychic soup—the phrase is Langer's, not mine." She took a mouthful of liquor before she went on.

"For months now, Larry has been a weekend parent who came home stressed from a Concorde flight and left in a flurry of business preparations. The children had only one set of grandparents—again the Strassberger family! Larry was acutely, sometimes morbidly, conscious that there were no Lucas grandparents to counterbalance their influence. Finally, there was you, Carl. You are the son of the house, the crown prince. You abdicated. Larry became the heir presumptive. The challenge to him was enormous. The burden was enormous too. Your father made it no secret of his high expectations. He made no secret, either, that the rewards had to be earned. Larry did not shrink from the task, but he was haunted always by the specter of recurrent depression and the mania of near genius which drove him.

"In this illness, there is always some element of paranoia. There has to be an enemy, to justify the fear in the downtime and the exaltation of victory in the uptime. As a therapist, I had to be aware always of the poison ivy in the garden of his mind. The ivy is harmless to look at, but it is poisonous to touch. In Larry's case, the poison ivy was a sense of desperation, of injustice in the scheme of things, of tribal forces in the family tipping the balance against him. It was this which tempted him always, if not to outright revenge, to some outrageous act which might balance the loaded scales."

Suddenly, the absurdity which Rubens had noted began to make sense; the pieces of the puzzle began to fall into a more rational pattern. Rubens had been telling me the truth. Larry's act of revenge had been plotted a long time ago.

"I've lost you, Carl, come back to earth!" Alma Levy commanded me abruptly. "Tell me what's on your mind!"

I told her of my last night in Milan and the session with Liliane Prévost and Sibilla. She was angry and let me know it. She called it an abuse and an invasion and much else besides. Then I told her of my session with Dr. Rubens in Geneva and his claim that 'once the Suez deal was disposed of' he and Larry had agreed to mount a takeover of Strassberger. I described, as well as I was able, Rubens's relationship with Larry: his analysis of Larry's need for respect, more than love, his conviction that Larry could be stabilized enough to function as resident genius in a new coalition of interest.

To my surprise, Alma agreed.

"Of course he could! He will recover from this breakdown. He was already halfway to it before he went to Paris to begin the Suez negotiations."

"But he is still ready to embark on a Judas bargain with Rubens!"

"I would put it another way." Alma was somber. "What you call a Judas bargain was the manic folly which finally broke him. I told you about this when we first talked in New York. In the manic mood, every extravagance is possible, every gamble is a sure winner, the credit card is a horn of plenty which pours out a never-ending stream of goodies. It is only when the bills come in that sanity reasserts itself and the guilt begins. In Larry's case, the burden of guilt was too much to bear. Dr. Langer told me that when he brought Larry to the Burgholzli for treatment, he listed him as an acute suicide risk."

"And now?"

"Langer tells me he's on the mend. We're seeing him together tomorrow morning. If our first encounter goes well, Langer will leave me alone with him. After that, we'll compare notes and decide the question of family access."

"What are you going to tell Madi?"

"Only that I have confidence in Langer and that I'll be seeing Larry tomorrow. I'd like you to tell her the same thing—no more, no less."

"Whatever you say. You're the therapist."

"After that scandalous episode in Milan, I think you need therapy yourself." She finished her drink and set down the glass with a clatter. "Now you may take me to dinner and entertain me. I need a complete break from mind medicine!"

* * *

Madi did not join us at the dinner table. The meal was over by ten. I said good night to Alma Levy and went to my own room to call my father. It was four o'clock in the afternoon, New York time. My father was in his office. The news he gave me was not good.

"The operation was a technical success. The orthopedic surgeon did a first-class job. However, your mother is very weak. There is fluid in the lungs. She is still in the intensive care unit. We wait and we pray."

"Would you like me to come home and bring Madi with me?"

"Not yet." He was firm. "Finish what you have to do in Zurich. That will be one less problem to deal with. If there's any drastic change in your mother's condition, I'll let you know. You can be back here in eight hours or less."

"What's happening in the market?"

"Nothing to make us happy. Two larger institutions—a mutual fund and an insurance group—unloaded a lot of shares today. That stretched us tighter than I like."

"I hope you're not buying on margin."

"Not yet. But it could come to that. The problem is that if we don't support our own stock, there'll be a drastic fall. We have to maintain market confidence. You know that. I'll tell you something, Carl. I wish you were here right now—and I'd even be glad to see that scalliwag, Larry. He'd be flying kites all over the campus, just to confuse the opposition."

"Do you know yet who's masterminded the raid?"

"Corsec has come up with some indicators but no proof. Do you think Larry is involved?"

"Possibly. I'll know better in forty-eight hours."

"That's a hell of a long time on the trading floor."

"Trust me, Father, please!"

"I do, believe me. I'm just beginning to understand how much I've depended on your mother. So long as she was there at the dinner table, I felt secure. Now I hate the thought of going home."

"She'll be back, Father, sooner than you know."

"I hope so. Without her, I see little point in the battle we're fighting now. All of a sudden, I'm feeling old and tired."

"Have you seen your doctor?"

"He's been shouting for me to see him. I'll get around to it, once your mother's on the mend."

"Just remember that she'll need a healthy husband to care for her."

"Carl?"

"Yes, Father."

"I never thought I'd ask this. Even now, I'm not sure I have the right words for it. With Larry gone, I need you at my side, at least while we organize our battle lines. The shareholders—those who have a continuing loyalty to us—have the right to reassurance. Larry's defection is an open secret now, even though there is no question of malfeasance. We have to demonstrate family confidence in the business. I know it's a lot to ask, but to be honest I'm not sure I'm up to the role of Lone Ranger. I don't want it anymore. I'm very tempted to go to auction, cash in my chips, and spend what good time we've got left with your mother. There, it's said. Think about it. I'll accept whatever you decide."

What do you do with a man like that? The roof trees of his world were falling about him, but he still had the grace to offer me a choice and the integrity to face me squarely with the interests of the shareholders. The least I could do was deliver a swift answer.

"As soon as I'm finished here, I'll come."

"Thank you, son."

"There may be things to tidy in Paris and London, before I leave."

"Do whatever is needed. I'll put the word about that you're back."

"Give my love to Mother."

"I will."

"And do something for me."

"Whatever you want."

"Call your doctor now and make an appointment for a full checkup. Deal?"

229

"Deal," said my father, in a tone I knew of old. He had not only struck a bargain, he was convinced he had the best of it. For myself, I had done what Strassbergers had been taught for generations. I had eaten the bread of righteousness. I found it dry as dust in the mouth, tasteless on the tongue. I understood why it had given Larry Lucas such violent indigestion.

Next day, the children were better, but Madi and the nanny were out of action. Alma Levy had a midmorning conference with Dr. Langer at the Burgholzli Clinic. I had time to kill, so I offered to take the children for a ferry ride on the lakes and feed them lunch somewhere in the old town. My life was on hold now. I might just as well make myself useful as a nursemaid to two very puzzled youngsters who were eager to see their father again but dazed by the long-drawn-out approach to him.

I am known as an agreeable uncle, but I am not exactly a creative one. I will happily indulge the whims of children, but I am sadly deficient in an entertainer's talent. I cannot juggle oranges or do card tricks or make coins disappear. I do not know where clowns and strolling minstrels and museums of natural wonder are to be found. I am slow of access to chocolate factories or makers of children's toys or exhibitions of dolls or ancient firearms.

So a boat ride on the lake seemed a safe bet. At best, I could improvise local legends and draw sketches on postcards for their friends at home; at worst, I could feed them soft drinks and sweets and make them sick all over again.

As it turned out, I found myself under inquisition from two very intelligent and very troubled young people. We had completed half the circuit of the lake and were homing down the northern shore when the tour guide pointed out the buildings and the surrounding meadows of the Burgholzli Clinic and gave his little lecture about the famous people who had done research there. Laurence Emil, seven years old, asked what he was talking about. Obligingly, he rendered the talk into English, explaining that this was a place where people who were "sick in the head" were brought for treatment. When he had turned away, the questions were addressed to me.

"Uncle Carl, is that where Daddy is?"

"Yes, it is."

"Will we go there to see him?"

"I don't know. Dr. Levy will be able to tell us that this afternoon. She's up there now, talking with your daddy's doctor and with your daddy too."

"Why did she get to see him first, instead of Mom and us?"

"Because the doctors have to decide whether he's well enough to see visitors."

"But we're not visitors. We're his family. Doesn't he want to see us?"

"Of course he does. But sometimes when people are sick, they are too tired or too confused to cope even with people they love."

"Is Daddy confused?"

"That's why he's in the hospital. The people up there have a great reputation as healers, all around the world."

"And they're sure to make Daddy better?"

This was Marianne's question.

"They're working on it right now, sweetheart."

"Why can't Daddy come home and get better with us?"

My nephew was back in the discussion now. I caught the querulous, mistrustful tone of the young misogynist. This was a question I had to deal with very carefully. It went to the heart of the problem, not only for this seven-year-old but for all of us. I began with a question of my own.

"Do you trust me?"

"Of course I do, Uncle Carl."

"Good. Because the first thing I have to tell you is that it's not a disgrace to be sick. It wasn't a disgrace for you to vomit and make a mess that Nanny and your mom had to clean up. You were sick; you couldn't help yourself. Yet you still felt ashamed. You were angry with yourself and angry with people around you."

"Sort of, I guess."

"It's even worse with a sickness of the mind. Conversation is very difficult. Even though people use the same words, the meaning for each one is different. Imagine yourself in the middle of China, all alone, trying to tell people what's wrong with you—or even something simple, like asking for a drink of water. That's the way your daddy feels. He gets frustrated and angry and afraid, too, because he loves you very dearly but he knows he's not making sense to you. He doesn't blame you for not understanding: but until he's cured it's better for you to be apart. The doctors and nurses are trained to deal with sick people; you're not. Do you understand what I'm telling you?"

"I understand—but I don't understand why Daddy and Mommy had to be cruel to each other."

"People are often cruel because they're frightened and helpless. It's like a puppy biting you when you're trying to take a piece of glass out of his paw. He's hurting. The only way he can let you know is by snapping at you."

"Then why is Mom getting a divorce?"

"Did she tell you that?"

"I heard her talking about it on the phone to Grandma."

"Did you ask your mother to explain it to you?"

"Yes."

"And what did she say?"

"She said that was what our father wanted. He loved us, but he was never coming back. But she's brought us all this way to see him. Does that mean he's changed his mind? If he hasn't, what's the point?"

Marianne added her own wise little-woman postscript: "I don't want to kiss him and just have him walk away for always."

To which Uncle Carl, the all-wise, the all-knowing, who had never begotten a child, who had not committed to either fatherhood or marriage, could manage only a weaselling answer.

"Listen, my loves! Nothing is fixed, nothing can be fixed until your daddy is better. Then everything will change, because your father will be changed and your mother will be changed, and maybe they'll be able to be happy together again."

"But we haven't changed at all," said Laurence Emil stubbornly. "What will happen to us? "

12

BY SIX THAT EVENING, Nanny was sufficiently recovered to supervise the children at supper. Madi, still poorly, was in bed, propped up with pillows, while Alma Levy told us both about her visit to the clinic.

"I met Larry, first in company with Dr. Langer, and then we had a long session alone. We walked in the garden, we sat under the trees and had coffee. He was pleased to see me. We embraced. He offered me his arm as we walked."

"How does he look? " Madi asked. "How does he seem in himself?"

"He is still depressed; but he has reached a plateau of calm. He is able to contemplate himself and his situation rationally and without desperation. He has the look of a man who has just recovered from a long illness—as indeed he has. He is prepared to acknowledge need and dependence, but you must understand that this is not a surrender. He is not beating his breast in penitence for the trouble he has caused. He still has the need to explain and defend himself."

"And where does that leave us, me and the children?"

"Better off, I believe, than you were before."

"You'll have to explain that."

"He explained it himself when I told him you had done what he asked and filed for divorce. And, by the way, he's happy to sign the papers you've brought. What he actually said was, 'Good! That means I can approach her like a civilized being, because we won't have anything to argue about. I can show love to my children when I have love to offer. I can stay away at the loveless times, when my heart is empty!'"

"Oh, God!" Madi's fists were clenched in frustration. "Why didn't I understand before?"

"Because he never said it and you wouldn't have believed it if he had. You've both traveled a long way in a short time."

"And now the children need help."

They both stared at me, shocked by the sharpness of my tone. I told them what the children had said to me during our boat ride and I leaned on young Laurence's last pregnant comment. *We haven't changed. What's going to happen to us?* Then I asked my own question of Alma Levy.

"Larry has consented to see Madi and the children?"

"Yes. Tomorrow morning. If you'll order a car for us, Carl, I'll drive out with them, leave them with Larry, and drive back with them when they're ready to leave."

"I'm dreading this," said Madi.

"There is nothing to dread," said Alma Levy. "You still have love for him."

"I'm not sure I have." Madi was on edge. Alma Levy was short with her.

"Then show him gentleness, at least. Let the children see that and let them show their own love. He will respond, just as he responded to me. But no arguments! No talk of tomorrow! And you do not say good-bye but *au revoir*. You tell him the door is open whenever he wants to walk through it to visit you or the children."

"That's the point." Madi was angry now. "It may not always be open. I can't promise that. I won't."

"Then change the metaphor, for Christ's sake!" I was irritated now. "This is a read-through with improvisations, not the first night of *Rigoletto*!"

"She understands." Alma was more gentle. "She'll be ready."

"I wish I could be as sure as you are, Alma!" Madi was not convinced. "We have this nice loving get-together. What happens at the end of it?"

"So far as you are concerned, nothing. You take the children back to New York."

"And that's the end of it with Larry?"

"It's as far as any of us can look." Her answer was cryptic. "Langer and I both agree that Larry is coping on a day-to-day basis in a protected situation. As his confidence grows, the prospects for both of you may enlarge. Tomorrow is, perhaps, more important for him and the children than it is for you. You are the strong one."

"Why do we have to see him at the clinic? Why can't we take him out for a picnic somewhere?"

"Because, again in our medical view, it is important that the children understand that their father is ill, that he is not to blame for his erratic behavior, and, most importantly, neither are they! Also, if the meeting doesn't work as well as we hope, Larry can retreat and so can you."

"And for this"—Madi was weary and bitter—"we've dragged ourselves thousands of miles across the Atlantic. My mother's dangerously ill. My father's vastly overworked and worried. He is a natural candidate for a stroke or a coronary, but here we are doing three verses and a chorus of "J'attendrai" for that husband and father of the year, Mr. Laurence Lucas! I think I'm going to be sick!"

The next instant she was out of bed and dashing for the bathroom. Alma sighed in resignation.

"Leave her to me! I'll catch up with you in the bar. You've got a special billing in this operetta."

"I've already got my script, my dear Alma. Father has asked me to come back into the company. As things are, I can hardly refuse!"

Alma threw up her hands in theatrical despair.

"And they say we Jews are *meshugganeh volk!* They should see what I see of the madness of the *goyim!*"

The scenario which Alma Levy laid out for me in the bar had been designed and written by Larry himself. It required me to drive out to the Burgholzli at one o'clock the next day and take him out to lunch alone at a lakeside restaurant—and this only an hour after his meeting with the family, within the confines of the clinic itself!

Alma freely admitted that there were contrasts and contradictions between this script and the one which had been written for Madi and the children. She also admitted that both had been devised by Larry and that his two medical advisers had colluded with him. They were even able to accept two quite different systems of logic.

In the case of Madi and the children, they were afraid of an emotional crisis if any argument broke out. In my case, it seemed they wanted to stage a tournament of reason. Larry felt a great need to explain himself to me, and through me to my father, in rational terms. He had even put a name to the exercise: a dialogue of peers, followed, if possible, by an honorable amends for the damage he had caused and a renewal of basic trust between us.

I thought it was just another manipulative ploy, though I could not see exactly where it might lead. With the best will in the world, how could you trust a man who was by nature unstable? Alma Levy did not contest my opinion. She herself had expressed the same fear to Dr. Langer, but he had reasoned her out of it. This, he claimed, was a positive gesture of goodwill on Larry's part. It was an essential step in the recovery process. His willingness to venture outside the protective perimeter, to risk a face-to-face encounter with the man who had recently been his pursuer, represented an enormous therapeutic gain.

For me, gain was the worry word. Whatever his qualifications, whatever his ethics, Dr. Langer was the appointee of Dr. Rubens, trustee of all Larry's interests, associate of another highly suspect character, Francesco Falco of Simonetta Travel. To all of which Alma had no direct answer. Instead she asked a very simple question.

"What do you lose by taking the man to lunch?"

"Time, patience, the cost of the lunch, and a hell of a row with my sister when she hears of it."

"Don't tell her until it's over. She'll be gone all morning. You'll have left the hotel before she returns."

"You have a plotter's mind, Doctor!"

"What do you expect, Carl?" She gave me a shrug and a world-weary smile. "Every mind I enter is a new labyrinth. At the center of each one is a roaring Minotaur. I'm supposed to slay it like Theseus. The sad thing is that most of the time the bull's roar is the wail of an infant magnified by misery, but I have to wade through miles of bullshit to find the child. So, please, just buy the man lunch and let's all go home!"

Although Larry Lucas had been the center of my attention for weeks now, it was with something of a shock that I realized it was nearly a year since we had met, in New York, at a birthday party for my father. I remembered him as a handsome, athletic, smiling fellow, radiating enthusiasm, a turner of heads among women, a boon companion among men.

The Larry Lucas who came to greet me in the reception area of the Burgholzli Clinic was like a wax replica of the one I remembered. His complexion was sallow; his skin seemed to have tightened across the facial bones. His lips were pale, his eyes sunk back into his head. He moved slowly, his speech was deliberate, but there was still a trace of the old raillery in his rueful smile. His handshake was still firm. His first words were an expression of thanks.

"It was good of you to come, Carl. I was afraid you might refuse. I wouldn't have blamed you."

"How did it go with Madi?"

"Better than I deserved or expected. She's quite a woman, your sister. The kids were great—very protective. They wanted to impress on me that they understood I'd been sick and they hoped they'd see me again very soon."

"I'm glad it turned out that way."

"So was I. Where do you propose we eat?"

"There's a place called the Black Swan. The concierge at the hotel recommends it highly."

"Wherever you say. I eat very lightly these days and, with the drugs they're giving me, I'm not allowed to drink."

"How are you feeling?"

"Better. This has been a slow turnaround. It takes a certain time for the medication to take hold. That was part of my problem. I wouldn't give it time. I wanted instant miracles. It has helped to be in the clinic. I hated it at first, but it was a relief to have other people make up my mind for me. Thank God I've still got a mind, or most of it anyway. They tell me the rest of it will begin to function very soon. I'm looking forward to this little drive in the country."

It was a pleasant excursion. The air was heavy with the scent of mown grass. The meadows were a patchwork of fresh stubble and rising corn and yellow rape flowers and stands of orchard trees. The restaurant was a sunny chamber which opened onto a pontoon deck where tables were laid under striped umbrellas. We ordered drinks: a vodka and tonic for me, apple juice for Larry. We settled on the food: hors d'oeuvres and grilled trout. We told the waiter we were in no hurry. I wanted Larry to begin our talk. I hoped I would be able to steer it toward the information I needed. Once again, he disarmed me.

"I can't tell you how sorry I was to hear of your mother's accident. She's a great lady. I've always admired her. I pray she mends quickly. How is your father taking it?"

"He's taking it hard."

It was a bald statement but I could not trust myself to extend it; otherwise I might have spun into a tirade against the begetter of many of our present woes, who faced me, mournful as a basset hound, across the napery. His next gambit was a cliché to end all clichés.

"I suppose you want to know the reason for this lunch?"

"It would help, yes." I gave him a sour grin. "Especially as I'm paying for it and I've had to travel halfway round the globe to catch up with you!"

Then he was laughing at me, a genuine, mirthful, schoolboy's laugh.

"That's it! That's the pure, unadulterated Strassberger response: On guard! Engage! And you're in there, thrust and parry, because it's Strassberger ground you're standing on and only Strassbergers have a right to set foot on the sacred soil. That's the next question I was going to ask you, Carl. What happens if your mother dies? What happens when the job gets too big for your father or he decides there's no point to it anymore?"

"I'd say, Larry, that was none of your goddam business now. You quit, remember? You wrote the severance letters. You're working up a takeover bid with Rubens."

"I did. I am."

"However, I'll answer your question. When Madi and the children go back, I'm going with them."

"Back to the business?"

"That's right."

He did not mock me this time. There was no laughter left in his eyes. The waiter walked into our small zone of silence, laid the platters of hors d'oeuvres in front of us, wished us a good appetite, and left. I addressed myself to the food. Larry nibbled a mouthful or two, then picked up the thread of the conversation.

"I'm sorry you're giving up your career."

"It isn't a career. It's a way of life that I enjoy. I have a modest talent but at least a recognizable one. I have the means to enjoy it. It's no big deal if I have to defer the enjoyment."

"You have more talent as an artist than as a banker."

"I know. That's why I abdicated and you got the job. Then you abdicated and I'm stuck with it again."

"And you hate my guts. Is that it?"

"No, I don't. You can thank Madi for that, because she was wise enough to stay with Alma Levy, who taught me something about your problem. You can thank my father, too, because he cared enough to send me chasing after you, so you wouldn't come to harm!"

"Don't patronize me, Carl!"

240

I sensed the deep stirring of anger in him. I knew I had to calm him if I could. I reasoned with him quietly.

"I'm not patronizing you, Larry. I'm here because you asked me. We're halfway through the first course and you haven't yet told me why."

"You're right. I haven't. Please be patient with me. I still fly off at a tangent sometimes. Let's begin then: you, your father, and me. You're out studying and painting rose windows and gargoyles and flying buttresses. I'm the wonder boy, adopted into Strassberger and Company. Pass me the ball and I run with it—touchdown, touchdown, touchdown! I marry the boss's daughter, a union made in heaven, blessed on earth. I beget two beautiful kids. I am twice blessed—no thrice!—because I have now endowed the grandparents with continuity."

He broke off while the waiter removed the platters and offered us each a small thimble of lemon sorbet.

"You're a very patient listener, Carl," he said.

"Because you're telling me something I've wanted to know for a long time."

"One of the problems!" He gave a small, dismissive shrug. "If you don't talk about it, people don't ask. If they don't ask, why tell? How do you describe hell to someone who's never been there?"

"Hell is an infectious disease. People catch it from you."

His head came up like that of a startled lizard. There was no anger in his eyes this time, only a kind of wonderment. After a long moment, he relaxed and gave a nod of agreement.

"You're right. They do—but that's the last thing you understand. Alma Levy used to say—and Dr. Langer agrees with her—that the betterment only begins when you stop looking inside yourself and start looking outside to other people. There's a problem, however, with that piece of advice. You're not looking inside yourself at all. There's nothing there to see. It's an empty blackness that goes on forever. You close the door on it. Then you're looking over your shoulder at the great birdlike shape that pursues you all the time and that one day, sure as sure, will fold its black wings over you and blot out every ray of light or hope.

241

When the darkness lifts—and it does—you don't see the normal daylight as other people do. You emerge into a kind of panic joy, a frenzy of relief in which you could tear your clothes off and run naked and shouting through the streets, or toss a lifetime's savings out the window and cheer the people who run off with it. Am I making any sense to you at all?"

"Yes, you are; but only because other people, like Madi and Alma Levy, prepared me to understand it. There's something, however, I still find hard to grasp."

"Tell me."

"This resentment, this need of another victim or a whole series of victims to expiate a suffering they didn't inflict on you."

The question was clearly painful to him. For a moment, I thought he was going to retreat into himself and close the shutters on any further intrusion. He recovered, however, and began to piece out his answer.

"The resentment is real; but it's general and not particular. There were days when I resented you so much that I would cheerfully have murdered you. You were three thousand miles away, painting happily in a château garden, and I was in one of my black weeks, trying to raise ten million for some cruddy experimental venture like a tidewater generator in Puget Sound. I needed victims, because I was a victim—come to that, I still am—but I'm learning to think that other folk have worse demons than I do and less hope of escape. Or perhaps the key is that I'm not looking for an escape anymore, just alleviation."

"Did you have to leave your wife and children to find it?"

"I did, yes. I'm staying away for other reasons."

"May I know what they are?"

"Sure. You've earned the right to know. How can I say it? Given this affliction of fear and frenzy, given even the fact that it can be controlled by medication and counsel and by a certain exercise of self-control, which I'm not yet very good at—given all these things, the Strassberger clan is too tight for me, too judgmental, too trenchant, too much everything I'm not. If I can't live in it, I shouldn't work in it. And by the same token, Carl, my friend, you shouldn't either. I know you'll tell me again to mind my own business, but I'm giving you the truth as I see it. With all the goodwill in the world, you'll never make a banker, and if you try you'll break your heart."

"So what am I supposed to do, stand by and watch my old man kill himself?"

"No."

"What then, Larry? You still know the business better than anyone. You know it well enough to want to take it over. What would you suggest for me?"

"They're bringing the main course now. Let's eat it while it's hot. I'll tell you over the coffee."

And tell me he did, in spades, clubs, diamonds, and hearts. He borrowed a pencil and an order pad from the headwaiter and dazzled me with displays of figures and graphs and diagrams. I could literally feel the adrenaline surging through him as he rode through the last trough of depression and swung up onto the rising wave of optimism which Alma Levy called hypomania. The drugs were buffering him against a high manic surge, but the underlying symptoms were clear. His mind was racing, his speech was faster, he radiated light and confidence. He finished his exposition with a flourish.

"You tell me your father is tempted to sell, yes?"

"That's what he said. He's tempted. But that's off the record."

"And if he put all the family shares on the auction block—which means the controlling votes in the company—there's what he'd get for them." He wrote the figure on the pad, underscored it heavily, and thrust it at me across the tabletop. "Forty-five dollars a share—fifty, tops, in a bull market, which right now we don't have. Am I right or wrong?"

"As near as dammit, you're right."

"What would you say if I promised I'd get you sixty-five?"

"I'd say you were out of your cotton-picking mind."

"I'd say Strassberger and Company would be out of their

243

minds to refuse it, with an ailing management, a less than competent succession, and quite a lot of dissension among the troops, especially in France."

"Fomented by you?"

"No. Exacerbated by old-fashioned, heavy-handed management and roughshod audit procedures after I went underground for a while."

"I became aware of the dissension myself. But to come back to this sixty-five-dollar figure of yours, who would be the fool to underwrite it?"

"I'd sell by tender because I know there's money on the table. I think you should at least tell your father."

"Why should he believe me?"

"You mean why should he believe Larry Lucas?"

"Either way."

"First, because I'm telling the truth; second, because the figure is genuine—all that's needed is a formal call for tenders to activate the offer—and, third, because this is my way of paying some of the debts I owe to the Strassberger family."

"You'll forgive my saying it, Larry, but we weren't aware that you acknowledged any debts to us. I think Madi and the children have clear claims on your love and care, but they're private to you as a family. So far as my father is concerned, there's money owed to you, if you want to claim it."

"And you, Carl? Don't I owe you anything? I took away your nice well-planned life and gave you one you didn't want at all. I feel bad about that. I'd like to make some amends."

His words made an extraordinary impression on me. Against all reason, I had to take them as truth. One part of my brain told me that this was a sick man who carried black devils on his back, and sometimes the devils turned into angels carrying him to undreamed-of heavens. But angels and devils alike were illusions of an unbalanced psyche.

Another part of my brain had registered the fact that his figures on Strassberger's value were accurate and that only a few weeks ago he had brought off a huge market coup. Did I believe he could create fifteen dollars a share extra value for Strassberger?

If he rejoined the firm, yes, he just might; but he didn't want to come back and I was sure my father wouldn't take him anyway. Me? I was drawn to him as I always had been, for his wit and his panache and flair for the dramatic.

I could not give him the lie, direct. I didn't want to part from him in anger. I signaled for more coffee and began again to question him.

"Help me to understand, Larry. Help me to explain to your children. I'm still their Uncle Carl. They ask me questions. They trust my answers. How did this flight of yours begin?"

"It wasn't flight, Carl! That's where you all got it wrong. It was a wild urge for change: What was around the next corner, over the next hill? Maybe the black bird wouldn't find me. Maybe the sun would shine more days in the year. You thought of me as a fugitive. I felt more like a kid playing hooky and chasing butterflies."

"But didn't you think what you were doing to other people?"

"Not much. You find that hard to understand? Let me try to explain. You Strassbergers all have a continuity, a past. You have parents, grandparents, ancestors. The dark bird is perched a long way back in the family tree. I don't have that. My parents were snatched away. I had to build my future on assumptions of a past. That was tough, but I did it. The wonderful thing your father did for me was to accept me at face value. His judgment of my talents was right. His judgment of my needs and my character was dead wrong. He couldn't see I was flawed. I was his creation. I was his daughter's husband. He used to tell me, over and over, 'You can do whatever you set your mind to, Larry!' Every time he said it, I used to make a silent scream of protest: *How can you say that when you don't even know who I am?*

"When he sent me to Europe on the Suez takeover, I was scared witless. I was the new boy from New York. The French put me through the hoops like a circus poodle. I was trying to put together a list of investors, and Vianney and his crowd would hardly give me the time of day. I felt like a leper with a bell around my neck.

"Then someone gave me the name of Dr. Hubert Rubens in Geneva. They also gave me chapter and verse of his family history: how his father had set up funk funds for war criminals and Nazi bigwigs and wartime profiteers and the looters of Jewish properties and estates. His father had retired long since, a victim of Alzheimer's disease. Rubens had settled into a bunker existence, a kind of armor-plated anonymity from which he ran the funds and trusts which the accidents of time and war had left under his control. The stretch and variety of his interests is enormous: South America, Africa, Hong Kong, Taiwan, the Arab states, Indonesia.

"At first, I found him a daunting figure—and he is daunting, because he has deliberately anesthetized himself to normal emotions. That was my key to him, as it is the key to all of us odd ones, Carl. We have to concentrate on survival, because we live in a state of recurrent siege. Anyway, I listened and Rubens understood. He agreed to invest and to bring in other investors. It was almost a magical process. Rubens made telephone calls and suddenly the air was full of angels with buckets of bullion. But they weren't phantoms, they were real!

"Somewhere in the process of working together, we began to understand each other. Very little was spelled out. We developed a kind of shorthand. He was trying to live with a past he hadn't created. I was trying to create a future built on a vacuum. Each of us had guilts. Each of us had fantasies too. There are no fantasies in the schedule of Strassberger assets, but there are a few on Rubens's list! Simonetta Travel is one of them. It is marginally profitable, with the possibility of large capital gains. Falco is a known rogue, but Rubens manages to live with him and control him. The concept of providing safe havens for dropouts appeals to his sense of humor, and it also is a modern analogue of his father's early days. Rubens suggested, more as a joke than as a serious project, that I should give myself the experience of finding a safe haven for myself if I ever needed it. I took him up on it, because all the time I was in Paris I was suffering bipolar swings and the Simonetta connection helped—just as Claudine Parmentier helped at the office."

My puzzlement must have been written on my face. I sat gaping at him, waiting for an explanation. He gave me a small, rueful grin.

"One of the problems with this ailment of mine is that it affects the sexual drive. In the downtimes, I'm not interested. I guess I'm looking for comfort and not congress. So it helped to know girls like Claudine and Liliane, who preferred lesbian love but were happy to have a well-turned-out male companion. In the high times I couldn't get enough sex, and sometimes at home, Madi's rhythms and mine were out of kilter. That didn't help either of us." He shrugged away the allusion. "That's just a sidebar, a footnote. No blame to Madi. She deserves a lot better than I gave her."

There were still questions I wanted to ask, but I could see the energy seeping out of him again. I asked point blank, "Are you up to this? You're looking tired."

"It's time to clean house, Carl. Let's get on with it. What more do you want to know?"

"How did a brilliant banker like you come to tie himself hand and foot to a man like Rubens, not to mention Simonetta's bolt-hole bargains for the brokenhearted? From what I learned, they cost a pretty penny as well."

He hesitated a long time on his answer. I signaled for more coffee. The waiter refilled the cups. There was another silence. Finally, Larry found voice and words for his answer. His voice was low but firm. The words were very simple.

"The Simonetta situation was a sideshow, nothing more. I used their services. I paid for them. Their new-life projects became like parlor games. The fact that I paid through the nose was unimportant. Rubens was a different matter. I trusted him. He understood, at least as well as Alma Levy or Langer, the financial follies someone like me can commit in the manic phases. One day he put it to me quite bluntly: 'Why don't you let me look after your money, Larry? I charge more and I'll tie you hand and foot, but you'll always eat well, you'll die a damned sight richer than you are now, and you'll have something decent to hand on to your children.'"

"He was asking you to take a hell of a lot on faith."

"He was, but he had backed me in the Suez affair. However, I did haggle with him, because he likes a haggle. I went through the same exercise as I did with you. I asked him to put a figure on Strassberger shares. He came up with fifty dollars tops. I asked him what they would be worth if he merged the two entities: Rubens and Strassberger."

"What did he say?"

"He asked first who could plot such a merger. I told him I could. He asked me who would run the new entity. I told him that was his affair. I couldn't offer stable management, because I live always at risk. I could consult, advise, all of that."

"His reaction?"

"He told me it made sense in theory. He asked me what I would charge for planning such a deal, as I had done for Strassberger. I said I'd want the same percentage as he was charging me for trustee management, plus an extra half percent as a reward for genius. He laughed in my face. 'What makes you think old man Strassberger would let you or me past the front door with a proposal like that?' I told him money talked all languages. The trick was to pick the right moment to start the conversation. He wasn't laughing now. He gave me that cold, baleful stare of his and then stuck out his hand. 'Go to it, then. We've got a deal.' I didn't shake his hand. I told him we didn't have a deal until he'd given me a best-offer figure for the shares. He said he'd given it: fifty dollars. I told him I wanted to go in with sixty-five. He told me I was crazy even to dream it. I told him I had accounts to settle with the Strassberger family. In money terms, at least, this would be one way of doing it. He suggested I take a long holiday in the Seychelles to get the beetles out of my brain. The idea had a certain merit. I knew I was coming up to the crest of a big high. So I took off. I got as far as Sirmione before I cracked up. Rubens moved in Dr. Langer, who brought me here."

And that, it seemed to me, had to be the end of the story. The rest was wishful dreaming, a phantom horse on which a beggar-man would ride to wealth and power. All I could find to say was, "It was a nice try, anyway."

"It was more than a try," said Larry calmly. "I spoke with

Rubens yesterday. I told him we'd be lunching together. First thing this morning, he sent me this fax from Geneva."

He fished in his breast pocket and brought out an envelope embossed with the legend *Psychiatrische Universitätsklinik Burgholzli*.

Inside the envelope was a facsimile message marked with the date and the place of origin, Geneva. It read:

> "For Laurence Lucas from Hubert Rubens:
>   It was a pleasure to talk with you. I am delighted to know from Dr. Langer that you are sufficiently recovered to contemplate early discharge and a restorative vacation. I commend your willingness to make a friendly contact with your family. I have given much thought to the merger proposal we discussed some time ago. It is my present view that we could make a once-for-all tender offer, valid for thirty days, of sixty-five dollars per share. You are authorized to convey this information to the person with whom you are meeting at lunch. We would require at least indicative response within thirty days of this date. Get well soon."

When I looked up from the paper, Larry Lucas was watching me. There was mockery in his eyes and a crooked grin on his lips.

"The message is authentic. The offer is genuine. I'd say you had a legal obligation to convey it to your father and the other members of the board."

"I will."

"And if you take my advice, you'll press for a speedy response. Available money like that doesn't lie around for long."

"What more can I tell them about the subscribers, apart from Rubens?"

"Nothing. From Rubens's point of view, I'm sure that's the cream of the joke. It is from mine, too. You can't sit in judgment on money—only on people. When will you go back to New York?"

"Tomorrow, if I can get us all on a flight. And what about you? Where do you go from here?"

"Where? God knows—but I don't know him well enough to have him tell me. That's where Simonetta comes in handy, you see. They'll plan it all for me: coral atolls in the Seychelles, the silk road to China, archaeology in Yucatán, sex tours in Thailand and the Philippines. And they'll supply a nice clean chaperone of either sex to take care of me. You're asking the wrong question, Carl. 'Where' doesn't matter because Larry Lucas is where it happens, and he's always the same. Up, down, or sideways, drunk or sober, with medication or without, coupled or alone in bed, he is what he is.

"The question he has to answer is quite different. Can he last the course? Is there enough thrill on the upswing to make the gut-wrenching downward slide worthwhile? Will the black bird ever fly away and leave him at peace in the sun? Not easy questions, Carl; but there's a harder one still: Why? Why did the Creator design a tooth-and-claw universe whose creatures live by devouring each other? Why do the gears of the cosmos slip so often? Why Siamese twins and anencephalic babies? Why am I, Larry Lucas, as drug dependent as any dropout junkie? Do you have answers?"

"No. I have only the same questions."

"So don't judge me! Protect my children, if you can, from the judgments other people will make of their father."

"I'll do my best."

"I believe you. Do you mind if we leave now? I've had more than enough for one day."

I paid the check and we walked out together. The lake was ruffled by a small spring breeze. A pair of swans cruised lazily past the redd fringe.

"Look!" Larry Lucas laid a hand on my arm and we halted to watch the stately progress of the birds. "Thank you for the lunch," he said quietly. "It was a pleasure to be with you. We could have been good companions, I think."

It was a long time since I had been so close to tears.

Back at the hotel, I stopped by the concierge's desk and asked him to book us all out to New York on a morning flight. The morning flights were full. We compromised on Swissair at one in the afternoon, which would get us into Kennedy at eight in the evening. I went to the bedroom to collect the tickets and take them to the concierge for emendation.

I found Madi moody and tense. Her only comment on her visit to Larry was, "Thank God, it was short for me and sweet for the children. Now we can get on with our lives." She showed neither resentment nor curiosity about my luncheon with him, and I made no mention of the financial proposal he had made.

I did, however, rehearse all the conversations with Alma Levy. I needed her professional opinion on Larry's mental competence. She delivered it with much more freedom than I expected.

"He's out of my hands now, Carl. I'm writing my last notes and closing the file. It's sad but inevitable. Langer is a good and ethical practitioner. He has chosen a therapeutic method which does show results but with which, fundamentally, I disagree. He is moving Larry forward, yes; but he is moving him like a locomotive, on rails, to a series of predetermined arrival points. Each arrival represents a triumph for the patient, an accomplishment, an assurance of ultimate cure. My own method, which is far more difficult—and more risky—is to encourage excursion, diversity, curiosity, a variety of goals and interests, so that if one arrival is delayed, or one project fails, there is always another. So far, Langer is succeeding. He is focusing Larry on the exercise of his most evident talents—finance! He admits freely that he is encouraged in this by the patronage of Hubert Rubens. He sees no ethical conflict in that because, to a large extent, it supplies Larry's psychic needs: protection, respect, an activity that forces him out of the cave of his own mind and into the turbulence of the social arena."

"And you have no answer to that?"

"I have no satisfactory alternative. I do not control Larry's life. To a large degree, Rubens and Langer direct it. Larry has handed them control by a legal contract. I have, however, exposed to Langer my reservations and my fear."

"And what is your fear, Alma?"

"Not for his sanity, Carl, which is the nub of your question. I ask myself where he may arrive on this one-track journey—"

She broke off. I waited. Finally, I had to prompt her.

"Talk to me, Alma. We're friends. I have to make recommendations to my father, to the shareholders. I have to face a cross-examination on every statement I make. Can I trust what he has told me?"

"You can, yes."

"Then what are you afraid of?"

"The end of the journey. The tracks recede across a flat desert landscape. As they recede, they converge. Finally, on the line which separates earth and sky, they meet."

"The vanishing point?"

"That's the limit of our vision. But what happens then, we can only guess. I feel very old this evening, Carl. Old and helpless. I feel I should quit practice and take a teaching post at some very dull university. Then I could spend my life churning out paper and never have to lose another patient."

I called my father to tell him of our travel arrangements. He had some good news. My mother was mending slowly. Tomorrow, with any luck, she would be out of intensive care, but it would be a long road to full recovery. He himself had kept his promise to me and scheduled a full physical examination for the following week. The market pressure on Strassberger shares seemed to be easing. They were trading more modestly around the forty-three-dollar mark. He would be glad to have us all home. He would send a stretch limousine to the airport for Madi and her tribe. He would send another car for Alma Levy and myself. I should drop her off at her own apartment and spend the night at his house. There was much to talk about; we should prepare for my formal installation—a short address from me to the board might be appropriate.

I was reminded of Larry's mordant comment: "Pure, unadulterated Strassberger response!" As soon as we were back on Strassberger ground—and he without my mother to temper him!—we should all march to his tune, and God help the hindmost!

Finally, I managed to contact Arlette in Nice. I told her I had made a number of attempts to reach her.

"I guessed you would be busy, *chéri*," was her only comment. "I was much occupied too, repainting the gallery, new lighting, putting in movable display panels. I think you will be very pleased when you see it. When will you be back?"

I told her I mightn't be back for a long while. I explained why. I asked her to tell my house couple at the studio, and arrange to pay them for me. I would send funds to her bank account as soon as I reached New York. She took it all with her usual calm, affectionate interest.

Then, bumbling fool that I was, I blurted out, "I love you, Arlette! I miss you so much it hurts. Will you marry me?"

"And be a banker's wife in New York?"

"Would that be so bad?"

"It would be hell, *chéri*, and if my guess is right it will be hell for you! When you can't take it anymore, come back here and be a painter again. Then ask me the same question. I miss you. I think we are good for each other."

"Do you love me, Arlette?"

"In my fashion, *chéri*. The problem is I'm getting out of practice in the language of lovers. Look after yourself. Call me when you can. Wish me luck with the summer shows."

I wished her the best of luck in the world—and wondered, with a certain gallows humor, whether Larry would ever come up with sixty-five dollars a share, to pay for my own upcoming season in hell.

On the evening of my arrival in New York, I sat up late with my father over a decanter of his favorite port. He looked more worn and tired than I had expected. After a few defensive conversational passes, he let down his guard and talked freely of the fears he still held for my mother and the bleak prospect of life without her. He told me flatly that he prayed he would not survive her too long. Madi and I would make our own lives. The grandchildren would not fill the void which the loss of my mother would leave in his life. The reason he had called me home was that he wanted desperately to retire and take the sunset road with the only woman who had endowed his life with meaning.

It was a perfect moment to tell him of my meeting with Larry in Zurich and the extraordinary proposal he had put to me. I showed him the fax from Rubens. I gave him my own impression of the man. I gave him Alma Levy's reading of the relationship between the two men.

My father listened in silence, chin cupped in his hands, weighing every word with the grim solemnity of a hanging judge. When I had finished, I expected an outburst of anger or contempt. Instead, he refilled our glasses, nodded thoughtfully, and made a toast.

"To your mother! She still brings luck into the house!"

"You mean you're interested in the offer? You believe Rubens could make good on it?"

"Yes to both questions, my boy! Yes! Yes! What I can't figure out is how Larry guessed that Rubens might go for the idea. I wouldn't—not in a hundred years." He gagged on his drink, then set the glass down carefully and wiped his fingers and his mouth with his handkerchief.

"Carl, my boy, I love you dearly. I love you more than I can say because you were willing to throw up your own career, which I know you love, and stand with me against the vandals in the marketplace. I know you hate the business. You'll never be a banker's bootlace, but you went after Larry and found him and now you've come back like the Angel of Deliverance.

"Larry—may God have mercy on the poor tormented devil!—Larry is a shining genius. He planted the idea and let it grow. Let me show you how it works. All those strange animals that Rubens controls—trusts, *Anstalten,* Panamanian companies, entities in the Antilles—have served him well for years, but they're falling out of fashion and they cost more and more each year to run, and they're more and more vulnerable to the tax man. So, says our Larry, if they could all be sold, severally or at one stroke, into a legitimate, international public company like Strassberger, then Rubens could grab a large chunk of capital gain and the new Strassberger-Rubens combination would come to market with a sudden new glow of asset value. Rubens obviously did his sums carefully, but Larry had the genius to figure the situation long ago—even while he was heading for his crackup."

"So what are you going to do about it, Father?"

"Give them what they ask: an indicative answer. Yes, we're willing sellers. Let's have the tender documents so we can present them to the board and the shareholders. Then we'll get the show on the road."

I confess I was shocked by his eagerness to do business with Rubens and Larry. I taxed him with it, sharply.

"You have no questions? No reservations about the company you'll be courting: Hubert Rubens and Larry Lucas? No thought of our own long fiduciary tradition?"

"None!" I was startled by the vehemence of his answer. "I've been a banker all my life. Strassberger paper has always been prime paper. I kept it like that. Now I can't do it any longer. The money game is out of control. It's a floating crap game. The money market is run by twenty-five-year-olds shouting the odds on every trading currency in the world. Can you cope with that? I can't, not any longer. How can I hold myself accountable to the calls of a kid in Singapore or Hong Kong or New York? I can't. I won't."

"But if you sell Strassberger, the name has to go with it."

"So what? If you don't breed yourself a son, the name dies anyway. Are you getting married?"

"I asked the lady. She couldn't make up her mind."

"Because you wouldn't make it up for her. Well, it's your life!"

"For the moment, Father, it's yours. You asked for it, remember? I gave it back to you, without question. My paper is still prime paper."

It was a cruel, cold moment and I could not for the life of me understand how we had come to it. It seemed to last an age until my father reached out and touched my hand.

"I'm old and I'm tired and I'm scared," he told me. "Forgive me, Carl!"

Next morning, I went to visit my mother in the hospital. Stretched out in the orthopedic bed, she looked frail and small, like a Dresden figurine; but her makeup was perfectly applied and not a hair was out of place. There was still the ring of authority in her voice.

"Tell me, Carl! Tell me everything that has happened to you. Don't stop if I close my eyes. I'll still be listening."

It was, as you may imagine, a long and tortuous tale; but if I paused too long, her eyes would open and she would urge me on with an imperious flutter of her hand. When, finally, the story ended, her first thought was of my father.

"I want him out of the business, Carl. As soon as possible and to hell with the price. I know he's afraid that I'll go before he does, but I won't. I've promised him I'll stay long enough for him to build us a beautiful house in Hawaii with a garden full of flowers and birds—and no steps to climb. He's been such an upright man. He's worked hard all his life. He's never learned to enjoy himself except with me. I've talked to his doctor, who tells me he's the kind of man who can topple over with a stroke or go out—*bang!*—with a massive coronary. If he's stricken and survives, I can be no help to him. So I'm glad you're back, Carl, though you mustn't stay forever. I'd like to see you married and happy. What about this woman you have in France? Are you fond of her?"

"Very. I've asked her several times to marry me. She feels happier and safer the way things are now."

"If I were in her place, I'd probably feel the same. We spoiled you, I'm afraid, Carl. We trained you to be so self-sufficient that you couldn't bring yourself to depend on anyone else—let alone express the need. I've thought a lot about Madi and her future. I've wondered, too, how much she gave or withheld from Larry in his lonely times. I'm glad you found him finally, and that you were able to talk freely together."

"I'm glad about that too, Mama. One of the few sermons I remember was about hell. The preacher said, 'Hell isn't fire and brimstone and devils with pitchforks. Hell is the absence of love—and the loss of all capacity to enjoy it.' That's what we've had, isn't it? A lot of love."

"Too much, perhaps," said my mother softly. "And we spent most of it on ourselves."

It took four months to tidy the sale of the Strassberger shares, although the essential act was consummated the day my father called Rubens and agreed to the deal. Rubens behaved with impeccable precision. Larry and I conferred on matters of detail. Some of our meetings were held at my house in Cagnes among the brushes and gallipots. He was a model guest, companionable, a very good cook, a patient watcher if I wanted to pause on a walk and set down a sketch. I made him a present of one he admired especially: Arlette, chopping vegetables for a pot-au-feu in the big rustic kitchen.

I noticed that Larry never brought a woman with him on these visits, although I invited him to do so. He simply grinned and said, "Now is not the time for me." I was slow to understand that his brightest moments in company were those on which his depression was deepest. When Arlette was there, she would flirt with him and coddle him, and when he demanded to know why she hadn't married me yet, she would give a big Gallic shrug and the perennial excuse, "He needs more training. And he's still a banker, isn't he?"

I kept in touch with Sergio Carlino, who was and still is an assiduous and witty recorder of the world in which he lives—a fringe kingdom of sybarites and cynics and politicians and captains of industry, dusted over with the gilt of old names and titles. He had kept his promise. Liliane Prévost was safe, passed from woman's hand to woman's hand into a fairly secure domesticity with an aging prima donna in the Paris Opéra.

When the deal with Rubens was finally consummated, my father rented a house and staff in Hawaii, chartered a jet, and flew my mother there. He vowed that he would find a plot on which to build her dream house. The card she sent me said it all:

"Now he's an expert on botany, Polynesian navigators, and island miniclimates. I'm trying to push him into buying the place we're in, which is very comfortable and more than adequate for our needs. Life is too short to be hustled by real estate agents, or plagued by architects and builders. I have my man with me. That's all I need."

Madi, now divorced, very rich, and even more independent, was faced with new dilemmas. She had suitors and male friends galore; but which of them could she trust as stepfather to Marianne and Laurence Junior?

I retired, as I had planned, to my farmhouse sanctuary and started work again. I also worked on Arlette, who with more reluctance than I expected, agreed to marry me after what she called a six-month trial.

I blew up and we staged a battle royal that raged for three hours and ended in three weeks' silence, after which she agreed to marry me as soon as we could get the papers and permission. However, there were conditions. She would keep and run the gallery, and we should be married by a Catholic priest in the Matisse chapel at Vence. I told her I'd marry her in a balloon if that would make her happy. She gave me an old-fashioned look.

"You could have any woman in the world. Why do you take so much nonsense from me?"

To which I had no ready answer. Enough that she would marry me; and she did. Sometime in sleepless nights the question haunted my pillow like a mischievous imp, but always by morning it was gone.

Epilogue

WHEN WINTER CAME AND CUSTOMERS were sparse at the gallery, we snugged down on the farm at Cagnes while I painted and Arlette wrote letters and made telephone calls to clients and artists around Europe. We lived well together. We were, we told each other, lucky and content.

Then, one day, when there was snow on the ground and the winds were whistling down the defiles of the Maritime Alps, I had a letter from Dr. Hubert Rubens. It was a strangely formal communication.

> Dear Mr. Strassberger,
>
> As executor and trustee of the estate of the late Mr. Laurence Lucas, it is my sad duty to inform you that Mr. Lucas passed away in Amsterdam, Holland, on the fifth day of January this year. The certificate of death was signed by the attending physician, Dr. Piet Haan.
>
> His former wife, Mrs. Madeleine Lucas, presently in Antigua, has been informed of his demise and of his testamentary dispositions, which she has no intention of contesting.
>
> Under the will, half the estate, some seven million dollars, passes in trust to his children, Laurence Junior and Marianne Lucas of New York. There are minor legacies, mostly to

women friends, amounting to half a million dollars. The rest of the estate is to be dedicated to founding and endowing world-wide research into the origins and the treatment of depressive illness.

It was Mr. Lucas's wish that Dr. Alma Levy of New York and Dr. Alois Langer of Zurich be invited to participate as foundation members of the Board of Trustees when it is set up.

You are not named as a beneficiary in the will, but there is a sealed letter, which, according to Mr. Lucas's wishes, I send you herewith by registered mail.

I offer you my sincere condolences on the loss of a relative and friend. I trust you will believe that I share your grief.

Hubert Rubens
Doctor of Law

Larry's letter was brief and poignant.

My dear Carl,

I'm tired of asking questions. I've decided it's time I found out the answers for myself. I'll be happy to pass them on to you, if there's any way I can communicate—which I very much doubt.

Fortunately for poor devils like me, the Dutch permit a civilized choice of exit from an intolerable existence.

Please keep an eye on Marianne and Laurence Junior. Madi's a good mother; but every child can use a good uncle.

For you, Carl, my erstwhile pursuer, I have nothing but goodwill and good wishes and thanks for the brief friendship we were able to enjoy.

I hear you've married your Arlette. She's better than you deserve and you're a better painter than you realize. Be kind to each other. The human psyche is a very fragile vessel.

My debts are all paid. Spare me a memory sometimes and pray that whoever or whatever is out there will receive me kindly.

Hail and farewell,
Larry

When Arlette came into the studio, she found me, with tears streaming down my face, slashing paint wildly on a large new canvas. When she asked me what was the matter, I pointed to the letters on the table and went on with my assault. She read the letters, set them down again, then stood, a few paces away, arms akimbo like a peasant housewife watching my attack on the fabric. Finally my emotion wore itself out and I stepped back from the turbulent mess. Arlette pronounced judgment.

"That's good. That's very good."

"I'm glad you understand it. I don't."

"The dam's broken and the river's in flood."

"I don't know what you mean."

"We're going to drink champagne, *chéri*. Here and now."

"What are we supposed to be celebrating?"

"The liberation of Larry Lucas. God give him rest!"

"I'll drink to that."

"Then we'll celebrate Larry's gifts to us."

"What gifts?"

"That's mine." She pointed to the canvas. "A newly minted talent for my gallery! To you, *chéri*, he gave the gift of tears. You needed that so badly. I needed it in you. Now I believe we can be happy together."

Redemption

Leon Uris

'A sweeping, passionate story' *Chicago Tribune*

As begun in the bestseller *Trinity*, Leon Uris continues his mighty epic of love and loss in Ireland's journey towards independence.

Set against the dramatic backdrop of increased unrest in Ireland and a world about to be pitched headlong into the nightmare of the First World War, *Redemption* follows the stirring fates of three great families – the Larkins, the Weed-Hubble clan and the Fitzpatricks – families whose passions, battles and loves are intimately tied to the history of Ireland herself.

From the majestic mountains of New Zealand to the shipyards of Belfast, the deserts of Egypt and the disaster of Gallipoli, the drama unfolds, climaxing in a dangerously unpredictable Ireland and the Easter Uprising of 1916.

Redemption is a magnificent novel from one of the greatest storytellers of our time.

'Uris is a master at weaving historical fact and fiction' *Life*

'*Redemption* rivals the best of his earlier work. Few writers who have tackled the Troubles have exhibited the scope or the . . . skills Uris demonstrates here.' *Publishers Weekly*

ISBN 0 00 649895 7